Over Forty in Broken Hill

Jack Hodgins was born in 1938 on Vancouver Island, the son of a logger and the grandson of pioneer farmers. After working his way through the University of British Columbia, he settled down to teach English in Nanaimo. His first book, *Split Delaney's Island,* a collection of short stories, was published in 1976, followed by *The Invention of the World* (1977), which won the Gibson Literary Award as the best first novel of the year. *The Resurrection of Joseph Bourne* (1979) won the Governor General's Award for Fiction. A second collection of stories, *The Barclay Family Theatre,* was published in 1981, a novel, *The Honorary Patron*, in 1987, and *Left Behind in Squabble Bay*, a children's book, in 1988. His novel, *Innocent Cities*, was published in 1990. Jack Hodgins was awarded the Canada-Australia Literature prize in 1986. He now lives in Victoria, B.C., where he teaches at the University of Victoria.

JACK HODGINS
OVER 40 IN BROKEN HILL

unusual encounters in the
Australian Outback

A DOUGLAS GIBSON BOOK

M&S

Canadian Cataloguing in Publication Data

Hodgins, Jack, 1938-
  Over forty in Broken Hill

ISBN 0-7710-4192-6

1. Hodgins, Jack, 1938-   -Journeys – Australia
2. McDonald, Roger, 1941-   -Journeys.
3. Australia – Description and travel – 1981-
4. Novelists, Canadian (English) – 20th century –
Journeys – Australia.*   5. Novelists, Australia –
20th century – Journeys.   I. Title.

PS8565.03253 1992   C818'.54   C92-094393-4
PR9199.3.A63Z47 1992

Co-published in 1992 with the University of Queensland Press, Australia

Printed and bound in Canada

A Douglas Gibson Book

McClelland & Stewart Inc.
The Canadian Publishers
481 University Avenue
Toronto M5G 2E9

for Roger McDonald

Contents

Acknowledgments   *ix*
"Only a few think I'm crazy"   *xi*

1 Sydney again, at last   *1*
2 Braidwood revisited   *14*
3 The road to Gundagai, and beyond   *27*
4 Hay, hell, and almost Booligal   *46*
5 The Walls of China, The Walls of Death   *63*
6 Over forty in Broken Hill   *80*
7 Camels, artists, and a disgruntled cook: Trying to cope
      with the dust   *95*
8 So this is what it means to be bogged   *109*
9 "Please call again soon": The siege of Charleville   *124*
10 The invasion of the prickly pear   *147*
11 Cassiopeia and the dreaded parthenium   *157*
12 Queensland vernacular: It's raining in
      Rockhampton   *177*

Acknowledgments

To Alfred, Lord Tennyson for "Ulysses"; to Phil Jarrat for his *Newsweek-Bulletin* article, "Tracks Winding Back" (Jan 30–Feb 6 1990); and to Ted Egan for "Northway to the Sheds", "Lime Juice Tub" and "Flash Jack from Gundagai" from his tape of shearing songs, *The Faces of Australia Series.*

Excerpts from *Over Forty in Broken Hill* have also been published in *Overland* and in *Island.* Thanks to Barry Oakley who encouraged this project and published a short early account of the trip in the *Australian.*

I want to express my gratitude to all those who offered friendship and generous hospitality. The fact that I've avoided using some names does not suggest that I think these people need the protection of anonymity, but rather that I respect the privacy of those who did not know – as I didn't know myself – that I would be writing this book.

QUEENSLAND

Clermont

Barcaldine   Rockhampton
        Emerald

SOUTH AUSTRALIA   Charleville

Cunnamulla   BRISBANE

Bourke

Broken
Hill   Wilcannia
        Nyngan

Lake Mungo   NEW SOUTH
        WALES

ADELAIDE   SYDNEY

Hay   Canberra

Gundagai   Bateman's Bay
Victoria   Braidwood

MELBOURNE

"Only a few think I'm crazy"

When the telephone rang, I had showered but not yet dressed. The voice belonged to the hotel manager, who stood listening to radio opera in his kitchen directly beneath me. "I have a call for you. If you hang up, I'll put it through."

"But I haven't the time to take it."

I was already running late. Because of the rain thundering down upon Sydney, my plane from Wellington had been delayed — forced to circle the airport. I'd arrived at the little Victoria Street hotel with only forty minutes to shower, shave, press something to wear, get dressed, and take a taxi downtown where I was expected to give a talk to a group of Canadian expatriates on a topic which was still unknown to me.

I hadn't yet dressed when the telephone rang, I hadn't shaved. I had less than a half hour left. Because the room was so humid, the slightest movement made me sweat. After a desperate search, I'd found a place to plug in my travel iron but had to get down on my knees to press my dress-pants on the carpet. The Consul would be there. Various members of the consulate. Someone from the High Commission. I had no idea what I would talk about; I imagined arriving and finding there'd been a misunderstanding, that I was expected to talk about national unity, or environmental concerns in the Arctic. I would be struck dumb in front of an audience. *If* I got there in time; *if* I got there at all. A taxi had already been ordered but of course I wouldn't be ready. He would drive on. Taxi drivers had little patience when they were called to the Kings

Cross area. I imagined cables to Ottawa: *Who agreed to pay this idiot's airfare?*

"It's someone named Roger McDonald. He telephoned earlier, too, before you arrived."

Long distance, from Braidwood. This was not a call to ignore. After all, it was Roger who had given me the reason for being here. At least part of my reason for agreeing to this evening's event, and others like it, was to get to this side of the Pacific and take him up on an invitation for another sort of journey altogether.

"Roger?"

"Jack. You arrived all right? I wasn't sure what time you were getting in."

"Just got in. The plane was late." Some of these wrinkles would have to stay, at least I'd got a straight crease down the front of the legs. "I'm off to give some sort of talk in a few minutes. I don't even know what this one is supposed to be about." How did you get into a pair of pants with only one free hand?

"Well, look, I won't keep you. I'll be up to Sydney on Thursday for a meeting of the Australian Society of Authors. Maybe we could get together in the afternoon?"

"Yes. Good. That's great. I'll put Thursday afternoon aside." One foot in, but how to get the other foot in without falling and breaking my neck?

"And Saturday lunch. You'll be my guest at the ASA lunch."

"Sounds fine to me. You got everything ready for the trip?"

"A few more details have fallen into place since I talked to you last. If you arrive down here a week Friday, we'll set out on Monday morning. April 2. We'll drive west as far as Hay, where I've lined up an interview with a shearing contractor." Hay? How far to the west was Hay? "Then we'll spend a couple of days at Lake Mungo Park before we go up to Broken Hill, I think. That's where most of the Maori shearers work out from, so there'll be plenty for us to do there."

I had only a vague idea where Broken Hill might be but I

was tempted to say: Why wait? Forget tonight's talk, tomorrow's reading, all those interviews. Why don't we set off for the bush right away?

After Broken Hill, it would be the Easter weekend. "We might go to the Flinders Ranges, I'm not sure. Or up to Sturt National Park." Afterwards, we would cross the Channel Country in Queensland, and then up to his brother's cattle station north of Clermont. "We'll eventually get to my mother's place in Rockhampton, I hope, and maybe go camping with her in Carnarvon Gorge. That's likely to take the full month."

There was a small mark on the front of the shirt. How could I reach the washcloth to get it off? I couldn't. And anyway, there wasn't time for it to dry.

"Now Jack, you don't happen to be a good mechanic by any chance, do you?"

What was that supposed to mean? "Me? I wish I was." I was heading into the desolate interior with someone who hoped that *I* was a mechanic? "I'm useless at that sort of thing." I put my free hand through the shirt sleeve, held my arm straight up in the air while the shirt dropped to my shoulder. Now, how to get the other arm in without wrenching a muscle?

"I'm no better myself. I took the truck around to the mechanics in Braidwood the other day for a check-up and they said, 'Whaddaya gonna do out there when she breaks down?' I said I've bought a book that shows you what to do, and they laughed. 'Oh, right. A writer's got a book. That'll do you a lot of good.' "

When she breaks down! I couldn't worry about that now. I had to get moving. I could worry tomorrow about setting off into the outback in a truck the mechanics laughed at.

"Well, we'll be a great pair," I said. "Maybe we'll be forced to learn something. We may both be terrific mechanics by the time we get home." *Maybe we'll die, too, when we blow a cylinder a million miles from a service station.* "Everybody I've told about this trip is envious." *Only a few think I'm crazy.*

I finished dressing. Towelled the sweat from my brow.

Told myself it didn't matter, it didn't matter, whatever the topic was I'd think of something, I'd make up something to say, all those years of teaching would come to my rescue. Surely I hadn't come halfway around the globe simply to make a fool of myself.

Down the staircase and out through the door. The taxi waited in the rain. I ran down the steps, leapt over the heaps of plane-tree leaves and the water racing down the gutter — then realised my room key had flown out of my hand. Where? Where? I couldn't see it. Not into the gutter, surely! I knelt, dragged my hand through the stream, sifted through the leaves. No key. I ran to the taxi. "Can you come out and give me a hand, I've lost my room key." But even as I talked I spotted it — up the slope on the pavement. I grabbed it up and jumped into the taxi. "Jesus, mate," the driver said, "I nearly drove off and left you. I thought you were down in the gutter looking for used syringes. You can't be too careful in this part of town."

I looked at my hands that would soon be shaking the hands of diplomats, civil servants, home-sick Canadians. It was time to calm down, get ahold of myself, relax, start to enjoy the adventure of being where I'd been wanting so badly to be for the past three years.

1 Sydney again, at last

Roger McDonald's *1915* was one of the handful of novels which had originally ignited my enthusiasm for Australian fiction. During a visit to Australia in 1987, I asked if I might meet him. We were invited – my wife Dianne and I – to spend a day with him and Rhyll on their Braidwood farm, not far from Canberra. A friendship developed during a subsequent trans-Pacific correspondence which covered everything from the price of wool to the difficulties of teaching writing and the intricacies of structuring a novel. Eventually we read and commented upon one another's latest work in manuscript. Then he wrote to ask if I'd be interested in joining him on a four-week camping trip through the outback of New South Wales and Queensland while he researched a nonfiction book on shearing. Invitations to the International Writers' weeks at Adelaide and Wellington meant that I was able to take up his offer much sooner then he might have expected, if he indeed expected me to take it up at all.

Of course I would have to be crazy not to jump at an opportunity like this. But an opportunity to – what? To travel where poisonous snakes were waiting behind every tree? If there were any trees. To perish of thirst in a desert? I'd read *Voss*; I knew what happened to people who strayed too far into that continent.

Books had told me what to expect. Red dust, heat, sheep, long distances between gas stations. Petrol stations, rather. Friends warned of venomous spiders waiting to finish me off. Bad jokes were made, about dingoes and their fondness for travellers in tents. Dianne reminded me of the flies. "They drove you crazy at Ayers Rock."

In Adelaide a group of Australian writers convinced me that if I startled a goanna it would run up and sit on my head. An English novelist advised that I "take a shovel" and "remember to dig the hole first." A writer from Berlin shook his head and proclaimed, "It is all just a dream."

Australians said, "You'll see more of Australia than most Australians do," but did not say they envied me. They approved of my guide, however. "Roger McDonald? Oh, that's fine then, at least he knows what he's doing. Well, I think he does. Well, I certainly hope he does! How well do you know him anyway?"

This was a man who, according to legend, learned to fly a plane as part of his research for one of his novels. He'd taken up horse-back riding for another. Vague hints about broken bones and other calamitous endings to those escapades only made you wonder how far he might go for a book about shearing sheep. He'd already spent some months cooking for shearers — would he want to take on the sheep themselves now, and insist that I do so too? It wasn't difficult to imagine disasters provoked by a pen full of ill-tempered rams incensed by the bungling attention of amateurs.

I'd been warned: Australians were the hardest people in the world to get along with. A man who had drilled for oil in nearly every country decided this. "After doing all your tests and examining the data you'd make your decisions and say, 'We'll run the line through here. Lay a charge over there,' and instead of just doing it you'd have one fellow saying, 'Well now, wait a minute, why're you layin' it there? I reckon it oughta go over here,' and another, 'You crazy, mate? The place you oughta put 'er is right over there.' Nothing gets done without an argument. They've got to make sure you don't think you know more than they do just because you're an expert. Egalitarianism gone mad."

It was because of this sort of exported image, in fact, that I hadn't even wanted to visit Australia at all the first time. The trip had been free — an award. I could hardly turn it down. But what if it would be like being trapped for four weeks at Don's Party? I expected to be sneered at, insulted, and pushed around by the sadistic louts who populated the noisy bars of Australian novels. (Why? It seemed they didn't need a reason. The colour of your shirt.) Part of the joy of that earlier trip was the surprise: Australians were generous, friendly, almost shy – at least on their own continent. Which is not to say that I mightn't have got the wrong impression.

What did I remember of Roger McDonald after three years? He'd met us at the last gate to Spring Farm in a black Snowy River kind of hat and a long oilskin coat of the sort worn by stockmen galloping across the landscape while hoof beats thundered out of Dolby Stereo. His face with its deep weathered complexion wore a welcoming smile – but the sort of tentative smile that only Australians can manage, where one end of the mouth was prepared to become a sneer if a sneer should be more appropriate. He'd had a fire ready for us, on the top of a hill of gum trees, and a billy can ready for tea. He'd cooked lamb chops on the outdoor barbecue. He'd led us with great determined strides over his property, and spoke of throwing manuscripts into the fire. Despite the letters it was not entirely impossible to imagine him riding up to the hotel on a half-wild stallion, a beer in one hand and a gun in the other, to demand that I submit to a test: drink three cases of stubbies and wrestle a kangaroo to the ground, mate, if you think you're coming on any trip with me.

The man who arrived at the Jackson Hotel on Thursday afternoon was not wearing a stockman's oilskin or a Snowy River hat (though his black Akubra was out in the car). But neither was he wearing what seemed to have become the Australian uniform: shorts and colourful summer shirt. He wore long cotton pants and elastic-sided boots and a blue long-sleeved cotton shirt over a t-shirt. A country person, I found myself thinking – cleaned up for, but not dressed up for, a visit to town.

We greeted one another, I believe, with some relief. There was no guessing what second thoughts he might have had on the drive up from Braidwood. How long before he discovered they were justified? Though I'd been raised in the country like him, I preferred cities when I travelled: Vienna, New Orleans, Sydney. I didn't especially like camping – the idea of living in tents and eating at picnic tables brought back memories of drizzling rain and mosquitoes. I was not a mechanic, I had no talent for cooking. It was entirely possible that I could spend this whole trip wondering if I was making Roger McDonald sorry he'd invited me.

But second thoughts were not permitted to show. The world was full of other things to talk about. The weather, for instance: "I'm glad that rain didn't last."

The annual Society of Authors meeting: "Could be lively." He enjoyed the company of gathered writers only up to a point. But there was something about this meeting he shouldn't miss.

My hotel room: "This isn't too bad, is it?" He peered into the bathroom as though I'd offered to sell it. "Quite pleasant, in fact." He looked out the narrow window onto the glass roof of the breakfast patio. I leaned back against a wall; there wasn't really room for two people to stand without colliding.

We seemed to agree: the sooner we got out of confined spaces like this the better.

"We'll have a bit of a way to walk. The closest I could park was a couple blocks down and around the corner." This did not surprise me. Dozens of battered old vans and sedans were lined up along the curb, all with FOR SALE signs in their windows so that youthful travellers could afford to fly home – HURRY! MAKE US AN OFFER! The youths themselves overflowed the backpacker hostels and sprawled all over the sidewalk – footpath, rather – reading letters or listening to music or chomping thoughtfully on pieces of fruit.

"They hadn't spread this far when we stayed here before," I said. "Anyway, I'm a sucker for all these lacy balconies and flowering trees. Reminds me I'm someplace *away*."

Downtown, we stopped in at Abbey's Books, where Roger had been invited to sign copies of his latest novel, *Rough Wallaby*, which was still amongst the Recent Arrivals. This was that breath-holding period when reviews might (or might not) yet be followed by impressive sales. After a decade, his first novel, *1915*, still sold well — had become something of an Australian classic, in fact: a story of two boys from the bush and two girls from the city who are all caught up eventually in the tragedy of Gallipoli. It was praised for its strong realistic narrative and sharply drawn characters; but it was also read as a tale of Australia's own "growing up" and initiation into the harsh realities of the twentieth century world. Something about it had captured the national imagination. As someone who knew little of Australian history or mythology, I simply thought it a superb novel.

Sales clerks were pleased to see him. Conversations took place — about the Society of Authors meeting, about the reception of *Rough Wallaby* and some of his other books, about the trip ahead. He would fold his arms and rest his weight on one leg — the other foot ahead — and speak leisurely, and with warmth; then, when he'd had his say, he'd lower his gaze to his forward boot, and did not seem to mind when there were silences. I've contributed my part to the conversation, he seemed to imply; now it's up to you. He listened with complete absorption, I thought, which might explain his enviable skill with dialogue.

In his earlier dust jacket photos, Roger looked like a sturdy black-haired Scottish boy, with a just-slightly pleased grin and the hint of a self-conscious frown. You could almost hear him saying, "Let's get this over with", even while privately enjoying the cause for attention, if not the attention itself. In real life, the boy's complexion had been roughly textured by years of outdoor weather, the features were stronger, the eyes willing to assess you openly, before falling away. But the frown-grin combination had survived. And the hair, though slicked into strict adult order, stubbornly re-established its natural inclination towards a boyish shape.

We stopped for coffee at an outdoor cafe, where he brought me up to date on his research plans. Within the next week he would have to drive to Dubbo — which was apparently not just a character in a Patrick White novel but a town to the west of Sydney. Someone he couldn't afford to overlook had surfaced there, who might throw new light on the famous "wide-comb dispute".

This was an event I would have to know something about if I were to make any sense of what Roger was up to in the month ahead. He filled me in – or at least introduced a topic which he would tell me more about as we travelled. This conflict in the shearing industry resulted from the introduction, by migrant New Zealand shearers, of wider handpieces into the sheds. This was in the early 1980s. Besides being opposed by the union, the wider "combs" were also illegal.

"Why?"

"Australians believed the wider four-blade comb did a poorer job than the two and a half inch comb. It's flat and wide, the sheep are curved – ridges get left." The wider combs were faster, naturally, but wages were not adjusted, so the owners benefited while the shearers did not.

As a result, all hell broke loose. A strike. New Zealanders kept on shearing – causing resentments that persisted in places even today. "When the wide combs were made legal, some good men left the industry altogether in disgust. Many are bitter even now."

Although many Australian writers spoke with an accent which seemed softly British to my ears, Roger's vowels were unmistakably Australian. Woide cowm. Wyges. Plyces. But not so pronounced as the Paul Hogan brand of smart-ass "Strine" which some Aussies adopt for people from "Overseas". He hadn't even said "G'day".

Perhaps the wide-comb dispute was an unusual topic for conversation in a Sydney cafe, while tourists hurried up the sunny slope to the strip joints and souvenir shops of Kings Cross. But even the tourist could have seen in Roger's face how interested he was in this. Despite his slow and rather casual manner of speaking, he was intense about it. The contentious issue was important, I understood – to us both – because the Maori shearers we would be meeting with in Broken Hill were part of the legacy of this dispute, though widely respected in the shearing world.

"I should probably go up to Dubbo next week on my own,

though," he said. "I'm not sure what arrangements they might have – "

"Yes." I wasn't ready yet to get started anyway. "I still want to rent a car and go off for a few days down the coast." This was something Roger couldn't understand anyone wanting to do, though he didn't mind that it was Bateman's Bay I'd chosen from the tourist booklets. "We drive down there ourselves, once in a while. But I can never stay for long." He smiled, a wide one-sided grin, and shot me a sidelong glance. "A lot of water sloshing against the shore."

A lot of water sloshing against the shore! "Well, yes, uh, I guess you're right, but I like coastlines, I've lived most of my life near the sea." I can't imagine doing without it for long.

"Well, it'll be different where we're going." This sounded like a threat. "I like it better – flat and red." A man of the plains.

The man of the plains drove the man of the coast in his dusty cream-coloured sedan out to the nearest available coastline to explore South Head and Watson's Bay, a part of Sydney I wasn't likely to get to on my own. We walked along the lengthy beach past the picture windows of the wealthy. We climbed the steep slope to the favourite cliff-top jumping spot for suicides. Was it my stamina that was being tested by this life-long mountain climber and bush walker, or my emotional stability? We confined our conversation to the world that pushed itself into our faces. Roger experimented with a camera he'd bought for the trip. More specifically, for his book. Shearers in action, I imagined. Shearers at leisure. Sheep before and after their humiliating ordeal with the "combs" whose history had turned an industry on its ear.

On the way back, he parked the sedan on a steep slope where we could look down over rooftops to the harbour. Immediately below us was a large private school behind a fence. In the paved schoolyard, rows of adolescent boys in uniforms stood at attention while older and taller adolescent boys in uniform shouted instructions at them. It was a sight that drove a cold, disturbing shudder through me.

"This is the school I attended for a number of years."

High fences, uniforms, military exercises, bullying seniors. Just looking down at those boys made me break out in
a cold sweat. Attending a rural public school had had its own
sort of terrors, but I'd always known there was something
worse. The down-island private boys' school was where
you'd be sent if you fell in with the wrong sort. I knew what
this would mean. Teachers with sneering English accents
would beat you with canes all day and rich older boys would
torture you all night. You would be doing everything in
crowds, you'd do everything according to rules, while someone grotesque watched over your every minute – you'd
never have a moment of privacy – all within stone walls
which were themselves within fences. In my mind, this was
indistinguishable from a reform school – a prison. In fact, I
was nearly an adult before I realised there was a difference.

"You had to do that? Line up like that in rows, in uniforms?
March around?" Was I about to hear him say those were the
best years of his life? Then I would be setting out on a trip
with an unfathomable alien.

He nodded. His expression was not one, I hoped, of fond
nostalgia.

"You liked it here?"

"I hated it."

I was more than a little relieved to see that he meant what
he said.

At a dinner party that evening in Balmain, the famous novelist on my left quizzed us about the planned journey while
bouncing her baby girl on her knee. Roger listed place names,
described the route we would take, explained his interest in
the Maoris who'd come to Australia to shear. I confessed excitement about exploring a brand new world of plains and
Outback towns and "the bush". She pulled an envious face.
"This is the sort of thing that – all my life! – has made me
wish I was a boy!"

Was this to be a boys' adventure then? I suppose it was.
There were echoes here of childhood overnights in a friend's
back yard, of adolescent hunting trips in search of the six-
spike deer. There were echoes, too, of the great American

myth – Huckleberry Finn escaping society. And of the great Australian myth – mateship in the bush. Both of these had raised troubling questions in recent years, but their appeal had not been spoiled. I could not think of a Canadian myth suggested here. Radisson and Groseilliers setting out in their canoes for beaver pelts and the frozen ports of Hudson's Bay? (They were known as Raddishes and Gooseberries in Canadian History classes.) What became of them? The former was captured by Iroquois, the latter was arrested by France for trading without a license; together they were responsible for founding the most influential trading company in the country's history – businessmen!

"It's Never Too Late to Have a Happy Childhood", a bumper sticker insists. As childhoods go, mine wasn't bad. That is, I had stable, loving parents, and a seventy acre hobby farm for a playground. Maybe I had it too good. I was too sensible to run off and join the circus when I was ten, or to get myself a job on a freighter instead of graduating from high school. I trained as a teacher, entered into a happy marriage, and started a family when others my age were hitch-hiking across the face of Europe. Maybe this trip would fill a gap in my life.

It wasn't simply that I'd fallen in love with a landscape on that previous visit, or felt like a child dragged too quickly through a wonderland, left with an appetite for more. Something more complex had been at work in me. I'd developed a powerful lust of a literary nature: a desire to live inside an Australian narrative. Having read and admired so many Australian novels – and having just written a novel myself with a section set in nineteenth century Australia – I longed for what seemed like the natural next step – neither to read nor write an Australian novel but to live one.

What did this mean? I wanted to inhabit a house like the Murphy home in Rodney Hall's *Captivity Captive*, which looked like a house with its walls taken down, with "the family sprawled or squatting on the veranda in the spaces between the posts which held up its flimsy iron roof." I wanted to speak with rough and simple people like David Malouf's

Jenny and Digger Keen outside their junky riverside store. I
wanted to walk, as Voss had walked, through desolation, and
eat goanna roasted over a fire, and visit the dusty sort of little
bush town that Walter Gilchrist and Billy Mackenzie grew up
in, before manhood and Gallipoli claimed them. I wanted to
breathe the air of a landscape in which, like that of Stow's
Tourmaline, "every pebble glares, wounding the eyes, shortening the breath . . . and nothing seems easier than to cease,
to become a stone, hot and still." And into this landscape I
wanted to ride, like poor deluded Oscar Hopkins, in something as wondrous as his glass church — sailing absurdly up a
tiny river into the baffled heart of bush Australia.
    As simple and as preposterous as that. A reader and a wri-
ter of stories, I wished to inhabit a story too. Since Australian
novels were what I'd been reading lately, then an Australian
novel was what I wished to inhabit. To travel through the
Australian landscape with an Australian novelist as my guide
would be about as close as a person could possibly get to
achieving such a goal.

Friday, March 23rd, was sunny and rather humid. Roger was
at the Hyatt Hotel debating copyright laws with other Australian writers. After breakfast I went out into the street
where sleepy backpackers chatted in groups on the footpath
or brushed their teeth behind the wheel of their battered
vans. Did they think that only seventeen-year-olds should
tackle this continent? I walked down-hill past the restored ter-
race houses and the blooming hibiscus bushes, and descended the 113 steps to Woolloomooloo Bay. Across the bay
I climbed another flight of stairs and entered the botanical
gardens. From a bench near an enormous banyan tree, looking out towards the gleaming white shells of the Opera House
roof, I watched joggers thumping past, a replica of the *Bounty*
sail by, harbour ferries come and go. Ibises moved here and
there around me, probing the grass with their long thin
crooked beaks.
    Three weeks of duties were behind me — ten days at the
International Writers' Week in Adelaide, a week at the Inter-

national Writers' Week in Wellington, and several days of readings and talks in Sydney. Now I was free to enjoy this city again, and of course, to record a few impressions in my notebook while I had this time to myself. Kings Cross. The Rocks. The ferry to Manly. Circular Quay. Apparently my pen had other plans. When I looked up from my notebook half an hour later, ibises were still poking around for whatever ibises eat, the *Bounty* had disappeared behind Mrs Macquarie's Point, a pair of lovers had laid themselves out on the grass not far from my feet, but none of this had been recorded. Instead, what I had written was this:

The hotel's owner himself brought Mrs C. her basket of toast, which he placed on the pink tablecloth before her. Madama Butterfly was broadcasting her anguish from the kitchen radio. "The Cross was quiet last night," he said.

He meant only that no one had been murdered, she supposed. Kings Cross was never truly quiet. From her room, she could hear the laughter, the shouting, the sirens from up the slope. She had seen it as well, in the evening: young men trying to get you in to the strip joints, prostitutes slouched against the walls in leopard skin shifts or in little-girl pinafores, old men sleeping on the benches. A young woman who was a member of a visiting volleyball team had been stabbed by someone's syringe as she passed down the street, and had to undergo tests for the AIDS virus. Last week a backpackers' hostel had burned to the ground, killing ten sleepers. Parents in West Germany would be mourning.

"And coffee please," she said. She did not want to talk about the Cross, or anything. Her husband would not sleep for ever in his bed upstairs, despite the sleeping pill she'd given him. She was leaving him, of course. Already someone was out on the street, standing beneath one of the plane trees, she imagined, waiting for her to emerge from the Jackson Hotel and get into his zebra-striped Holden panel van.

What was this? The beginning of something fictional. Unbidden. Not to mention inconvenient. This was neither the time nor place to get inspired.

The name of the young man waiting outside was Kieran. Or at least that was the name he had used on the notice she'd found taped to the window of the little shop at the top of the block. "See Kieran in the zebra van." The notice had announced his desire to find a travelling companion, someone to share the price of petrol on a journey he planned to make to the west. Mrs C. had turned to look for the van only out of curiosity. She'd had no intention of going anywhere. She and E were to enjoy Sydney for another week yet before flying home, once his conference had ended.

Spilling down the street from the Cross almost as far as the hotel – a three-storey structure with iron-lace balconies – were the backpacker hostels where young people sat out under the plane trees and the blooming hibiscus bushes talking, or writing letters. Car doors were opened all down the curb; people inside brushed their teeth, or lay sleeping on foam mattresses. "For Sale $1200" was taped to a window. "Make me an Offer." Fords, Holdens, Volkswagens – dusty, hand-painted with flowers or stripes or the flags of various countries – all were for sale, presumably so that the young people who'd bought them and used them could afford to fly home. "We MUST sell today!" You imagined planes losing patience and taking off without them.

"I shall be stepping out immediately," Mrs C. said to the hotel owner when he returned with the coffee pot. "But my husband will remain in bed for some time."

"Yes, of course," he said. He might have heard this sort of thing before.

"So you will soon see me walking off with my suitcases and leaving him to settle the bill. And to cope without me as best he can."

Which was to say, she thought, that he would fall apart. She crossed her legs and picked up a knife in order to butter the remaining slice of toast.

Perhaps I should leave him a note, she thought, to the effect that I'm running off with a twenty year-old boy. Perhaps the owner would be happy to give him a message. "Your wife has dumped you in favour of a ride in a striped panel van. She said she could not bear another day of your company. She has gone off to live amongst the goannas and the tiger snakes, sleeping in the nests of emus, eating barbecued wombat at the campfire of some family of blacks. She will take a new name – a long name, full of o's. Charlotte Dongalongaloo."

E would not believe it. He would say, "She has too much imagination for her own good. She likes to be comfortable. She is somewhere sipping a tia maria while the air-conditioner hums."

I shut my notebook on this. I hadn't crossed the Pacific to

become slave to a fictional world, as I would have been happy to do in my study at home. It was time, clearly, to get this trip on the road. Australia itself, I imagined, would soon erase all interest in this infant story from my mind.

Of course I knew better. For me it was quite usual to discover that I was accompanied by fictional presences while I travelled – taking from the journey what they wanted, commenting upon it in their own way, making sure I was never tempted to forget there was more than one way of responding to whatever was going on. Why should things be any different now? Almost certainly I would become interested in the abandoned husband. Perhaps he and a friend from Braidwood would set off together into the outback to find her – stepping into the unknown, as I was about to do myself. I couldn't help but wonder what lay ahead for all of us. I'd convinced myself that I wanted to live inside an Australian narrative, but I could not escape the fact that while I was doing this, some kind of narrative was intending to live inside me.

Saturday, after we'd lunched at the Hyatt with the Australian Society of Authors, Roger set off to get his car for the three-hour drive to Braidwood. We would meet in Canberra the following Friday, and drive to his farm to make our final preparations. I went out onto the "footpath" to walk downtown, forgetting that Australia closed down on Saturday afternoons. While waiting at a crosswalk for the sign to change, I was startled out of my touristy gawking by a sudden barrage of honking from the car that moved across the intersection. A cream, dust-covered sedan.

It was Roger, of course, and he was not only honking like an exuberant teenager, he was grinning as well, and waving. Private school boy let loose for the holidays at last. Country boy fleeing the city. The envious novelist with her baby on her lap had been right, of course. Two grown-up boys were setting off on an adventure. There went one of them now – already started.

2 *Braidwood revisited*

Pilgrimages, quests, explorations, crusades, and banishments — it may be that no journey has ever begun without someone saying: "Just a minute, there's something I've got to do first."

Roger had described himself as an inlander. Oceans, forests, and mountains have always been my world. I've lived my life on Vancouver Island, within walking if not spitting distance of the sea. After spending any length of time inland I've eventually experienced a powerful, almost painful need to smell the salt-chuck, to glimpse moving water, to let my vision lose itself in the mysteries of forest. Before joining Roger in Canberra, I'd arranged to spend a few days travelling alone down the coastline south from Sydney — through Wollongong, Nowra, and Ulladulla down to Bateman's Bay, a small cray-fishing and oystering town at the mouth of the Clyde River.

In Bateman's Bay a man with a knitted tea-cozy on his head stood fishing off the sea wall boulders. When he'd reeled in something small, he tossed it to me. "A leatherjacket." Striped yellow and blue, this was something I might otherwise see only in an aquarium. In my hands the gasping creature had the rough gritty feel of sharkskin, a giant's armour. If that little fellow had been long enough, the fisherman said, he would have cut off its head just behind that top-knot spike, then peel back the skin. "Delicious." Too short to be eaten, however, this coastal creature was gasping in the waterless world of my hand. I resisted the temptation to see symbolism here, and tossed him back in the sea.

The fisherman had only recently moved to the coast — he'd lived for years in the bush and had no plans to return. He did not envy me what lay ahead. "It has its own kind of beauty out there, I reckon — it's ugly as hell."

The novelist Trevor Shearston also stayed close to the sea. His cottage at Moyura Heads was half-hidden behind leafy bushes, not far from the beach. We walked onto the dunes to look out across the long golden beach where he was accustomed to fishing for his supper. White overlapping bolts of watery lace unrolled from the collapsed waves off the wide blue ocean. Cliff-edge casuarinas leaned their heavy boughs away from the breeze.

"What do you do — how do you fish? Wade in?"

"Yeh. And cast." He pointed out variations in the ocean colour. Two dark stains. This afternoon, fish would be over there.Though a man of the coast, he didn't share the other fisherman's disdain for the rest of the country, even as we looked upon this remarkable scene. It was true that he'd sought out this marine solitude, that he was content to entertain only the occasional guest and visit Sydney no more than a few times a year, but he had once travelled all around the continent. He had been, as he put it, "a folkie".

He and a friend used to sing in pubs, he said. Travelled the country. This was in a campervan, which they'd parked just wherever they'd happened to be at night. He was never in any danger. He'd never felt crowded. As he talked, I imagined an Australia nearly as empty as the surface of ocean before us, yet as interesting as the sea-edge life at our feet.

Snaking upward into the Coastal Mountains, I was too intent on keeping to the narrow pavement to pay much attention to views — which I could tell, at the edges of my vision, were spectacular. Even to risk a glance was to cause the bottom of my stomach to fall away. You wanted to throw yourself over just to end the suspense. No-one had warned me this climb would be so steep. No-one had told me Australia even possessed anything so close to the perpendicular.

It seemed this was the wall that must be scaled to gain entry to the rest. On the far side of the mountains at last — no, there was no far side to these mountains, they just rose to their summits and forgot they were supposed to plummet again, they levelled out and became a plateau that would stretch, presumably, across the remainder of the continent. When the world levelled out, that is, I rejoiced to feel the heat and humidity give way to dry cool air. Instead of the green chaos of brilliant forest, here was a long undulating stretch of dry brown grass. A few cows. A few horses. The occasional clapboard iron-roofed house. Grass was chewed to the roots, except for tufts of what must have been unsavory weed. A bull stood in sunlight, stunned by his thoughts. Maybe he was dizzy — knew that the edge of the world was nearby — trying to keep himself fastened to the earth.

· Roger met me at the Budget office on Lonsdale Street in Canberra, where I turned in the "hire car". The bits of hay stuck to his black pullover sweater suggested that the streets of the capital, like the streets of Sydney, could take him or leave him just as he was.

"You get enough of the coast for a while?"

I'd had enough. "Ready to go."

Not quite ready yet. We spent the day in Canberra buying some of the things we would need: large plastic containers for all the water we would have to carry, gas cylinders for boiling the billy on the side of the road, gas lamps, groceries, an Itty Bitty Book Light.

Itty Bitty Book Light? I'd never heard of such a thing but Roger was certain we needed one. One each, in fact, so that we could read in our tents at night. We raced from bookshop to bookshop, asking clerks if they stocked this valuable item.

"Itty Bitty Book Light?"

I couldn't believe a manufacturer would take a chance like that. What adult would ever ask for one?

Yet Roger did not blush when he said the words. Clerks did not roll their eyes when they heard him. Perhaps a people that saw nothing ludicrous in referring to their most violent game of sports as "footy" saw nothing silly in two grown men asking for Itty Bitty Book Lights. Footy. Mozzie. Uni. Truckies. Greenies. People who called Christmas Chrissie could not be embarrassed by any sort of infant talk.

This contraption was indeed small, as its name implied, though it came in a box the size and shape of a hardcover book. A fragile plastic thing of folding arms and swivelling joints attached to a battery case with a long black cord – it was made to clip onto the back cover of a book, its little electric bulb arched over and down like a street lamp outside a doll house, so that it could shine a light on the page. When I walked out of a shop with one of these under my arm, I could not believe that passersby weren't stopping to jeer, or at least nudging one another and giggling.

In case we decided to be lazy at times, we set off to a department store in search of folding chairs. Unfortunately the most comfortable were also the most embarrassingly gaudy in colour, bound in shiny plastic. There were only two choices: one was a two-tone blue, the other grey with a pink stripe – the colour of the small parrot I'd seen fly up in noisy flocks from alongside the road: galah. We set one of each out in the aisle. Roger quickly claimed the blue – sat in it – and indicated the grey one was mine.

"Why?"

"Because I want this one."

"Well, I know what these colours suggest. And I know what people mean when they call someone a galah." This was what reading Australian fiction could do for you. I sat down hard, as though to suggest I preferred the pink and grey one anyway. And folded my arms.

I was not the only one who looked the fool at the moment. We spread wide our knees, and leaned back. And grinned. We pulled old-men faces. "*You finished with the funny papers yet, Merv?*" No question, these chairs were meant for a couple of senior citizens, to set out under the canopy by their caravan where they could watch the kangaroos hop by.

This was no time for pride. We bought them anyway. Who that we knew would ever see us sitting in them? Besides, by the time we'd finished making fools of ourselves in the aisle of the Target department store, we'd become quite attached to those chairs. The rest looked far too ordinary now for us.

It didn't matter to me whether we ever used them. The important thing was that they had been an opportunity to find out that we didn't have to take ourselves too seriously. Already this trip had taken on a mock-epic flavour. Whatever myths our journey might appear to echo, it was important they be undercut with a healthy dose of irony, mocked with a little irreverence, turned upside down so that any loose scraps of stiff solemnity would fall out fast.

We arrived at Spring Farm after dark, having picked up both Elinor (the eldest McDonald daughter) in Canberra for her weekend at home from school and Anna (the second daughter) from a friend's party, to be welcomed by Stella (third daughter) who was disappointed to discover I did not have snow on my ears or icicles hanging from my nose as she had hoped.

Rhyll had spent the day in Braidwood waiting for repairs to be done to the truck we'd be taking. A new fuel gauge. You did not go to the places we were going without knowing how much fuel was in your tank. The problem was that the new gauge was proving to be unreliable. Rhyll didn't think we should leave without doing something about it; Roger felt this was not a reason to worry.

The truck in question was parked in the open garage across the grassy lawn from the house. I saw it for the first time next morning. It wasn't quite what I'd expected. A pale yellow, rust-spotted '71 Holden one-tonner with a wooden tray on the back. I don't know that I'd expected a high shining Landcruiser four wheel drive, or a Toyota utility truck with 'roo bar and spot lights and water bags hanging in front of the rad. Maybe I had some idea that we'd be riding in a pickup truck of the sort I've wanted to own all my life but have found no rational excuse for buying – a high-cabbed round-fendered, deep-bedded '56 Chev, maybe? For some reason, I hadn't yet noticed that in this country the closest thing to a pickup truck looked like a family sedan with the back half sawed off and replaced by a sort of bathtub (the newer models) or a stone-boat (Roger's). Hardly a glamour vehicle, especially when the cab roof was so low it appeared – from outside – to be cutting off the top of the driver's head.

Maybe it would not have been possible to grow affectionate towards a Landcruiser or a Toyota 4x4. This truck, like some old horses, looked as though it needed someone to take it along on an adventure – perhaps its last. There must have been some crusaders who rode sway-backed old nags, pilgrims who walked in holey shoes. I did wish, though, that one or the other of us had some mechanical skill.

What it needed most before it went anywhere was a good scrub. Anna and Stella gave it that. A bucket of hot water. Scrubbing brushes. A hose. Even the rust patches started to shine.

Spring Farm was such a pleasant place that I began to wonder if I wanted to give it up in favour of the unknown. Shaded by a grove of trees, the McDonalds' house provided a combination of openness and privacy – the cool veranda and the large glass-walled country kitchen were inside and out at once, while the more private rooms were mysteries behind doors. I already had an affection for the sprawling openness of much Australian architecture. I wondered if there was a connection between this and the famous Australian hospitality. Had the climate which encouraged an architecture of verandas and louvres and patios – houses without walls, so to speak – also encouraged an openness of spirit to go with it? Had Canadian homes, which began as fortresses against the weather, become fortresses against the stranger too?

Spring Farm was more than home, it was also a business – Rhyll's. When she wasn't writing poetry she was raising sheep. In the area surrounding the house, Roger had created a private botanical garden. Tall rows of poplars rustled not far from native ribbon gums. Tiny Douglas firs from Canada lived precariously within protective sleeves at the foot of a hill crowned with twisted eucalyptus. Rows and rows of uniform pines were a startling green, unnatural in this setting of

brown grassy hills. Roger referred to this potential timber as
his retirement fund.

His place of work was a study created out of an old garage,
a sensible distance from the house. The walls of this large,
high-ceilinged room were decorated with maps, with snapshots of people – including those he'd cooked for, celebrat-
ing at their "cut out" party – and with photographs of low
red barren-looking landscapes. Plenty of floor for pacing,
plenty of reference material laid out along the counters,
plenty of cool silence. The actual writing machinery, the desk
and paper and computer, looked down on all of this from up
in a loft. The writer in his floating tree house was twice removed from most distractions of the world.

The weekend provided an opportunity to practise certain
necessary skills. Out on the grass, I demonstrated (eventually) that I could set up Roger's mother's little igloo-shaped
red-and-white tent without tearing the canvas or breaking the
poles or collapsing in a heap of frustration. The drive to
Braidwood offered plenty of opportunity to learn how to hop
out, run ahead, open a gate, close it again, make sure it was
properly hitched, and run back to jump into the truck, or the
family car. Although I'd referred to myself as Roger's "sidekick" Roger preferred that I think of myself as his official
gate-opener. This was all right with me, though the metaphor
was inappropriate. It was not this foreign hanger-on who
would be opening gates that would otherwise have been
closed.

Driving home from a bush walk in the coastal mountains,
we stopped in Braidwood where Roger picked up the truck
from its final visit to the mechanics and suggested that if I followed in the family sedan with Rhyll and Stella I could jump
out and open each gate for both vehicles to drive through.
When he'd driven off, we discovered he'd taken the keys to
the sedan with him. No amount of dancing up and down on
the main street brought him back. We leaned against the car.
We looked at our watches. We paced. We paid quick point-
less visits to a number of shops. Rhyll phoned home to tell the
girls what had happened, in case he went the entire distance

and forgot us altogether. (Not entirely unlikely, she suggested, and laughed. Rhyll McMaster's laugh was a low, level, gentle, and sexy rumble that would continue, like underlining, just beneath the comments and exclamations of others.) It would take an hour to get all the way to Spring Farm and back, but we could hope he'd notice soon that we weren't behind him.

I didn't particularly want to be involved in a situation where my host would find himself feeling foolish in front of an audience. How did I know his embarrassment wouldn't turn to anger and that he wouldn't turn his anger on me? Maybe I would find out today that the man I was about to go travelling with threw tantrums when things went wrong.

Most of an hour had passed before I recognised the Holden coming down the street. I was interested in nothing but the look on the driver's face.

"What happened?" he said, when he'd got out of the truck. He was smiling. Half smiling. "Why didn't you follow me?"

"You've got the key."

He felt in his pocket. He seemed relieved to discover the problem was such a simple one. "I couldn't make out what that look on Jack's face meant," he said to Rhyll.

"I was just trying to gauge the look on yours," I said. "So that I'd know whether I ought to make myself scarce."

"So what took you so long to figure out that we weren't behind you?" Rhyll said.

"I stopped at the first gate and waited. When you didn't pull up behind me I started to read the paper."

Rhyll heaved in a long deep sigh and took the keys. "Roger and the *Sydney Morning Herald*." Evidently this was a combination impervious to the existence of the outer world.

When we'd returned to the farm I asked if there was a second key to the truck. "Just in case something like this happens when we're a million miles from anything." I was given a key. No one suggested I was being overly cautious. To a certain extent – everyone seemed to suggest – I'd better be prepared to look out for myself.

Certain language must be mastered before any trip can

commence. I was greedy to become bilingual. My introduction to the speech of this continent took place in an incidental fashion throughout the weekend — at the kitchen table, out walking around the farm, driving to town, down the Old Corn Trail, having coffee with friends at the Altenburg Cafe. I picked up whatever swam by. No, the truck we would take was not, unfortunately, to be called a "ute", a term I had learned from novels. The rusted yellow '71 Holden was not a ute or a lorry, and obviously not a road train or anything else excitingly foreign — it was just, disappointingly, a truck. A "one-tonner". I knew already that it had a bonnet rather than a hood, but I now discovered that what I thought was its rear-view mirror was its rear vision mirror, its windshield a windscreen, and its glove compartment not a compartment at all but a box.

The insulated chests in which we would keep ice, drinks, and perishable food, were not "coolers" but "Eskies". (Named after Eskimos? How would I break the news that you were not supposed to say "Eskimo" any more? What would Australians do with "Innuit?") When we drove down a road just to see what was there, or stopped to look at a farmer's crop, what we were doing was sticky-beaking. We would be sticky-beaking much of the trip ahead. And while we were sticky-beaking around the country, the places we would hope to put up our tents were "caravan parks" and not the "trailer parks" I thought them to be.

"If Canadians call caravans 'trailers' then what do they call the two-wheeled things you haul machinery in behind your car?"

"Trailers as well."

"So how do you distinguish between the two?"

"I don't know." Suddenly it seemed I was in the thrall of an inadequate language. "We used to say 'house trailers' but you don't hear that any more. Now everybody's got a — what they call a recreational vehicle." Just saying it was enough to make me cringe. I refused to explain that most people just called them RV's. Or that I had relatives who roamed the continent in RV's bigger than Greyhound buses, each pulling a compact car behind, and a boat-and-trailer behind the car. So far I hadn't seen any such thing on these roads, thank goodness.

Shop clerks in Braidwood, like the clerks in Canberra, said "You're right" instead of "You're welcome" to your "Thanks". This was not, so far as I could tell, a way of acknowledging the old saying that the customer was always right. Rather, it seemed to be roughly equivalent to "That's all right". Not too distantly related to "She'll be right, mate", and "Too right", and "Right, then, this ratbag's got kangaroos in his top paddock if he reckons I'm goin' walkabout with him." The word "right" enjoyed a longer, more satisfying run past the tongue and teeth that it's ever been allowed on the North American continent. Here, it sounded (to my ears) something like "ryyyyte", or sometimes even "royyyyte", so that you imagined the speaker might want to lick his lips with satisfaction after saying it.

Of course I knew that the places we would be visiting in order to interview shearers were stations rather than ranches, but I hadn't known that the families who owned them were sometimes graziers, sometimes pastoralists, and squatters only if their ancesters had grabbed the land in the early stages of colonyhood.

"A small farmer?"

"A cocky."

This was derived from cockatoo. Cow cockies, fruit cockies, scrub cockies.

"Someone who can't make a living off the land but keeps trying is called a battler. He'd have a 'battler block' somewhere out in the bush and work in a shop in town."

"And I keep forgetting to ask someone. What's a panel beater?" I'd seen the sign on large blank corrugated iron buildings here and there but could never guess what might be going on inside. A crowd of people all beating – panels? Panels of what?

"You don't have panel beaters in Canada?"

"Not to my knowledge."

It was too silly to say this out loud. I'd wondered if panels might possibly be an Australian word for carpet – surely carpets and tapestries were made up of panels – so that a "panel beaters" shop might be full of people slamming tennis racquets against hanging rugs. Or some modern version of this process – the name a holdover from earlier days. Not very likely but it was the image which had occurred to me nevertheless.

"It's where you'd take your car after a collision – to have the dents taken out. What do they call a place like that in Canada?"

"A body shop. You'd take your car to a body shop."

"Body shop? Body shop?" Roger laughed. It seemed to me that he took a sort of contemptuous delight in this bit of news. "Sounds like a chain of cosmetic merchandisers to me!"

Some things you were glad to learn before setting out. Not to take it personally when Roger disappeared into the *Sydney Morning Herald*, for instance. To remind yourself that his occasional absent-mindedness was only a match for your own. (That I was strangely comforted by this might suggest a curiously inadequate instinct for self-preservation.) To be thankful for his willingness – from long practice as a husband, father, and object of the mechanics' fond scorn for an appealing incompetent – to laugh at himself where another might take himself more seriously. I was pleased, too, to discover ahead of time that Roger's eagerness always to get a quick and early start at things was less likely to make you a nervous wreck once you noticed that his last-minute phone calls and just-remembered tasks made it impossible for him ever to meet his own deadlines.

"Where has he got to now?" Rhyll would roll her eyes, ready to get in the car.

"He's on the telephone again," one of the girls would say.

Rhyll would sigh, and shake her head. "Roger?" No answer. "If we're not leaving right now, I'm going back in to bake a cake." I thought this was a family figure of speech but she meant it literally. Even when the cake came out of the oven there were still more phone calls to be made, more last-minute things to be taken care of. I was glad my family wasn't here to witness this, and to let it be known how familiar all of this seemed.

April first. Sunday afternoon. Time to pack the truck — which stood ready by the gate, gleaming from its wash. No crusader's steed had ever been given such careful grooming. No pilgrim's shoes had ever been so lovingly re-soled. So what if the petrol gauge didn't work, and the long-handled crank for raising and lowering the spare tire in its cradle had broken? The truck was ready to take on its load.

We set everything out on the grass by the gate — tenting equipment, sleeping gear, suitcases, water containers, cardboard boxes of food, Eskies — ready to be fitted into the shallow wooden tray and covered over with the strapped-down tarp.

Out in the machinery shed, we went through Roger's check-list." "Two extra fan belts. Do you know how to put a fanbelt on?"

"I could if I had to," I said. "I think. At least I know where it goes. We could figure it out if we had to."

"We'll take this bucket of chains, in case we're bogged somewhere and need to be pulled out."

Roger said that in his books Jack Absalom recommended a plastic air bag which attaches to the exhaust pipe and inflates beneath the vehicle, lifting it clear of the ground. We would be doing without this amazing invention.

A plastic air bag? I had no way of knowing whether this was a case of excessive caution. I remembered, suddenly, the image of the four-wheel drive pulling itself out of a creek in *The Gods Must be Crazy* and winching itself right up into a tree where it hung like a side of beef.

"Two jerry cans of petrol — just in case."

"And you put out the water containers we bought?"

"And a third. Here's the WD40."

"A spare tire?" (Impossible to think of the word as "tyre", though I knew that "tyre" was what it must be to Roger.)

"We've got three spare wheels ready to load on the truck."

"They'll take up most of the room."

"We'll be glad of them if we need them. Jack Absalom

says we should take extra gaskets. You want to grab those down off the wall?"

I suspected that this would not be the last time Jack Absalom's name would be invoked. Apparently this man was the supreme authority on outback travel. There was no point in producing the little paperback I'd purchased in Kings Cross, a guidebook on Going Bush. Not in the face of Jack Absalom's reputation with the present company.

When the truck was finally packed, with everything fitted tightly into its place, and we stood back to think if there might be anything forgotten, I recalled that moment when we were parked above the private school in Sydney, with its fences and drill yard and uniforms. "I hated it." Wherever it was we were going now − dusty plains and woolsheds full of sheep and small towns baking in the sun − I had the feeling that in some peculiar way that schoolyard was really what we both were leaving behind. Don't fence me in.

3 The road to Gundagai, and beyond

5:30 am. The sound of an engine starting in the silence just prior to dawn calls up from childhood a hushed excitement that chills the bones. A sense of parting the curtains of night for a secret venture into a sleeping world. As we started down the lane, I thought of mornings when I'd been taken from bed to sit wrapped half-asleep in the back seat while the family drove down-island to catch the steamship to Vancouver. And of early morning hunting trips with my father and his friends, setting out into the mountains where willow grouse and deer were unaware of the fate sneaking up on them. Excitement and gnawing anxiety both – "My God, how fortunate can you be?" and "What have I gone and got myself into now?"

Was I ready for this? I'd put on a long-sleeved shirt (for morning chill) over a short sleeved t-shirt (for daytime heat). Brand new Reeboks, blindingly white. A new kangaroo-hide bush hat (purchased in Kings Cross) rested between my shoulder blades. Also purchased in Kings Cross: a fat Olympic Stripe notebook in which I would nightly try to make sense of the day. In my suitcase under the tarp were new shorts in case I ever got up the nerve to wear them, a new bathing suit in case I underwent a complete personality change, and my paperback copy of *Going Bush* just in case the combined wisdom of Jack Absalom and Roger McDonald should ever fail us.

Obviously I was a foreign traveller setting out, but Roger was a man going off to work. His equipment rode between us on the seat: spiral notebooks, camera, maps, insulated bag for keeping film safe from sun. Figs to munch on. His Akubra was propped between the back of his seat and the window.

Tawny suede hills and darker creases began to appear as we moved down the long dirt road. Gate after gate must be opened, then closed. A soft mist hung in the air. Pale clouds had moved in from the coast. A hare leapt out from somewhere and went hopping down the track ahead of us. A fox streaked across and disappeared. Then everything was still and rigid again, in this silence. Hereford cattle stood staring out of the brown sepia landscape as we passed – like the naked gum trees they stood at silent attention in honour of our setting out.

Beyond sleeping Canberra, we drove up through the brown landscape to Yass, where we turned left onto the Hume Highway and started down the road which led to Gundagai. I wasn't sure why "the road to Gundagai" had a familiar and romantic ring to it. Something to do with a song.

Above Gundagai we looked down on the Murrumbidgee River, which we would be following, more or less, all day. It wandered in tight curves along the snaky gully, its edges flanked by a crowded guard of eucalyptus trees. Passing up the opportunity to visit the statue of the dog on the tucker box, we drove down in to town and stopped for coffee at a small cafe – chosen by Roger as much for its name as for its location: the Niagara Restaurant and Coffee Lounge. Did people in fabled Gundagai think fabled Niagara was more exotic? Or had a homesick Canadian expatriate named the place? (The drawing on the paper serviette was from the Canadian side of the falls, though backwards.) We drank coffee and munched down raisin toast in a booth where people must have sat for coffee and raisin toast in the thirties or forties, in the same leather-and-arborite decor.

Outside, buildings blared with an excess of brightly coloured signs: BROADWAY RESTAURANT, TUCKERBOX FOODMASTER SUPERMARKET AND DISCOUNT LIQUOR, HOTEL GRESHAM. If the light from the sky did not hurt your eyes, the signs on the storefronts would.

Some distance down the Sturt Highway, heading west, the

curved and gently hilly landscape began to flatten out, as though submitting to the heavy weight of the glaring sky. Beyond Wagga Wagga (pronounced Wawga Wawga, as I'd been instructed by a Wagga Wagga resident in Adelaide; or simply Wawga in the Australian way of shortening any word or name that could survive the amputation) it appeared as though the flattest stretches of southern Manitoba had been left too long beneath a scorching sun. Spotted with low green tufts like an ancient worn-thin chenille bedspread, the plains were broken by only the occasional eucalypt. Although there was little sign out there that anything lived or moved, there was plenty of evidence along the road that several things recently had. Kangaroos, wallabies, and possums lay with limbs or half a body stretched out onto the pavement, as though arrested in the act of reaching for something that would never be attained.

Emus seemed to have more sense than to try. A family of three large birds strutted regally through the dried grass alongside the road. They ventured a little closer when we stopped. The working man was as pleased as the foreign tourist by this. He tapped on the cab roof to attract their attention. "They're supposed to be curious." Out came the cameras. But the emus – who looked to me as though they'd wandered onto the wrong planet and were mystified by their error – were not so curious as we'd hoped, nor so eager to have their photos taken that they came right up to the truck. Perhaps they were insulted by our interest. (On their own planet, they were considered quite normal.) Away they hurried – or strutted as fast as it was possible to strut without sacrificing their immense dignity – dark feathers all afloat.

We talked about writing, of course. Two writers passionately dedicated to fiction were setting out on a journey which would end in a work of nonfiction. The driver was the more experienced at it; the visitor was curious to learn how it was done.

After university, Roger had, like myself, become a teacher. But while I was busy manipulating a teaching career in order to make writing fiction possible – leaves-without-pay and an eventual shift from high school to university – he'd discovered almost immediately that he hated teaching, and gave it up to work as a television producer. He'd published two books of poetry and then abandoned poetry in favour of novels. In order to eat while writing these novels, he'd worked as a publisher's editor, he'd written television scripts and novelised adaptations of television scripts. More recently he'd subsidised his fiction habit by the writing of nonfiction books.

Naturally I wanted to know if he'd discovered the ideal existence. For a novelist, that is. If so, I would pester him with questions, and watch him in action, and find out how this ideal existence was won.

Clearly he enjoyed the work. But he confessed that for the novelist there were frustrations. "There's the difficulty of having to re-imagine, in memory, some situation which you could just make up for fiction. Or alter to suit your own purposes."

Certain practical matters intrigued me. "Have you decided whether you'll use the real names of the shearers you're interviewing?"

He'd already interviewed enough of them to know that not everything he would write would please them.

"I may for some. I'm not sure."

"It isn't as if they don't know what you're up to. They could be careful what they say."

"But they're people who don't read books. I'm sure they haven't thought about it, they just think I'm going to make them famous."

Conversations like this did not last long. Landmarks interrupted. Also it was necessary to raise your voice to be heard above the engine, the humming tyres, the air slapping past the cab. And because it had got very hot, you had to roll the window down once in a while, jacking up the noise level to a roar. To get seriously into a conversation meant rolling up the windows, raising your voice, leaning towards the centre of the cab, and holding your finger in the slats of the broken vents. The pen I'd jammed in to prop it open had long ago dropped inside, where it lay rattling its plastic rattle like a constant rebuke.

It didn't seem to bother Roger that the new fuel gauge was untrustworthy – rose only to half-full and descended from there apparently at whim. He knew how much petrol the tank held, he knew how many kilometres we would get to the litre (approximately). We'd simply have to keep careful books at every fill-up. And not take foolish chances.

To bring in the noon news it was necessary to wallop the radio with the heel of a hand, then roll the tuner up and down the dial until something came in that wasn't static. The effort was unrewarded. Apparently radio stations in this region had little interest in the rest of the world. Wool prices, agricultural wheeling and dealing, the weather. The recent federal election rated only a brief mention – would a certain cabinet minister keep his post? Latest words from the Prime Minister and the leader of the Opposition, Mr Hawke and Mr Peacock – squabbling in this antipodean aviary.

I knew better than to hope for news of home, where the same politicians who had ignored the protests of nationalists when they signed the free trade treaty with the US were now watching in confusion while the country pulled itself apart.

Paddocks of forage sorghum flew past on one side, giant red gums on the other – the river side. A barren stretch of dry grass and white skeletons of ecalyptus trees – long dead but still standing – was very much the sort of thing I'd been led by photographs to expect out here. Russell Drysdale paintings: dead trees, red earth, little else. Where were the skinny elongated humans angling across their dusty yards?

Roger's childhood had been spent in country not far to the north of here – Bribbaree, Temora, and Bourke. What would a country child do with a landscape like this? Climb trees, I supposed.

"Fish for Yabbies. Swim in the dam."

I assumed that those upright zig-zag trees which clawed so picturesquely at the glaring sky had been sucked dry of their life by the harsh yellow sun.

Wrong. "Ring-barking", Roger instructed. Those trees

had not died of drought or over-exposure at all. Farmers had killed them off. Had killed them off deliberately in fact, but had not bothered to fell them. Why should they? It wasn't that those skeletons stood in the way of anything. Getting rid of the grass's competition was all that mattered. Let all the moisture go to the grass, and then to the sheep. "Sometimes they stand for a generation before they fall, or someone cuts them down." This was no peculiarity of a single lazy farmer, I understood, but just how things were done in this peculiar land.

Strange beauty. And sensible too, I supposed. I tried to imagine my parents emigrating to this land and discovering this to be the accepted way of claiming it. It wasn't possible. My father — perhaps the most un-lazy man on the planet — had spent his life (when he was not up a mountain logging trees) carving one field after another out of the thick Vancouver Island forest — felling, cutting, dragging, burning, fencing, ploughing, planting — tidying up the ragged world for man and beast. He would never consider that you'd claimed the land for yourself or your stock so long as you hadn't cleaned up all of man's and nature's mess and set things in proper order.

It didn't take us long to set up our tents on the rich green grass of the caravan park outside the town of Hay. We'd been on the road for nine hours but at three o'clock there was still plenty of time to catch some shearers at work — in particular, to find the Grazcos contractor Roger had arranged to interview. As soon as the tents were up (our claim staked) we got back into the truck and continued still farther west for a few kilometres past the little town. I was about to get my first opportunity to watch, at close range, how a nonfiction writer went about gathering material for his work.

"Mungadal." Merino Stud. The carved merino ram which stood on the top of the sign by the gate looked, in the manner of all stud rams, as though the twin curved horns were pressing so hard against the sides of his skull that his head must hurt. He was painted white — clean and puffy and tidy in the manner of sheep seen munching down the rolling green pastures of New Zealand, say, or Wales. No such rolling green pastures were to be seen in this vicinity, however. This elevated fellow had little in common with the living sheep who had to drag themselves through the dust and saltbush of New South Wales. The white painted fences on either side of him were just as deceptive – they stretched barely far enough to make a good impression, then abandoned the rest of the unimaginably large station to the no-nonsense barriers of barbed wire and weathered posts.

To the left of us, all but naked plain – burnt stubby grass and dust. To the right, behind the fences, a dirt road led across parched earth where the short dusty growth might have been only a film, the downy surface of suede. Beyond one bone-jarring grid and then another, however, we entered the world of riverside gums.

The river seemed a rather poisonous-looking brown-green colour here, creeping past beneath the trees – a mixture of the colours of the leaves and the trunks along the muddy banks, though not merely from their reflection. The water was thick and soupish, almost unmoving. That such a narrow sluggish watercourse was a river of considerable importance suggested something significant about the country.

I imagined a score of venomous snakes looking up with interest upon our arrival. Could tiger snakes, like horses, smell human fear? I was not encouraged by a bleached and broken sheep's skull which lay beside one of the little patches of inedible melons which grew here and there in the dust.

A large gabled barn stood up on crooked stumps, the sun glaring off the great overlapping scales of corrugated iron down its sides. The two halves of a wide door had been flung wide open. Inside, in the shadows, a man sat on a bale of wool thumbing through a magazine.

Before going inside, we went round the side to where rams which had already survived the ordeal of the shed were queued up in a narrow fenced lane to have their horns clipped and something shot down their throats. As if the indignity of waiting naked like army inductees was not bad enough, they displayed what seemed to me an alarming number of bloody nicks and scratches. Had we stumbled into a crew of butchers, or was this considered normal? There had been cases – somewhere – where a shearing handpiece in the hands of even a fine shearer had somehow opened a sheep right up, so that its insides fell out on the floor. There had been cases where sheep had been killed by blows to the head from a shearer impatient with their struggles, and then shorn dead. But Roger assured me there was nothing in what we were seeing to cause alarm. Half a dozen gashes and scrapes were perfectly usual.

Two of the station hands came over to explain what was going on. One of them was a young woman in tight jeans, with a deep freckled tan and long hanks of sun-bleached hair. The tall fellow in khaki shorts and wide-brimmed hat did most of the talking. These rams were to be graded by an expert, he said as he reached down to hoist up his crotch.

One half of them would be culled and sent to Saudi Arabia alive, he said, worth no more than $25. Insulted sheep bleated. Shorn of their dignity and grossly exposed, they still had some of their pride. He hoisted his crotch again.

Of the other half, about 3 per cent would bring in up to $1,000 at auction. Others would go for anywhere down to $499. Again he cupped his hand beneath his genitals and gave them a little bounce. You couldn't help but wonder if this peculiar habit was somehow linked to the job.

John Cain welcomed us, and took us inside. He was a tall lanky man in his early forties, dressed in jeans and a short-sleeved shirt. His dark hair was only beginning to grey. Whenever he said something he thought was particularly interesting or funny, he raised his eyebrows and bugged out his eyes (which vibrated with pleasure) and looked just a little above your own eyes while he laughed. He was the contractor who had agreed to be interviewed for Roger's book, the local representative of Grazcos, which, at seven million sheep a year, was Australia's largest shearing contractor.

Inside, the sound was what you noticed first – the sound of humming combs at work, the sound of men talking with raised voices, the sound of yapping dogs. There were dogs everywhere − some running back and forth, some curled up against a wool sack, some chained to the front bumper of a ute parked just outside. One of the chained-up dogs had been recently hurt − cut open by a fence − and had not yet recovered his courage. A sleek chocolate-brown dog of uncertain breed, it cowered and looked away if you glanced in its direction; it stood up and moved to one side if you came too close.

The shed which enclosed all this noise was constructed on the post-and-beam principle. The large sheets of corrugated iron were laid over a skeleton of round posts adzed where cross pieces of lumber joined them. Straight ahead was the widest wing, divided into pens for the crowds of sheep waiting their turn at the shears; to our left was the wool presser's hydraulic press, where bags of wool were filled and sealed and labelled; to the right was a corridor of fourteen shearers at work.

Roger set about taking photos. The interview would happen later, so John returned to his magazine. He made it clear I was free to snoop around all I wished, or ask questions. I tried not to look too much like a kid set loose in a brand new playground, but I was determined to cram it all in, and to understand as much as possible as well.

The shearers on the left side of the hall used electric combs, those on the right used combs run by the spinning shaft along their wall. All of them bent over the sheep between their knees. One leaned through a harness attached to the ceiling, apparently to reduce the strain on his back. It seemed that the belly and crotch were shorn first, then the top knot, then the throat, and then finally down over the shoulders and right on down the length of the side − the "long blow". The sheep was gradually rolled from one side to the other. Astonishingly, aside from a few nervous kicks at the beginning, none of the sheep protested the treatment or tried to escape or even seemed to notice when nicks were gouged out of their hides.

When a sheep had been completely "undressed" the shearer pushed it through a hole in the wall and down a chute.

He wiped his hands and sweaty face on the cloth which hung from a post. Then he went in through a gate to grab himself another sheep, and to drag it out onto his own small portion of the floor, polished a yellow lanolin shine. All this was done with such a fluid sequence of confident motions that watching these men was not unlike watching a fine ballet dancer on the stage, or a superb athlete displaying a thrilling variety of skills.

Young men in jeans and sleeveless shirts that I thought of as undershirts — but which were called "singlets" here — grabbed up the bits of dirty or "daggy" wool and tossed them into open bags. They gathered the fleeces to their chests and tossed them onto the slatted wool-classer's table with arms thrown wide apart. They grabbed long handled brooms and went about gathering up the stray bits of wool, rather like hockey-players stick-handling the puck through the constant movements of the other players.

(Both Roger and John referred to these youths as "razzabats", which seemed a rather peculiar term to me but no more peculiar than everything else I was being introduced to that day. "Razzabats" was what they were until I came upon the term "rouseabout" in a book several days later. Absurdly, I then adjusted my own pronunciation to suit the written version — no more able to continue saying "razzabat" than I was able to start calling Roger "Rogah" like everyone else.)

A good shearer would do thirty rams in a run, John told me. A run was the two-hour stretch between breaks: starting time to smoko, smoko to lunch, etc. They were paid twice as much for rams as for ewes or wethers, because they had to take more care. Some of these men would be earning $230 a day.

The smell of lanolin and sweat and dust was not unpleasant. This was probably because the ceiling was high and a breeze ran through the opened doorways. Perhaps I was surprised because I was used to barns and stables that were closed in against the weather. This was an open-air country, where inside and outside were not so rigorously kept separate.

Since we were coming up to quitting time, some of the rouseabouts were bringing tomorrow's rams into the shed – a thousand of them. Above the sound of four thousand feet on the slatted floor – like heavy rain on a roof – was the noise of dogs yapping, men yelling, fists banging on rails to keep the sheep moving, filling up every pen. Noisiest and busiest of them all was the wool-presser, an intense, pleasant, eager young man named Mark.

This wool-presser was trying to be everywhere at once. One moment he was carefully stencilling the name of the company onto a wool bale, the next he was racing off to give someone else a hand. When he returned to his post, I asked him if he was expected to help the others so much or had he taken on this sort of thing on his own. What was the nature of his job? He crouched down and gathered in his two small black-and-white chained pups – one against either side. "I press the bale, do a bit of cleaning up, help on the board, do the table." Years ago, he said, it had been decided – by the union, I understood – that the presser should do nothing else but press, but he had never been content with that himself. Trouble is, "if you're a real good worker you can work yourself right into the ground. There's no end to the work you can do." At that he went thudding off again, to grab up a broom and help the rouseabouts clean up the floor of the shearing wing.

"I think we've hit the jackpot," Roger said, as we got back into the truck to drive away. He looked, at that moment, every bit as delighted as I felt myself.

"Back to the park now?"

"Just time for a shower. John's invited us to meet him at six, at the pub. Looks like you're going to get inside one of those old hotels you like so much."

In fact, the Commercial Hotel had quite a bit in common with old hotels found in small towns anywhere in Canada – peaked roof, two storeys, verandas right around. What I'd

hoped for (thanks to the movies) was a sort of sprawling and
exotic airy bird cage where indoor and outdoor flowed back
and forth through louvres and latticed screens, reminiscent of
old-time opera galleries and balconies for presidential procla-
mations. Although this one did not have lacy ironwork railings it had any number of doors you could go in and out of.
And it was decorated with plenty of colourful signs: VICTORIA
BITTER, SUNDAY ROAST, VACANCY, NOW OPEN, FOSTERS LAGER
FOSTERS LAGER FOSTERS LAGER. Farther down the street, still
more gaudy signs blared off the fronts of stores. HAY LI-
CENSED TUCKERBAG, AMCAL CHEMIST, PARAGON CAFE.

Angle parking here was reverse-in to the footpath. A peculiar scene. If nose-in angle parking suggested the tied-up
horse contentedly waiting for its owner's return, this backed-
in parking made me think of rows of impatient mounts, all
straining for the sound of a starter gun to set them in motion.

When we entered, only two men were seated at the front
bar. They turned, decided we were of little interest, and went
on talking. We ordered – one beer and one coke. Unlike bar-
tenders in Australian movies, this one did not scoff at the person who ordered the coke. He was more interested in
watching me sort through a pocketful of heavy coins in search
of the right amount.

Surely here I would be able to watch Roger in action. I'd
got so interested in soaking up all that woolshed business that
I'd hardly noticed how he went about doing his job. Just taking photos and talking softly to this person or that. I really
ought to have stuck closer to him, to listen in. I vowed that in
this place I would try not to be carried away by what was
around me, I'd keep my eye on the nonfiction writer at work.

The nonfiction writer didn't have to do much to get our
first visitor to talk – just shake his hand and offer him a beer.
This man was someone John Cain considered the best of his
shearers – "the gun". Showered and changed and polished
up, he was pleased for the chance to talk. He wasted no time
in laying out his credentials. For instance, he'd recently married a woman twenty-five years his junior.

A small man with a round face, he barely moved when he

spoke – his beer glass held halfway to his mouth, his eyes held hard on yours, his lips smiling. He talked too fast for me to catch much of what he said, but I gathered that he was enjoying his married life. This would explain why he would not be staying with us long.

Of course he had been through a bad marriage breakup, he said. But he'd had ninety girlfriends before he'd married his new wife.

He quickly tossed back each glass of beer and placed it on the counter. I wondered if he chose to drink from a small glass to make sure those who expected him to talk for the sake of some book were constantly keeping the glass replaced. I knew I had better remember the importance of the famous Australian shout.

When John Cain arrived, he suggested we move to the back room – which could be seen through the gap which had been opened up in the wall so that the bartender could handle both bars at once.

A small crowd had already gathered in the back room – some playing darts, some staring at the television hanging off the back wall, some perched on the stools along the bar itself while others stood just behind. We took a table against the side wall.

One of the people at the bar was a young woman who'd only recently started a job as a rouseabout. The job – and her weariness from it – was entertaining the crowd. "Oh Jesus, don't tell me that," she said, "I'm ratshit as it is, I'm the tiredest rousey this side of the black stump." She showed off the tape which had been wrapped around her hands to protect them from blisters. She was dressed in jeans, and wore her long reddish hair in a pony tail.

When the newlywed excused himself to go home to his wife (grinning meaningfully), the young woman rouseabout joined our table for supper, having gone off somewhere to alter her appearance first. Her red hair was down – long and shiny – her make-up had been applied with a professional care, her jeans had been replaced by an attractive blouse and skirt. For a while I didn't realise she was the same person.

The colloquial speech at the bar had been replaced with something a little more self-consciously classy. When I asked her about her new job, she answered in a movie star way, blowing smoke at the ceiling, posing against the back of her chair, pursing her tight thin lips, speaking in a bored manner ("Oh, Jesus −"), speaking not to me but to some idea in the back of her head.

Her judgments and complaints were directed off, like her smoke, to every side. Everything was unbearable, her manner suggested, but everything was also more interesting than you could imagine, full of things that could not quite be said, and somehow infinitely boring to a glamorous and beautiful woman who came − apparently − from elsewhere. The City.

The toilet on the station where she was currently working came in for some abuse. It was a pit toilet. She wouldn't use it. She was scared of it.

"That's the last pit toilet in the state," John said. "They're illegal." She ought to be honoured to use it, his tone implied.

"Well I'm not using it," she said. She snapped out the words and pursed her lips, and switched her hair back and forth, as though to suggest someone would be sorry. "I'm scared I'll fall in. I won't go near it. That's it."

One young man stood leaning against the bar, talking to no-one. Beneath a hat which was far too big, he stared into space and looked pleased with himself, satisfied simply to look the role he'd chosen.

One of the women at our table had only recently returned to Hay, where she'd been raised. She drove a taxi now but wasn't sure she was glad to be back. To begin with, she'd had to leave school early because she'd hit a teacher with a baseball bat. "Now the twins've got the same teacher."

"A baseball bat?"

"Yeh."

The Australian "yeh" is an incompleted "yes" quite unlike the American "yeah", and requires a slight pinching of the nostrils so that it sometimes has the quality of a sneer. As with many Australian comments there is a sort of question mark at the end − not necessarily implying doubt on the speaker's part but suggesting offence at the questioner's possible doubt. She could have been saying, "You think I'd lie about a thing like that?"

"I didn't mean to hit the teacher. I was aimin' at this friend I hated."

Now that she was driving a taxi, one of her goals was to run this same old enemy/girlfriend down. "Almost got 'er th' other day too!"

Other groups came in and stopped to joke with John Cain – other shearing crews, I gathered – then settled at other tables or joined in the game of darts. One serious couple had a table to themselves, eating supper, looking at the television they could not hear, not sure what they'd stumbled in on. I recognised that tourist feeling. Perhaps I was finding out already what writing nonfiction could do for you – shift you over from being the puzzled anonymous observer trying to guess at the meaning of what you witnessed to being the welcomed and privileged guest. For a change, you didn't have to observe from the fringes of things.

How was the nonfiction researcher doing? No trouble getting these people to talk. It may be that he'd earned their trust by talking about his time as a shearer's cook. Certainly it would count for more here than just "a writer working on a book". He hadn't used his tape recorder yet or reached for a notebook, but listened hard – arms folded, his gaze on the table, or on the toe of his forward boot.

"I imagine you remember the wide-comb dispute."

"Yeh." John Cain remembered it, but looked away. "All that's better put behind us is my way of looking at it. People have got to get along."

This calm patient habit of looking down while the other person spoke probably encouraged ease and frankness – nobody watching your face to weigh words against body language. But I wondered if Roger had heard what my eyes had seen – how this question about the wide-comb dispute, however softly put, had made more than one person a little uneasy.

John would rather talk about Anzac Day – he'd already

started the countdown. Did I know what he meant? I did.
We'd witnessed the New Zealand version three years ago in
Christchurch. Much pomp and ceremony. Gallipoli haunted
everyone for a day.

"Twenty-fifth of April. I've got it arranged. I always take
three days off."

"Three days?"

He always drove down to Albury, where he used to live, to
spend the day with his old mates from Vietnam. "The third
day is to recover from the first two before I go back to the
shed."

Drink and recovering from drink. The grog was an occupa-
tional hazard, several agreed. Too much grog had got too
many shearers into trouble. One shearer had recently spent
some time in jail − for beating his wife. "Unfortunately, the
man had a gun in his hand at the time."

"He wrote me this letter from gaol. 'Can't you get me another shed, John? This one don't have no sheep.'"

Voices joined to tell of a shearer who'd got drunk and
killed several other shearers with his rifle. Heads were
shaken. Mouths set. There were certain dangers built right
into this life.

The novice rouseabout complained about someone named
Prong. She wasn't satisfied with his work. She didn't like
working with him at all. When all his personality faults and
bad work habits had been discussed, I wanted to know why
anyone would be named Prong.

I should have known better. John slid back and pointed at
his own crotch.

The young woman did not understand. "What? What?"
The taxi driver's delighted grin suggested she understood
perfectly.

John leaned across the table. "He's got a huge one!"

Horror and delight. "What!" Both hands flew to her face.
"Oh God, I'll never be able to talk to him again! I'll never be
able to call him THAT! Why didn't someone tell me?"

By ten o'clock I began to feel the day had been long
enough. Gundagai seemed so distant that the Niagara Res-

taurant might as well be overlooking the falls that shared its name. We'd been up since 5; we'd been on the road for 600 kilometres (600 k's, as they said here); I couldn't force another coke down my throat. But Roger had just been introduced to some old fellow at the bar. Someone apparently with a yarn to tell.

At eleven the day had become too long for Roger, too. It was time to head for the tents.We were warned that the police kept an eye out for people who came from the pub, so Roger handed over the keys to the truck. It was up to me to get us home. A block or so down the main street, it seemed that the lights had not come on, though I'd pulled the appropriate switch. We stopped to check. High beam yes, low beam no. If the truck was beginning to fall apart like this at the end of the first day, what would it do when we were out beyond civilisation altogether?

We agreed to worry about the headlights in the morning and drove with our lights on high beam back to the caravan park. A moon sent down enough light to paint shadows of the big red gums across the grass. Roger pointed out the saucepan and the southern cross – which would have turned over by morning – from amongst the patterns in that foreign sky. He was tempted, he said, to forget the tent and sleep out under the stars. For someone from the coast of British Columbia this seemed the ultimate folly – a clear invitation for the sky to dump buckets of rain.

Once I'd crawled into my little red and white igloo tent I scribbled a few notes in my journal. Not many. Since this journey was for the sake of Roger's book and, for that reason, not mine to write about, I needn't worry so much as usual about getting things down. Instead, I began to wonder how my fictional Mrs C. was handling her journey west. She and that zebra-striped van were probably not so very far from Hay, though certainly not in this caravan park. Might have stopped at that pub, for a while, some time earlier today. She had not, however, been there to sit at my table as other fictional characters had done on other trips, offering opinions on everyone around.

I still didn't know why she had left her husband, though I
suspected it was not dissatisfaction with the marriage. Something dangerous. She was protecting him from something he
didn't even know about. How had the husband reacted when
he'd discovered her gone? Anger! Her timing was bad. When
he ought to be delivering his important paper at the university, bolstering his reputation amongst his international col-
leagues, he was having to inform the police, to coax
information out of the backpacker youths who might know
the driver of the van, to set out himself to find her. To bring
her back. Save her from the terrible dangers he suspected she
was walking into. Naturally her journey into the interior
would be symbolic, but so, inevitably, would be his pursuit.

"You didn't recognise me at first, did you?"

E waited while the man in shorts decided whether he would tell
the truth. "Your accent brought something back," he said. "I wasn't
sure what."

"I've put on a little weight. Hell – who hasn't?"

The man in shorts hadn't. He was slim as a boy. All bones. Alex?
Alan? Started with an "A." He had given E his card in Honolulu,
with this address on it. Mr A Brackett. "In case you're ever in New
South Wales." He probably had not expected anyone to drive this far
south to find him. A hermit, living in this shack, looking out on the
most beautiful sandy beach E had ever seen. You could make a killing with a lodge up there on that cliff. Fly people in. Fish right off the
beach.

This fellow wouldn't, though. He could not be the private investi-
gator he had claimed to be in Honolulu. He was one of those ageing
hippies. There were chickens in his back yard. "Chooks," he called
them. A vegetable garden. Home-made pottery everywhere. A gui-
tar. The man was a drop-out. No interest in the world. How the hell
did you convince someone like this to help you find Charlotte?

I made an attempt to read a little. After all, I'd promised
myself that I would read Australian books on Australian soil,
and right now I was separated from Australian soil by nothing more than the thickness of a groundsheet, the floor of the
tent, and a pad of inflated rubber. Travel was often an opportunity to read books on the site, so to speak, of their concep-
tion. I'd read some of my overlooked Hardy in Dorset. I'd

reread some Faulkner on Faulkner's own front lawn. This time I would read some of the Australian books I hadn't got around to yet. Thomas Keneally's *By the Line* was the first book I pulled from my bag. "Next door to us lay the Mantles' narrow little brick place," I read. The opening sentence. I read it again. I'd long been an admirer of Keneally's work. But between me and the page a great distance inserted itself, filled with the day's events. Niagara, forage sorghum, emus, heat, sheep, the taxi driver's attempts to run down a childhood enemy. "Next door to us lay the . . ." I discovered that the Itty Bitty Book Light had not been intended for thin paperbacks. *By the Line* buckled under its awkward weight, collapsed, and fell on my face. I decided to get some sleep.

4   Hay, hell, and almost Booligal

Sheep. Shearers. Dust. Heat. Was there something wrong
with me that I would choose the Outback rather than re-visit
Vienna or Venice? I could be lying on the beach at Manly. I
could be dining at Stephanie's in Melbourne. Yet I was happy
to travel across endless expanses of reddish-brown dust to
watch people clipping the wool off a lot of sheep. Like a child,
with racing heart.

"All a dream!" I thought of the mischievous disbelieving
twinkle in the eye of Hans Joachim Schädlich, the German
novelist who'd taken part in the Adelaide Festival. When
most of the international guest writers were herded into a bus
and driven to the beach – coastline of the southern ocean –
he looked out in the direction of the Antarctic and shook his
head. "It is all a dream." He said it again as he looked across
the wide expanse of sand baking in the sun's fierce glare.
"Yesterday I was in Berlin. Today – this impossible dream."
When the two of us agreed that this dream was far too hot for
northerners, we gravitated towards the little general store in
search of cold drinks and shade. He stopped, suddenly. "General Store," he said, reading the sign above the door. "Gen-
er-al Store." He might not have encountered the term before.
He looked at me with a sly grin, and looked out on the vast
stretch of sandy beach. Then he said, in his slow, careful English, "Why – why would there be a gen-er-al store in the
middle of a desert?" He chuckled. What could be more astonishing than to discover the incongruous, the unexplainable,

the preposterous, while wandering around in a world so unlike home as to seem like a dream?

Perhaps what I was responding to in the Riverina was the "oppositeness" of everything to what I was used to in my own little piece of the world, a world of mountain and green impenetrable coniferous forest, a lush rainy Pacific coast world of giant Douglas firs and ancient cedars and wild thick undergrowth. I grew up in a rural logging community where we thought of ourselves as living "in the bush".

But what a different sort of bush it was from this Australian world that went by the same name! At home, to say "Oh, they live back in the bush" was to suggest a modest house – perhaps unpainted, probably old, a shack – up a winding gravel road deep into a world of crowded salal and oregon grape and salmon berries and willows and thick stands of cedar and fir. If there were pastures, they were small fields carved out of the forest which every year had to be fought back all over again around the edges. In Australia, "the bush" seemed to suggest the opposite – an abundance of open space, dirt, tiny dry bushes, few trees. Even the slight difference in the way the word "bush" was pronounced suggested the other differences. At home, "bush" is a word that goes past so quickly it seems dismissed. There might be no vowel in it at all – only a crowded forest of upright consonants, appropriate for an overgrown vertical world. In Australia, not only does the vowel play out its full role but the "sh" adds a note of importance and even menace. It is a word which is not let go of easily. Hearing it said, you can almost taste it yourself, a delicious word, to be relished.

What I was experiencing in this unglamorous world was that same sudden inexplicable rush of joy which overtakes me every time I discover that my sense of wonder has not deserted me – is still as basic and immature as it was during my infancy when I saw, for instance, my first Canada goose beat its wings up off the surface of a pond and begin to fly. It is something that has not been far away for most of my life, this sense of something within me beating its wings and lifting above the earth – making the entire world a wonderland.

Maybe I was discovering now that it had been lying dormant awhile, waiting for this trip to shake it awake.

The second day, I would be a tourist in the town of Hay. To see an Australian version of the small town "in the bush". Once I'd completed a few errands, that is. After I'd delivered Roger to the woolshed for his interview, I had to find a mechanic who would take a look at those headlights. I would also pick up some brochures and pamphlets about Lake Mungo National Park, our next stop. At ten o'clock I wanted to make my weekly telephone call home (Monday morning for me – Sunday dinnertime for them, already a ritual). I needed to buy some sort of quilt for that hour or two in early morning when the air was too cold even for my sleeping bag. (A "doona" Roger called it – I imagined this to be something like a duvet, made especially for people who slept on desert dunes.) "If you come back to get me at five, I should be finished. Tea at the caravan park tonight – we don't need another late night at the pub."

The mechanic at MG Auto was a friendly talkative fellow, who was interested in our travel plans but could not find anything wrong with the lights. They worked just fine for him. The only thing more humiliating than being shown by a mechanic that the problem is not a problem at all is being told this by a mechanic wearing a pair of shorts – the costume of a little boy. He scraped some melted solder off the wires but clearly thought the fault was in the driver's imagination rather than in the truck. "You bought 'er after you got to Australia?" His look suggested I'd been had. Or maybe he thought I'd stolen it. I explained the situation. He listened respectfully, smiling – no doubt wondering why the Australian owner would send his Canadian mate to have the lights repaired. I began an explanation – research, interviewing, shearing book, etc – and he kindly decided to believe me. He also refused to take any money – except for a couple of fuses I bought "just in case" – and sent me away with his best wishes. His young assistant, who'd been washing his hands in a pan of gasoline through much of this conversation, dried his hands on a towel, gave me a curt nod, and told his boss he was about to "shoot through". Then he hopped into his little white truck – a real "ute" – and shot through.

I did the same. Or rather, where he had shot through, I merely took off.

Why did Australians see themselves as shooting through where Canadians would be taking off? If the Canadians weren't taking off they might be "hitting the road" – either ascending or descending in the process of taking leave. Shooting through suggested much more energy. It also implied escape – shoot through to what? Perhaps most important was that it suggested a horizontal image for a decidedly horizontal world.

According to the leaflet I was given at the Visitors Centre, the explorer Charles Sturt passed the townsite of Hay in 1829. Of course the town did not become an important centre for transportation until Cobb & Co. began to build their coaches here. Now Hay was a town of three thousand people, almost equidistant from Adelaide (685 k), Sydney (735 k), Melbourne (405 k), and Canberra (500 k). The surrounding Shire spread out to include a number of other neighbouring villages, including the town of Booligal which Banjo Paterson made famous in his poem "Hay, Hell, and Booligal".

I was encouraged to fish for Yellow Belly, Silver Bream, Red Fin, and Yabbies in the Murrumbidgee River, to hire an eight berth houseboat to observe the wildlife along the banks, to visit a number of shaded parks, to tour the Bishop's Lodge, to visit a winery, or tour the Hay Gaol Museum. By the time I had attended to the truck, mailed a few postcards at the Post Office, bought myself a doona (which smelled, I later discovered, as though more than feathers had been scooped up off the chicken house floor to fill it) and made my weekly telephone call (competing with the mother-and-son team who took turns screeching into the neighbouring telephone in a language which was apparently as incomprehensible to the listener on the other end as it was to me), I did not have time to take all the brochure's advice. I was, however, interested in visiting the Old Gaol because someone in the pub had mentioned that it had spent time as a POW camp during the Second World War. An Italian prisoner of war named Colonel Edgardo Simone had escaped by cutting through the bars with a file and climbing the walls with a rope made of towels.

Colonel Simone was not the only one to have escaped. So had the attendants, apparently. No-one was around to answer questions, or even to take my money. The museum was open but deserted. I had the place to myself.

I'd expected the Hay Gaol Museum to be a museum of itself — that is, a maintained relic in which I would be able to see the file which Colonel Simone had used on his bars, perhaps even his rope of towels. I expected to see pictures of prisoners, instruments of torture ("these electric prods provoked John Doe into a confession on this very spot"), and displays of the uniforms worn by sheep thieves and murderers. I had no idea what mementos to expect from the building's days as a maternity hospital, its days as an insane asylum, or its days as a "Total Security Institution for incorrigible girls committed to the care of the Child Welfare Department" but I was eager, anyway, to see.

In fact this was an all-purpose museum, a receptacle for Hay's history. Cells were not merely cells but had been converted to display rooms for clothing and tools and machines from the previous century. History had, in effect, been taken prisoner. Appropriate enough. Once you'd imprisoned thieves and murderers and prisoners of war and wayward girls and the insane, what was there left to do but to capture all of history and lock it up? We all know the mischief history can do if left to roam free, revising itself, changing its protective colouring, disappearing down the cracks of memory, falling into the hands of novelists.

My footsteps echoed horribly — the only sound, aside from my breathing. When you walked down the narrow stone-walled corridor towards the sunlit door at the far end, you walked past miniature display rooms filled with old bottles, hospital gear, fire arms, tools, Aboriginal artifacts, laundry paraphernalia, books and photographs. If I didn't find the souvenirs of Colonel Edgardo Simone I'd been hoping for, that may be because the tension of being the only living human in that large, thick-walled, fortified, and gated complex soon filled me with an undeniable urge to imitate the man and get out as fast as I could.

My friend Edgardo was not the only POW to be overcome by a desire to get out of Hay. Two others went over the wall of the Supply Depot while they were part of a work party, and sauntered down the main street of town trying to look inconspicuous. But a young man named Frank Pepper was watering the footpath at the time and thought the two men looked – according to the *Riverina-Grazier* of August 21, 1942 – "more like Italians than Australians." He followed them for a closer look, perhaps in case his eyesight had misled him or Australia's immigration policy had changed. He gave the alarm and followed them on his bike but a sergeant on horseback got to them first and brought them back to their fate.

In the little corner cafe I was left to stand while mother and daughter waited one another out – who would pull herself away from the American soap-opera to serve the customer? Eventually the daughter brought me a sandwich – wordlessly, and without taking her eyes from the television set. Mother and daughter exchanged a few words in a Mediterranean language (descendants of Edgardo?) before settling again to the business of caring about other people's problems. Lovers were obviously parting, but not without accusing one another of horrendous sins against the heart – all in an accent which jarred my forgetting ears if not theirs. All those harsh "r's!" All those flat "a's!" I wondered at the phenomenon of "New Australians," or "migrants" as I had heard them called, learning to speak their Australian English off an American television drama. Neither of these two women would say enough for me to hear what the effect might be, but if they were responsible for the sign above the door I needn't worry. They were already cognisant of the ambiguities of the English language which made it so maleable in the hands of the advertiser: "Freshly Cut Sandwiches" inspired false confidence in the unthinking one, and did not at all promise that the sandwiches themselves would be made today, or even this week — only that they would be severed with a knife before your eyes.

Walking the streets of this little town was hot work, but if I'd felt like a swim to cool off, there would be no point in visiting the public swimming pool. It was closed. "For the Season", presumably. This was late autumn for the residents of Hay. Would they be surprised to learn that their late-autumn weather was much hotter than I usually experienced at the height of summer, when pools would be crammed with thrashing bodies, desperate to cool off?

Roger was pleased — if puzzled — to learn that the mechanic had found nothing wrong with the lights. Just a little melted something that he'd scraped off the wire. But then, we had not yet discovered — would not discover until after dark that evening — that the traitorous low beams which had co-operated for the mechanic in the little-boy shorts, making me look the fool, had decided, in the time since, not to repeat the performance for either the owner or his foreign sidekick. Making me look like a fool and a liar. (I might not have taken the truck to the mechanic at all. Did Roger wonder this?) This vehicle had taken a dislike to me, I understood, in the way some pet animals will turn on an apparently benign guest as though it sensed secret perfidies. We would be forced to use high beams throughout the rest of this trip, whenever lights were required.

At 5:45 am a truck door slammed. An engine growled into life. Voices mumbled in the nearby tent of the couple who'd come in late the night before. I could hear Roger rustling around in his tent, unzipping it, crawling out. Time to get up. We had been invited to have breakfast with some of the shearing crew we'd met the day before, now moved to another shed. This was on a station 40 km north of Hay (on the old Cobb Road towards Booligal) and 24 km west on a dirt road to the Lachlan River. This meant crossing the One Tree Plain. Who would not get up before dawn in order to draw something called the One Tree Plain into the spheres of his life?

Kangaroos hopped along beside us in the half-light. We passed a small isolated camp – a caravan, a utility truck, a motor bike, a trailerload of equipment, a tethered horse. "Drover's cook," said Roger. "Waiting for the crew to catch up to him." Somewhere a cook was waiting for us as well. Off to the right, the sun sent a pink fanfare glow up the sky to announce its imminent arrival, then rose from behind the long straight line of dark horizon, a neon disk of orange pink. Not a single tree broke the perfect table-edge of light- and shadow-flooded earth. Wherever the "one tree" was that had given its name to this expanse of world, it was not between us and the enormous blaring sun. Shadows were thrown by squat grey bushes no higher than knees.

(Joseph Furphy had mentioned no trees in *Such is Life* when he described this stretch of land as it appeared in 1883. Instead, the "mile-wide stock-route from Wilcannia to Hay was strewn with carcasses of travelling sheep along the whole two-hundred-and-fifty miles . . . I remember noticing once, in passing along the fifty-mile stretch of that route which bisects the One Tree Plain, that, taking no account of sheep, I never was out of sight of dying cattle and horses – let alone the dead ones.")

He was describing a drought year, when presumably even the saltbush had offered no nourishment to sheep. Today, it grew plentifully enough, if not closely together, where trees did not grow at all. We knew this was saltbush we were looking at because we got out and – with not a chance in a million of being seen by human eyes – tasted its dry grey tiny leaves. After several thoughtful nibbles, I concluded that sheep raised in these parts might as well be lapping up the salted water of the open sea. Surely their flesh was salted enough to hang untainted forever, long before any butcher got his hands on it – already cured on the hoof. Roger assured me that saltbush mutton was in fact delicious – raised to gourmet status in parts of France.

We turned off the road at the One Tree Hotel – a famous nineteenth century landmark, now a ruin. Not quite a ruin – new windows in the single-storey structure suggested a caretaker if not an inhabitant. No-one peered out at our curious prowling, though. No signs of footsteps, transportation, or litter. The corrugated sides of two empty water tanks outside the door promised ICE COLD BEER in high white letters – false advertising. That place had nothing to offer but heat and flies and dust. Heat, even this early, fell like a collapsed heavy ceiling upon our heads, promising even worse ahead. (No use wearing my kangaroo hat; it only made my hair sweat.) Flies starved for human company could be imagined screaming with delight as they rushed to set up their crowded colonies upon us. (The hat was good for something – fanning and swatting, to spoil their fun just a little. The ones that got to your ears were the worst.) Dust stretched all the way out to the wide round brim of the universe, nearly the same colour as the rusted tin roof. Horse-drawn wagons stacked high with bales of wool stopped here in former times, but you had to dredge up energy from every corner of the imagination to think of being a wagon driver desperate enough to see this as a place of rest and laughter and cool refreshment, a tiny spot of civilisation before moving on.

We moved on – westward now. A few eucalyptus trees grew here and there, as though to prove it could be done. When we came, finally, to the Lachlan River, trees grew closer together. Ribbon gums. Stringy-barks. "Look, Jack!" A black wild boar went snuffling off into their secret shade.

Presumably, he had a better sense of his destination than we did. Off we went for several kilometres down one red road, smooth as any pavement we'd left behind. "This has got to be it. There's nothing else." Faint tire tracks laid ruler-straight lines in powdery dust, but took us nowhere at all.

"This has got to be right. Look at the map. But it isn't."

We returned to the river to look for other possibilities. There were none. We tried the same disappointing road again, and perservered this time beyond gates and confusing junctions and promising clusters of trees that concealed nothing but imagined buildings. "Shearers would have eaten by now," Roger said. Meaning: we're late, we may not get any breakfast. He knew how the cook would feel. On we went beyond good sense – there was nothing else to do but follow those tracks as though we'd been hypnotised. And came, suddenly, to a gate, a compound of iron buildings in a grove of trees.

Light glared down so hard out of a steel sky that the buildings were reduced to white space in a composition of paprika coloured dust and pale green trees. A windmill did not turn. A corrugated water tank looked pitiful, high on its spindly legs. A bleached skull glared back from powdery earth at the sky, beyond mercy. Shearers' quarters was a wide roof standing on white matchstick posts, its doorways hidden in the veranda shadows. Cookhouse and screened meat-house stood close together; the woolshed, where clippers were already humming, was fifty metres away. A dazzling little colony in a parched empty world.

The cook had kept our breakfasts for us. We were instructed to sit at the long wooden table in the dining room – a table populated with tall plastic jars and containers of salt, pepper, tomato sauce, mustard, and other embellishments – where she insisted on laying out a table cloth across our end. Then she placed plates of eggs and bacon and sausage in front of us, over which she had ladled a sauce which seemed to be made from a mixture of mushrooms and onions. Presumably it had not been charred for those who ate it on time.

Standing at the work table in the middle of her dimly-lit and slightly smoky kitchen, she talked to us while she prepared Smoko. Sausages were wrapped in pastry and laid in rows upon a baking tray.

She loved her job. "For the first toime in moi loife I c'n be moiself?" Of course to any ears but mine her accent was only slightly broader than others, but this was what I heard. I heard the question mark as well, at the end of almost all her sentences, where an Australian ear might not.

Again and again, she hoisted up the strap of her white singlet, which kept falling off one shoulder and creeping down her arm.

Once she had been married into the high class, she said. "I could put on the dog when I had to?" To prove it, she named the names of the famous who had sat at her table. But she had turned her back on all that now and lived with one of the young rouseabouts who was working out in the shed.

Into the oven of the blackened old cookstove went the sausage rolls. Breakfast sausages were thrown to the dogs outside the screen door. Roger was shocked. When he was a cook, he said, he'd made a point of never throwing anything out. "Not all those sausages were burnt," he told her. "Some of them could have been used again for the sausage rolls."

Roger's eyes took in every detail of these two large rooms, examined the food that was being prepared, evaluated the equipment this woman had to work with. He pressed question after question upon her – about costs, volume, menus, the preferences of shearers. Occasionally he scribbled in his notebook, but made no show of it – he scribbled when she addressed an answer in my direction. This appeared to be just a shop-talk conversation between cooks. Still, his animated face and pleased grin showed what pleasure he was taking in this. After all, he was talking to someone who was doing what he had only recently done himself, and had taken pride in doing well. She knew this, and responded with energy. Was there ever a cook who did not rise to another cook's display of interest? She might have been waiting all her life for this perfect audience.

"Yes? I do that too? Now, did you find there were things that they just did not like?"

She was eager to talk about more than just cooking. She wished to express her joy in all the present circumstances of her life. About her de facto husband, she said, "He mykes me feel beautiful?"

This wasn't difficult to believe. You remembered the high schoolgirls who "matured early" – the loud ones who smoked and dated the airforce and laughed their hoarse sexy laugh while they looked you in the eye and dared you to make a pass. Time may have added a few lines to her weathered complexion but she had such large dark eyes and features so sharply defined that you had no trouble imagining how a young rouseabout might make her feel beautiful still. Perhaps it was for him that she'd cut her dark shiny hair in that youthful fashion that used to be called a pixie cut. Perhaps my own age was showing. Though one young rouseabout lived with her, others here called her "Mum". She liked to mother her boys, she said, but she also liked to flirt with them. They understood. "There are ways of saying things, and there are ways of saying things?"

Snick, snick, snick. Oranges were quartered and set out on a plate. She hoisted her strap again.

She seemed to have set herself up as a counsellor. They came to her with their troubles. "For instance, that boy you'll see out there in the shed? He was in tears last night? We went for a little walk and then he was foine? I just told him you've got to grow up, you're a man now, you've got to stand on your feet."

For shearers with marital problems — and apparently this was not uncommon amongst men who spent so much time away from home — she had a simple solution. "Just come home with your doodle out and she won't be able to resist."

I imagined puzzled shearers' wives comparing notes: "Has your husband started coming home, uh, half undressed? Where do you suppose they get these silly ideas?"

Chomp, chomp, chomp. A melon was chopped into slices.

"Once we were working down at Wentworth? We had a few drinks after work? Well they didn't have my favourite drink so I had a couple of cans of something else? Then we were driving home in the car and I fall asleep. Then I decide I want to go wee? Open the car door to step out. 'Where you goin'?' says driver. 'To have a wee,' says Cook. 'Bullshit,' says driver. Someone closes the door. Driver says, 'I can see the headlines: SHEARERS' COOK KILLED WHILE TAKING A PISS AT SIXTY MILES AN HOUR!'"

She set out a tray of sandwiches. She sprinkled a high round coffee cake with cinnamon and sliced it into wedges. She hoisted her shoulder strap. It was time to get the station wagon and drive the food across the yard to the shed for Smoko.

All this food, as well as a kettle of tea, a pot of coffee, and a large container of fruit juice, was laid out on top of filled wool sacks just inside the wide doorway to the woolshed. The shearers seemed happy enough to take a break, and descended upon the food as though they hadn't eaten for days. Then most of them drifted apart and ate, in silence, on their own. Some lay on the floor and lit a cigarette. Dogs pulled at their chains.

I asked one of the shearers about the strange sort of foot covering he and some of the others were wearing. He said they were special shoes made of something like felt. Carpet underfelt. "Shearing moccasins." These were supposed to be kind to the shearers' feet but, he said, "you watch a shearer when he walks, he's always walking on his heels. And he's never any good at running." I could not make out whether it was the job or the shoes that did the damage and this young man seemed too shy to endure a cross-examination.

He was not too shy to tell me about his plans, however. He was getting out just as soon as he'd paid for his 75 acre farm down in Victoria. He'd been shearing for six years – "too long".

Six years for him represented forty thousand sheep, he estimated. That was 180 sheep a day. And yes, he'd gone into it for the money. "I reckoned it was gonna be hard work." The look he gave me made it clear he had not found any reason to change his opinion.

He reached for a second piece of cake. I did the same. "I suppose the sort of cook you get in a job like this is pretty important," I suggested.

He agreed. He'd met a few bad ones in his day.

"How do you define a bad cook?"

"Well – y'finish up, half the crew's got food poison."

Apparently he'd experienced this himself, but had survived.

"I guess that cook doesn't work again, eh?"

He looked at me, then looked away. "Sometimes."

A serious-looking shearer did not speak to anyone else but he was willing to tell me a little about his job. At first it took you eighteen months to get your muscles into shape, he said. Until then, your muscles ached every day. For the first month you couldn't sleep at night.

This tall, broad-shouldered, dark-haired man who spoke to no one was unusually gentle with the sheep, said the cook. "Some men, they hit them when they won't sit still? Not him. He talks softly to them, never hurts them?"

He was about to turn in his singlet and blue pants for another uniform, she told us. "He's religious? He prays before he comes to meals? Nobody says anything about it? I think he's training to be a priest."

Was I discovering what shearers thought about while they worked all day with those sheep? They planned their escape.

When the men returned to work, Cook went with them. The spoils were left sitting around on their wool bales while station hands came in to pick over what was left. These were older, chubby men in hats and shorts who'd driven in on motor bikes from doing whatever station hands do – mustering sheep, fixing fences. This, Roger explained, was a tradition with some contractors. The cook always made sure there was just a little too much food, so the owner's men (and the owner himself if he chose) would have something to eat as well. This seemed a peculiar habit to me, since the food was not paid for by the station or even the contractor, but by the shearers themselves.

Up on the board where only a few years earlier her presence would have caused a walk-out as well as a scandal – "ducks on the pond!" – the cook had taken up a broom and gone waltzing around the room, gathering up bits of wool from the shiny pine floor. Doing a rouseabout's job. Her loose white shirt strap hung off one shoulder halfway down her arm, exposing much of one breast.

We followed her back to her kitchen once the station hands had picked the trays clean – time to start preparing lunch. "Then, after that, round three. One down, three to go."

She felt sixteen at times, she said, by way of explaining

how much she liked her job. For a while she'd reversed her
age to make herself feel better. When she was 43 she'd said
she was 34. "Now I'm 44 so it doesn't matter. From now on,
well, it's just generally not going to work?"

"I noticed you grabbed a broom over there in the shed," I
said. "Is that something you like to do often?"

It was. She had her reasons. First, she liked doing it.
"Plus, I get bored? Plus, it's helping the guys? Plus, I like to
have a joke? Besides, as one of the fellas once said, 'You smell
better than these blokes.'"

She'd had many jobs before this, she said. "Housekeeping.
Plus a geriatric hospital. Plus hospital cleaning. Plus garden-
ing for the council. Plus hostess for a while." Unfortunately,
she had to leave her teenaged daughter unattended for weeks
at a time while she was away from home working at this job,
a fact of life which bothered her live-in rouseabout more than
it bothered her. "It's a little thing they call trust? And I trust
her very very much?" This was because she and her daughter
had an understanding. "My daughter said, 'You trust me and
I'll love you.'"

When we parted, she asked Roger to say hello to all the
other shearers' cooks he met. "And ask them to send me
their recipes." I could tell he was unlikely to carry out her re-
quest. He was convinced, he said as we drove away, that
she'd grow tired of her job in a year. The pleasure she took in
feeding her "boys" and the heady power she'd discovered in
offering advice would soon pall. She'd be left with nothing
but the evidence of her own ineptitude − wasted food and
high costs. Sooner or later the shearers were bound to complain.

I was sorry to hear that. It seemed to me that this dusty
male world needed her. Seen in the brighter lights of town,
perhaps, or with the eyes of visitors come in from a different
world, she may appear a little threadbare, imagining for herself an importance she hadn't really earned, a less skilful cook
than she thought − but she expressed a kind of naive and exuberant zest which must, surely, brighten the day of the
shearers. Besides, there was the subtext humming along

beneath her chatter: a life had fallen apart in circumstances which were probably worthy of the daytime soaps (you could not imagine her marriage falling apart without colossal public battles, embarrassing dinner party scenes, melodramatic confrontations) but it was being put back together in a way that would do just fine, at least for now. It was not hard to think of the humiliations which must have been suffered by a wife who'd brought little but her sexy beauty into a marriage and then found herself having to act the hostess for the kind of people her successful husband wished to impress – people who would only roll their eyes at her efforts. It must have been a great relief to find herself worshipped by a youthful rouseabout who made her feel beautiful again, appreciated by a crew of men who needed what she could offer. What a world of meaning there was in her simple: "For the first time in moi loif I c'n be moiself?"

As we drove out across the dusty plain, leaving the baked corrugated iron of the Thelangerin buildings behind us, Roger said that John had invited us to stay on and go wild boar shooting with the shearers after dark. "But I told him we'd better move on, we want to get to Lake Mungo while it's light."

What? What? We'd turned down an invitation to hunt wild pigs in the Australian bush? With pit-lamping shearers? A chance to acquire the sort of story one could be telling still at age 90? This old black boar came snorting out from behind this saltbush, heading right for me. I held my spotlight on him while Roger raised his gun and took aim. Behind us, a dozen shearers froze. As novelists, we may have lost the opportunity which would enable us to write our *Moby Dick*, our *Bear* our *Old Man and the Sea*.

Roger did not seem to have this sort of second thought. "They'll fill themselves with grog before they go. They'll be staggering around with their guns in the dark. How safe do you think it would be?"

Not very. I suppose there was some relief in having someone else to be cautious on my behalf. I could safely regret the missed adventure. And in the meantime I would withhold

judgment until I saw what Lake Mungo National Park had to
offer us in its stead.

5   The Walls of China, The Walls of Death

When Johann Ulrich Voss makes his expedition to the interior of the Australian continent, his voyage (in the hands of Patrick White) becomes a struggle against evil, a quest for good, and a passage into both annihilation and immortal legend. Of course *Voss* is only one of many novels to trace the search for El Dorado, the quest for immortality, the hunting expedition after wisdom. The explorers may have been men who allowed the boys within them to seek adventure, but novelists insist on giving more meaning to their expeditions.

At no point did we take ourselves so seriously as to make this sort of comparison. We were hardly Burke and Wills, or Leichhardt and Gilbert. And yet such noble seekers came to mind when you caught your first glimpse of the Walls of China. This astonishing phenomenon has about it the feel of a place which humans trek long dangerous distances to find. A vision of another planet, perhaps. The site where answers to eternal questions might be found − a dry, silent, stretched-out scalloped mystery.

We fought no hostile tribes, but we did have the '71 Holden to remind us that things could still go wrong. Not satisfied with withdrawing the use of its highbeams, it seemed to have decided somewhere along the dusty road between Balranald and Lake Mungo National Park to let the radiator give us a scare. The temperature warning light came on. We stopped, and walked out amongst a stand of mallee while the engine cooled.

When mallee first appeared beside the road − like large

rhododendrons, I thought, with all those scraggly trunks growing out of a common set of roots – I wondered at the dark stain in the dusty earth beneath each bush. Had a fire gone through? Everything looked charred. Now I saw that this tree sat in the dark pool of its own debris – fallen leaves, shed bark, dead limbs, its own shadow. Nothing ever rotted here; it sat where it was and baked.

What did I expect to find on this visit to one of the country's newest parks? An exaggeration of the already piti-less lunar landscape we'd been passing through, I suppose, with what the tourist booklets called its "brutal, powerful, awe-inspiring, unsettling, stark beauty". In fact, it was hard to imagine how extreme Lake Mungo Park would have to be to deserve special attention in these surroundings. I knew enough to expect: a lake-bed which had been dry since the last Ice Age, a mountain range of white dunes made from the sand which the wind had scooped up out of the lake in all the years since, the site of the oldest human skeleton ever found – forty thousand-years old. Coloured photos suggested deso-lation.

This desolation could be glimpsed at a distance off to the right as we drove at five o'clock into a treed area of the park. We located the camp ground: fire pits, picnic tables, plenty of uncluttered flat space. We chose the most isolated site, where the only other residents were safely distant. A modest cara-van and a small community of tents were huddled together on the far side of the loop.

There was no breeze at human level, though a soft con-stant hum could be heard in the upper branches of the casuarinas where the limp needle-leaves (which made me think of hanging swatches of grey-green horse hair) barely moved. The fine red dust beneath our feet was sprinkled with tiny twigs and nuts and the occasional saltbush – every step crackled beneath you. There would be no sneaking around in this brittle place.

There was no escaping the flies, either. The Rid bottle was unpacked first and set in a conspicuous spot on the table. But this milky substance, applied to the rims of the ears and other exposed flesh, did nothing more than discourage them – certainly didn't scare them off. That is, they continued to buzz, and attempt to land, and make fly-pasts, and even alight for a moment – only to think better of it and take off again, enraged, to circle the victim in search of a less distasteful landing spot. I needed no lessons in the Australian salute – my arm adopted the attitude of a windscreen wiper blade, with little hope of rest.

Determined not to let the flies spoil anything, however persistent and annoying they might be, I would try, try, try, to ignore them. I would even try to acknowledge their right to exist, and do what they were meant to do. I might have succeeded, too, if one of them hadn't flown straight into my mouth and bounced off the back of my throat. I coughed, gagged, dredged up phlegm, stomped around the campsite spitting into the dust. I imagined the fly's wings plastered to the wall of my esophagus, its legs flailing. I imagined the fly already in my stomach, seeking escape. I gave it all the help I could – raised holy hell, in fact, with the campsite's peace. While Roger watched with a tentative sort of amusement, I did everything I could to turn myself inside out. But nothing changed. I could only gargle with water, wipe my lips, and hope to forget about the incident as fast as possible.

Perhaps eating would take my mind off this uninvited guest. A fire soon roared in the fire pit. While dark fell rapidly around us, Roger hauled out the giant iron pot from the back of the truck and prepared to put his skills as a cook to good use. Into the pot went the leg of lamb we'd bought in Balranald.

He would have preferred, in fact, to have bought a leg of mutton. I was grateful those Balranald butchers had neglected to stock it. My last taste of mutton, forty-five years ago, had left a coating inside my mouth that couldn't be got rid of for days.

"And," Roger said to the young fellow behind the counter who would not sell us a leg of mutton but had agreed to sell us a leg of lamb, "I'll have it bound."

Bound?

"That'll take me five minutes. Is there something you could do and come back?"

Bound? Why would he want a leg of lamb to be bound? I imagined a network of string like the one that keeps a ham from escaping its fate, but could imagine no reason for it.

"Five minutes," Roger said, with some scorn, as soon as we'd left the shop. "I could do it in four and a half."

When we'd picked up the parcel of meat in five and a half minutes, I asked Roger how this mysterious process was done.

"A sharp thin knife. Just slide it down alongside the bone and slip it right around."

Bone! Bone! The leg of lamb had not been bound, it had been boned. That is to say, de-boned. The long 'o' was different here from what I was used to. I wondered if I could somehow contrive to have Roger say "I stood up with my bow and arrow in the bow of my boat." Faced with both bows, what could a poor Australian do?

Once the de-boned leg of lamb had been browned, Roger tossed in potatoes, carrots, zucchini, and red capsicums. He also added some damper, the bushman's unleavened bread. While this bush tucker cooked, the truck radio – slammed into action – delivered the news that World War I veterans were preparing for a trip to Gallipoli for Anzac Day. A curious coincidence, to be hearing this in the company of the man whose literary reputation had been earned by his novel about these same men. It was as "the writer of *1915*" that Roger was introduced amongst the shearers. People recognised the title – though sometimes it was his television adaptation that they knew.

The newscast went on to tell of cabinet ministers learning what portfolios they would hold in the re-elected government. The opposition leader's future sounded rather uncertain to me – as it should be, if I were to believe the tales of palace coups and other shady shenanigans I'd been told about in Sydney. When you felt helpless to get rid of the politicians who were making a mess of your own country, you took some satisfaction in seeing foreigners toss their own brand of scoundrels out on their ears.

With the abrupt death of the news, a wonderful silence fell over the campsite. A warm breeze had come up. Moonlight fell through the long-haired boughs of the casuarinas, painting shadows on the dusty ground. Pale rabbits could be seen moving through the dark, pausing to watch this peculiar spectacle of two grown men on plastic-coated folding chairs exclaiming over the taste of something out of a pot.

Indeed the magic of either the pot or Roger's technique had rendered the lamb delicious. No roast of beef could have competed with this, no exotically decorated breast of pheasant. (I wouldn't go so far as to wish I might taste what miracles might be performed upon mutton.) If this was the sort of meal Roger had served his shearers, I was surprised they'd ever let him quit.

If "leaving the world behind" were one of our goals, we had achieved it. The dim lights of other humans across the camping ground were of no consequence here. Civilisation – even small towns like Hay – were far away and in another sort of world. Out there, in the dark, not far from us, was the shoreline of a wide lake which had been dry for fifteen thousand years. On the far side, eleven kilometres away, was the mountain range of sand dunes they called the Walls of China. All of it waiting in silence for us and the morning.

We walked out immediately after breakfast to the edge of the dry lake bed and looked across to the Walls of China. "Desolation" seemed an inadequate word. There was almost a biblical feel to this great flat dry expanse of tufted dust, the even greater expanse of harsh blue sky. A row of fence posts – unconnected to one another – set off in a line across the bottom, leaning, rotten, remnants of days when this was a sheep station. I tried to call up the sounds of sheep bleating and dogs barking, here, or the image of a horsemen galloping across the dusty paddock after some breakaway group – but could not.

It was equally difficult to imagine water lapping at the

shoreline below us, or seabirds swimming past – ducks, pelicans, sweeping the muddy bottom for food. You knew there had been a camp of Aborigines somewhere along this beach, but could not imagine so much life in this immobile silence – smoke from a fire, children laughing, dark figures wading in to spear fish, bending to pick up clams.

The only sign of present life was the ubiquitous rabbit – and even that was a doomed and tainted life. Rabbit pellets were everywhere, the pale dusty-green colour of the saltbush. Bits of rabbit fur were everywhere too, dry as shreds of bark. And everywhere there were rabbits hunched in the shade of individual saltbushes. Ragged, thin, blurry-eyed, sick; the rabbits were dying.

"Not dying fast enough for me," said Roger. He was scandalised to find so many of them taking so long to succumb to the myxomatosis which was supposed to be ridding the continent of this pest. Had they built up some immunity that slowed the disease but did not stop it? Did it cost too much to get rid of them faster? "There's probably a reason for letting so many infest the park. Maybe they hope campers'll write to their Member of Parliament demanding more money be put into the program."

This was rapidly revealing itself to be a place of death. Even the visitor centre at the entrance to the road across the lake-bed seemed to support this. Attendants did not show themselves – they might have died off. Wall legends told of disappeared water, disappeared tribes, disappeared prehistoric animals – giant kangaroos and wombats, long extinct. Skeletons were described. Photos were displayed of Aboriginal people being herded to other sites. Where were they now? Coloured posters showed you how many venomous snakes existed – far more than I wanted to know about. Worse, they showed you how difficult these killers were to spot. You were not likely – everything suggested – to get out of this place alive.

The old woolshed next door, though beautiful, was too clean, too dry, too odourless. The Chinese labourers who'd built it, the graziers who'd owned it, the sheep who'd suffered their indignities within it − all were long gone. History, like moisture and all other life, had been sucked out of the rough pine lumber and the dropped-in squared-off logs and the planked floors by the steady vacuum of the relentless sun. Not far away, a windmill stood motionless on the bleached floor of the lake. Too hot, I thought, to move.

This was where journeys ended. This was where movie makers in love with symbolism brought their aged heroes to dusty deaths. This was where lives, lived out in hope, disintegrated and came to nothing. The movie camera would find a way to turn human aspirations into those shreds of rabbit fur that lay about on the ground. We'd been dropped down in one of those places where nature has gone a little overboard with its symbols.

And there was more to come. When we'd driven across the vast lake-bed speckled with bladder saltbush (the shadow of one bush providing shade for a lounging kangaroo) we parked the truck near a cluster of eucalyptus at the base of the long mountain range of sand dunes − "lunettes" the brochures called them − and started the climb. At first the sand was pale pink, wind-wrinkled, and powdery. Here and there on the slopes, bared islands of ivory-coloured striated clay revealed themselves, sometimes rose up into wind-scraped lumps and knobs that held aloft a small acacia clinging for its life.

Roger set out like a mountain climber to conquer the peaks. (Flies had set up camp on the damp back of his shirt. I didn't want to think about my own.) I dawdled, ogling. Above the knobs and shrubs and upright figures that reminded me of the Alberta badlands' hoodoos, we walked out upon pure sweeping sand dunes, pale and clean − long curves of baking surface, shadowless. A kangaroo had passed through recently. Why hadn't I imagined that kangaroo tracks would include a thick stroke from the tail?

While Roger strode ahead with hands on hips, seeking some panorama to be part of, I trudged behind, sweating. A soaring wedge-tailed eagle carved an arabesque of shadow past me, then flew off. I couldn't bear to keep my bush hat on,

so drenched was my hair with sweat inside it; I couldn't bear
to take it off, the sun was such a burning weight on my head.
What must this be like in the summer? That striped
leatherjacket in Bateman's Bay might have thought something similar, gasping in my waterless hand.

My shoes were pink with the powder I trod through, brick-
red in the patches that had got damp at the campsite water
tap. Here was a good enough reason for buying white —
something for the trip to write itself upon. Shoes would eventually be transformed.

"Here's something more for your sensual overload,"
Roger said as I caught up to him. I thought I could see, in his
pleased expression, his reason for reaching this summit first
— or one of his reasons: he could present it to me now, like a
gift. He stood in what I recognised as his posture for giving
the other person the floor: turned a little to the side, with
arms folded and one foot planted ahead, like someone who'd
just drawn back a curtain. The crest, finally achieved, was a
long sharply cut edge of sand dune, a saddle curve across between two peaks from which we could look out over an endless world of more dust and spots of green and distant
scattered trees. It was all an adult playground after all, so that
middle-aged middle-class men playing at being boys could
feel what explorers must have felt, looking out upon the far
side of hard-won vantage points. Burke, Wills, Leichhardt,
Mitchell, Blaxton — the expectation of this moment must
have been what kept them going.

When we'd returned to the truck, we set off on the 60 km
one-way journey through the park. There would be, according to our information sheet, fourteen more designated stops
where we might read the information on erected plaques and
enjoy the changing view.

"Fourteen? Aren't there fourteen stations of the cross in a
Catholic church?"

"I don't know," Roger said. "Are there?" I suspected the
Presbyterian minister's son knew better than I did, but
wasn't saying.

"Different stages in Jesus's journey to Golgotha."

It made you suspect the park officials of playing games. Wasn't Golgotha, too, the "place of skulls?" Was the visitor being put through a required number of stops – the required number of "stations" – before achieving the local equivalent of a crucifixion? (That is, to be sun-dried like the rabbits on this frying pan earth, perhaps.) Or was redemption the goal? Even resurrection? Perhaps the mere relief of having survived the trip was all the reward that was needed – home free at last! (Baseball players were required to visit stations before achieving home – scholars had already noted the religious implications in this American game. Perhaps, because Australians did not play or watch much baseball, some spiritual need was being supplied in this peculiar manner.)

The truck began to heat up again. We would make this one-way circle tour past fourteen stations-of-the-place-of-skulls with Roger having to race the motor every few minutes, whenever the red light came on.

The pale road followed the lake-bed along the base of the sand mountains, then abruptly turned red and soared up into the sand dunes and beyond. At the first "station" someone had perched a dead rosella on top of the sign, its eyes picked clean. Later, when the road had entered a stretch of casuarina and mallee and long pale grass, one, two, four big grey kangaroos came bounding out of the trees to the right at an angle, about to cross the road in front of us – and did so, only a metre or so ahead, and kept on going on into trees on the left. In that held-breath moment, I was aware of the face of the last, with an expression of grim determination upon it. What could have caused such blind, foolish haste? Later, an alarmed emu raced across the grass beside us, its dark feathers floating, its periscope neck ahead, its long legs stroking as though through water. Then it crossed in front of us, like the kangaroos. Everything alive seemed full of alarm.

Perhaps they were spooked, like myself, by the corpse of a large kangaroo lying not far from the road – its skeleton intact, its hide still stretched across its bones, a hole in its stomach through which its guts had been eaten out. If this was a place of death, there was none of the sort of rotting I was accustomed to, in the rainy woods. Like the rabbits, the corella, and the mallee bark, this kangaroo was sun-sucked dry as dust. Mummified. Twigs and bits of bark crackled underfoot. Nothing, anywhere, was soft, or damp. Even the live saltbush was brittle. You could not be surprised that this was where they had found the oldest human skeletons on the globe. The only surprise was that you were not finding – or becoming – the newest as well. The alarmed rush of the emu and the fleeing kangaroos seemed to the alerted imagination to be, in retrospect, suicidal.

And yet, for those who survived the stations, there was life again, however modest, at the campsite. A wagtail flycatcher twitched its tail and darted about in a bush. A plump topknot pigeon looked out on the world. A flock of green-necked parrots descended upon one of the casuarinas for a noisy while, then flew on.

We took books and lunch to the roofed-over picnic shelter at the edge of the lake. The flies were a little less aggressive in the shade. Everything seemed bleached-out and colourless in the midday sun. Dark stripes of cloud shadows moved across the pale tufted powdery lake bed. Somewhere a crow would not stop calling – that long complaining and mournful sound of a neglected self-pitying child.

Thomas Keneally could wait until I got home. The book I decided to read here was D'arcy Niland's *The Shiralee*. The story of a swagman wandering around the outback with his small son seemed an appropriate choice. There was pleasure in discovering things I could understand now that I could not have understood a week before. When the hero "walked into the Grazcos office" I had some idea why he was doing that. When "the billy was singing, a little thrum, and the seething strings of bubbles were starting upwards," I felt my own reaction to Australia was somehow being "certified" by the printed word.

But it seemed ridiculous to be slipping into this published world while the awesome Walls of China were visible across the lake-bed. Waiting for us to do something about them. If the world was so determined to be too much with me, I could not relax until I'd somehow absorbed it into the fabric of my imagination.

Someone was hiding in the woolshed, looking out through the cracks between the logs upon this desolation? Perhaps my Mrs C? After fleeing Sydney in a zebra-striped van, perhaps she and the driver had been joined by a friend of the youth's in the Commercial Hotel in Hay – a wife-beating jackeroo who'd just been fired for coming to work drunk and slugging the grazier who'd employed him. The three of them had stopped in here for a look around on their way to Broken Hill. Three cases of Victoria Bitter had been emptied last night with alarming speed. They'd given her the van to sleep in, but convinced themselves that she would be disappointed and insulted if they ignored her. The driver had kept his key.

The heat was beginning to fry my brains and my pen didn't seem to care.

> With her knees pulled up to her throat, she leaned against the wall and watched through the slat. Their shouting voices boomed out from inside the visitor's centre. Was there no-one anywhere to hear? Glass crashed. They hoped to uncover her trembling beneath a display case of bones. Someone laughed – Kieran. But it was the other one who stepped out first into the sun, and stood blinking. With his hand pressed open against his forehead, he looked out across the dusty lake-bed for a moment. Nowhere to hide – he must have been thinking this. He turned to consider the woolshed.

"Where did *Rough Wallaby* get its start?" I said.

Roger's latest novel was still fresh in my memory from both manuscript and published versions. It is set somewhere west of the coastal mountains and brings together an astonishing variety of characters on a station known as "the Pool" for the swimming hole where "once you've been under you're never the same." A Sydney socialite, a radio talk-show host, a tragic Scandinavian stunt-man, horse breeders, dreamers – their story is told in a style which relies far more on the vernacular than any other Australian fiction I'd read.

Roger was lost in yesterday's *Sydney Morning Herald*.

"I mean, with so many characters it's hard to imagine what occurred to you first."

He didn't have to think about this. "An image, I think. This newly-married couple flying inland." Regina Delippett and the Scandinavian who would eventually bury himself alive. Flying inland. Fleeing west. Leaving the coast for the plains.

We talked about where stories come from. Why some seem right, some not. Why some would drive you crazy trying to resist you, while others seem to write themselves. All this was less mysterious than the outlandish landscape encouraged us to pretend, though we agreed that you wrote whatever you had to write and could not afford to worry about what others might say about your choice.

So long as you weren't forcing it, Roger said. The last time he tried to force a novel, the results were incomplete, unhappy. Fiction didn't really work until you found some emotional contribution which came from your own life. This was the lesson he'd learned. You couldn't just manufacture fiction. It had to intersect with something in your own life, drawing on your own experienced emotions.

Even if your story should be about two friends who go off to battle in a war that was fought long before you were born, or an aviator who became internationally famous only a little later.

I'd said as much to students often enough. Fiction did not begin until it triggered some deep, exciting, mysterious, and even frightening participation somewhere in the secret recesses of your emotional well. It must rise up and haunt you, thrill you, grab you by the throat — in the manner of a sudden memory of your first encounter with one of those childhood figures who became the abiding archetypes that stomp around in your brain for the rest of your life, demanding to be set free in a rush of papery words.

This was not the same as saying "write about what you know" — widely misunderstood to mean "write only about yourself".

"Reminds me of something that happened when William

Golding spoke to our classes," I said. When one of the students quoted this ancient advice to "write about what you know", an indignant Golding raised himself high on the invisible pedestal of his Nobel Prize and thundered out: "Who is the fool who told you that? Is the man in this room?" Those of us who were instructors held our breaths. Had any of us been guilty? When it seemed that the culprit was not in the room with us (or was being protected by sympathetic students), he ran down the list of his own titles on the chalk board behind him. "I have never been a school boy marooned on an island! I have never been a Neanderthal man! I have never built a cathedral spire!" Though he may have been taking the student a little too literally, his reaction was not likely to be forgotten soon by anyone there.

A shiny blue Landcruiser pulled in to the parking area and stopped. A young couple got out and slammed doors and walked out to the viewpoint at the edge of the lake.

"Newlyweds," Roger said.

"Pretty well-off for beginners. That's an expensive vehicle."

"It isn't theirs. It's her father's — borrowed."

"Imagine coming here for a honeymoon! Heat, flies, dust, dead rabbits, dead kangaroos — great start to a marriage."

"It's his second marriage," said Roger the fiction writer. "Look at him. Some cocky's son from down around Balranald. Thinks he's pretty flash. Did you see the bride?"

"Not really."

"Have a good look when they come back. She's one of those — I think of them as the typical Australian woman."

The "typical Australian woman" when she turned and started back towards her father's borrowed 4x4 was thin, plain, and colourless in this harsh light, with a weak smile on her weak features.

I'd seen that grim weak smile before, I'd seen those thin colourless worn-out features. While we were driving from Adelaide to Ballarat three years before, our hire car had developed trouble. It was Mother's Day, a Sunday afternoon, and hot. When we finally found a service station that was open for business, in the tiny rural town of Dimboola, it seemed at first that there might be fifteen mechanics there, all at work. In fact there was only one – a boy. The others were local men just borrowing tools. All around the station, inside and out, happy men ducked in and out from under the raised bonnets of the cars and trucks in which their silent wives sat grim and fuming. "Happy Mother's Day to me", their furious eyes snapped to every side. However the looks on their faces might be described, "surprised" was not one of the possibilities.

So I knew that it was compassion I'd heard in Roger's voice. It seemed as though the climate, and perhaps young men like the swaggering cocky's son, had drained all life or merriment or energy right out of this young woman who walked past us, just as the sun had sucked all life out of that woolshed and out of all this baking landscape. Perhaps she had already glimpsed the Mother's Day afternoon drives that awaited her.

The next morning we started down the dusty road towards Wentworth – perhaps an instinctual return to the river, this time the Darling where it was about to meet the Murray, which had already absorbed our Murrumbidgee somewhere along the way. (All of them perversely flowing inland in this peculiar world.) The road fled through dry mallee (whose appearance of growing out of dark stains of their own shed lives was even more appropriate here than I'd earlier imagined) and past the occasional scraggy grass clearings. The temperature light came on again and again, but went off when Roger raced the motor in neutral or when we stopped to let it cool off and to replenish the water.Eventually, however, the light did not go off. We stopped again, puzzled, not a little alarmed.

Roger tugged at the fanbelt. It seemed tight enough.

I checked the hose joints. No leaks that I could see.

With the cap off, the water level was down but not very much.

Since this exhausted our catalogue of things to do, we could only wait and imagine a long day of stops and starts –

limping down the track. In my fascination with the symbology of the fourteen stations of the place of skulls, I had not thought to worry about the effect of this via dolorosa upon the already-suffering truck.

Eventually a blue truck pulled up in front of us, a shiny new ute with a single bale of wool in the back. A stocky gentleman got out from behind the wheel, arranging his face into an expression of serious concern. "Got trouble there, have ye?"

His white hair had been slicked back with water. He wore a clean white shirt and blue shorts of a synthetic material – dressed up for a trip to town.

"Overheating. We can't figure out what's wrong."

"Fanbelt's tight?"

Why did I think that someone so far out in the wilderness should know about engines? He might have thought the same about us.

"Fanbelt's fine. Hoses are fine. The water's gone down but not much."

The traveller moved in and looked down into the open radiator.

"Bubbles come to the surface when you run the engine?"

"I don't know," Roger said. "What would that mean?"

"Means you've blown a gasket."

"The head gasket?" I said. The dreaded head gasket.

He nodded, grim. And stood back to survey the entire situation.

I'd owned a few ancient cars in my early days as a teacher. A blown head gasket was the sort of thing that caused garage mechanics to shake their heads, fight hard to hide their grins, tell you you'd have to wait four days while they caught up on these other jobs. Our trip could be already coming to an end.

Our visitor moved in again when Roger started the engine. We all stared into the open neck of the radiator. Foam rose to the surface, bubbles spilled out. The creased country face grew solemn with confirmed suspicions. "You're goin' to Mildura?"

"Wentworth."

"There'll be someone in Mildura could have a look at this

for you." He looked down the long long straight and dusty red road towards Mildura — sixty kilometres away. Then he looked beneath the opened bonnet again. Then he looked into the thicket of mallee beside the road. Obviously this was not going to be one of those situations where the stranger would say, "Well I just happen to have all the right tools in the ute to do what needs to be done to get you safely on your way."

"You'll be right then, you reckon?" he said.

"We'll get there," Roger said.

"I've got to get this bale delivered, you see."

"We'll be right. Thanks for stopping."

We watched him get into his truck, pleased with himself for having successfully sounded as if he knew what he was talking about in front of these two mechanical illiterates, but privately certain we were doomed. We watched him drive away. I imagined our mummified bodies laid out by the road, dry as that dead kangaroo. Bits of our clothing would lie here and there, like those tufts of rabbit fur. Our skeletons would be put on display in the visitors' centre, along with the poisonous snakes poster and the drawings of extinct giant animals.

"I don't think he knows anything more than we do," I said. "He just wanted to sound helpful."

"A blown gasket's probably the one thing he's had trouble with so he thought he'd say it just for something to say."

Roger looked as though he would like to believe me. "It's probably just the thermostat's stuck open."

I wondered why someone would be delivering a single bale of wool. "Did it fall off a truck, do you think, or would he be someone with just a few sheep?"

To give him credit, Roger — on this occasion as well as on others — did not betray amusement at my ignorance. "He's probably spent months gathering that up. There's some that do that — battlers back here in the bush. From fence barbs and saltbush around the countryside."

We might have hoped for the attention of a more competent Samaritan in our hour of need.

Our Good Samaritan was waiting for us in Wentworth. This mechanic not only diagnosed the problem in a very few minutes (a new radiator was mandatory) but he promised to have this new radiator, which he ordered from some other town down the road, installed by quitting time. This seemed rather unlikely to me – something of a miracle, in fact. Or was I discovering that outback living was less disadvantaged than the island living I was used to? In my experience, any mechanic with pride would insist that he had to finish working on four or five other cars before even thinking about yours. However, we were only too happy to surrender the truck to the cheerful mechanic in his service station (last "station" of our Mungo episode!) and to hand over our camera bags to his even more cheerful office manager (who had their two children in the private Day Care of her office – one in a small crib, the other sourly looking up from a heap of blankets on the floor) while we walked down over the levee to the caravan park along the river bank. Water, willows, grass, passing houseboats. In this little oasis, it was already hard to believe in the stark otherworld frightening beauty of the Walls of China while we waited for the truck to have the organ transplant which would see it reborn within the afternoon.

6 Over forty in Broken Hill

We stayed that night in a caravan park on the north bank of the Darling River, just before it joins the Murray River. This was at the end of Wentworth's short main street, beyond the dike, spread out on either side of "Sturt's Tree". The name of this explorer survived in highways, streets, a flower, a university, and even a stony desert. This was one of the most evocative of all Australian images – the tree trunk marked by a sliced-off oval with carved markings in it – calling up all at once the courage of the explorers in a hostile land, the importance of trees (with their proximity to water), and the similarity they all bore to the most famous marked tree of all, where Burke and Wills came within moments of saving their lives – a tragedy with the power to break the hearts of an entire nation, or to capture the imagination at least.

What were we doing camped on the river side of the dike? (Or levee, I was not sure what the high bank of dirt was called.) Some of the caravans were surrounded by low sandbag walls, but it was almost impossible to imagine any sort of flood in this hot country. Sydney might get the occasional rain but surely this sky had never entertained a cloud. And this river, which had collected water from any number of smaller rivers draining an area of over six million square kilometres, had still not gathered enough speed or width or depth or force to inspire visions of disaster.

Houseboats puttered by behind the screen of trees. The voices of tour guides, magnified by speaker systems, carried ashore. There was no real bank – the water was barely centimetres below ground level, lapping at the roots of the great eucalyptus trees, even seeping in amongst the layers of shredded bark in the dark hollows between them. Along the grassy edge grew limp leafy trees that reminded me of weeping willows.

"Now tell me what these trees are called so I won't go home and say we camped beside weeping willows."

"Those?" Roger barely smiled. "They're weeping willows."

While Roger was on the town side of the dike, dealing with the mechanic, I set out the camping gear, erected my tent, and then headed for the shower to get rid of the Lake Mungo dust. Afterwards, I put on shorts but not shoes. Although Roger preferred his khaki long-sleeved shirts and elastic-sided boots, I'd seen plenty of Australian men without shoes, even occasionally on city streets. I'd seen a few, in company, sitting in a living room chair with one bare foot up on a knee, fingers absently picking at dry skin between the toes throughout a conversation. Not a pleasant sight though apparently acceptable.

I hadn't been back on our site for more than a few minutes, setting up the table and the folding chairs, refilling the water containers from the tap, when a stocky man came out of the next-door caravan and called to me. "Wouldn't go walking around like that, mate. Not without me shoes."

"Snakes?" I imagined thousands of venomous snakes along the riverbank – indistinguishable from the shreds of bark. I had probably already walked past several who were waiting for me to pass by their way again. I knew from that poster in Mungo that they were practically invisible. (I must have assumed before then that they would, like the rattle-snake, politely give you fair warning. No such fair-minded-ness here.)

"Burrs," my neighbour explained.

"Burrs?"

"Grass is full of them."

"I haven't felt anything yet. This grass is quite soft."

"Across the road, I meant. You go walking across that

grass over there you'll be picking burrs out of your feet for a week."

All in a moment – so easily! – I was made to feel silly, foreign, dumb. He had that tone to his voice, that look in his eye, that showed me how ridiculous I looked. Australian men could walk around in shorts – often dirty or grease-stained – with their beer bellies hanging over the waistbands and their fingers playing with their naked toes. But I looked ridiculous and ignorantly foolish just because I'd not put on my shoes. How did this bugger know I wasn't from just down the road? How did he know he could talk to me like an idiot child – even before he'd heard a word from my mouth? "By Geez, Mabel, there's a Canadian out there! Bloody fool's beggin' for trouble."

"Well go and give the boofhead hell, Bruce. Go on."

To make things worse, while I was trying to explain that I didn't intend to cross the road to the supposedly dangerous part of the grass, Roger returned and seemed to feel, perhaps from the tone of our voices, that some sort of emergency had arisen. "What's the problem here?" The neighbour explained in a voice that suggested Roger should take his responsibility more seriously if he insisted on travelling with an ignoramus. I turned away to some task, ignoring the conversation, confident that I would never discover the nature of my sin.

The friendly possums which came out of hiding after dark and into our circle of lamplight were less judgmental than our human neighbour. One mother possum with a baby on her back placed her front paws on my safely-shod feet, moved them up my now-safely-clad-in-denim legs, and locked her pink bulge-eyed gaze on mine. Perhaps she had listened in on the earlier conversation and felt sorry for me.

The expression "to play possum" meant nothing in this country; for these animals to be so friendly, they must never have encountered any reason for playing dead. I didn't know until some time later that "possum", in the lexicon of Australian slang, is a word for the trickster's victim. The grass across the road was probably as soft and safe as my own front lawn. Bruce and Mabel had spotted an easy mark. Next morning, when a pair of squat smug Kookaburras on a nearby limb cackled uproariously for what I thought was an excessively long time without taking their beady little eyes off me, I was tempted to take it personally.

We drove the Silver Highway to Broken Hill. The truck seemed to have accepted its organ transplant without difficulty. The temperature light did not come on. We drove through groves of cypress pines and neglected wheat fields into wide expanses of brown flatland decorated with colourless grass and saltbrush. Whatever photographs I took would be lying. Wherever you looked in this country, three quarters (or more) of your vision was filled with sky. The minute I chose to put a frame around something I wanted to remember, I distorted the truth.

If Larry McMurtry is right when he insists a writer's style is influenced by his childhood landscape — his own style as level and unadorned as the low rolling Texas rangeland — what sort of effect would this flat world have upon a budding outback novelist? Sentences long as roads and flat as tables and so bereft of emphasis as to be razor thin, slipping across the pages without a burp. Words with too many upright letters would seldom get used — chains of words would keep their heads down low, "h's" and "b's" and "l's" as rare and lonely as scraggy gum trees decorating a desert. How could a writing style be ochre-red, and rubble-surfaced, and hot? I had no doubt it could, but would have to wait until I got home to my collection of Australian fiction to check it out.

I had imagined Broken Hill to be the quintessential Australian Outback town. Perhaps it was the name — something sad about it, something mysterious. Broken hearts. Devastated hills. Perhaps the photographs in coffee-table books had something to do with it: red dust piled up against a corrugated iron fence, lonely railroad station on a rusted plain. Perhaps it was the postmark on Roger's letters while he worked as a shearers' cook for the Maoris operating out of that city.

The brochures I'd picked up at the Hay visitors centre were filled with gorgeous photographs of the western end of the state (paddlesteamers on the Murray, trees along the edge of the Menindee lakes, camels in the dust of Silverton, the old courthouse at Milparinka) but did not permit a single glimpse of Broken Hill. They were keeping the place a secret.

And indeed we entered the town as though intruding upon a secret — everything was hidden by the heaps of rubble rising high above the fences which surrounded the mine compounds. Five mines operated within the city limits. Instead of building their town at a distance from their place of work (keeping the workplace out of sight, if not out of mind, like the rest of the world) these people had built their houses and stores and hotels wherever they would be tolerated in and around the mines. As a result, the tiny miner's cottages seemed to cower in their uniform rows; at every intersection commercial streets opened onto views of grey "hills of mullock" heaved up out of the earth; even the glamorous old hotels were dwarfed by the ugly mountainous backdrop which rose immediately behind them.

If Broken Hill was not exotic, it was certainly unique. Streets had been given names like Oxide and Sulphide and Bromide and Talc and Chloride. Only a few were named for the explorers whose names could be found on corner signposts in every town in the country, but to make up for this niggardliness each appeared twice — where back lanes had been developed for residences, they echoed the name of the nearest street. Thus Wills Street was followed by Wills Lane. (As Lane Street was followed, so help me, by Lane Lane.)

We found the Grazcos headquarters on one of these lanes. It was also the Taurau family home. This was a cement version of the miner's cottage: a low concrete fence surrounded the front yard, a veranda across the front of the building was partly hidden behind a dropped screen. A Grazcos sign leaned against the front veranda, near a single flowering bush. It was difficult to believe that any number of New Zealand shearers lived in this little building, along with a family of six.

A small child's face appeared behind the screen door. Then a second.

"Hello," Roger said. "What's your name?"

"Marshall."

"Martian? You're a Martian?"

"No – Marshall! Marshall!"

"And who's this?"

"That's Ramira!"

Ramira ran away.

"Is your father at home? Your mother?"

In a moment Marama Taurau came to the door. Roger already knew her, of course, from his period of cooking for her husband's shearing crews. She'd known we were arriving today, but her husband would not be home for another hour. This would give us time to find somewhere to set up our tents, though she doubted we would find any space. "There's a biker's convention in town; the caravan parks'll be filled." And even if they weren't filled, they might be dangerous. At the very least they'd be noisy. If we found there was no room for us in town, we were welcome to return and sleep, like several others, "at the back".

You only had to remember that the *Mad Max* movies were filmed in the vicinity of Broken Hill to wonder if you wanted to run into a motorcycle club that chose this spot for a convention.

Indeed the first caravan park we found was so filled with tents and motorbikes and people spread across the grass that it might have been the scene of a midway circus. Leather-clad figures stood in clusters talking, or tinkering with their bikes. Although he had no space even if we had wanted to settle down in the midst of this mayhem, the manager felt compelled to explain that these bikers were not a threat to anyone. They were members of something called the Ulysses Club, which meant they were all over forty. Apparently he believed that bikers mellowed with age, or lost their taste for terrorising people, or became more easily outwitted.

They seemed a benign and cheerful bunch. The black leather, the beards, and the studded belts suggested little in the way of threat. You could even imagine some of them with grandchildren at home, fat little hairy infants they liked to

take for joyrides on their bikes. When their glances briefly
passed over our truck, there was no indication in their faces
that they wanted to crush it between their hands, or hoped it
would be parked next to them in the campsite so they could
beat us to death with chains. They looked pretty tame. Middle-aged folks, adventuring.

Nevertheless, we drove on to the farthest corner of town
where the Lakeview Caravan Park, a slope of fenced-in grass
and small trees, overlooked the great Outback itself – an
endless stretch of brown rocky plain. Not a single motorbike.
No view of the lake which gave the place its name, either, but
we took comfort in knowing it must be out there somewhere,
probably hidden behind the pyramid of rubble from the nearest mine.

Back we went to the Taurau house, with my city map open
on my lap. "Down Argent to Chloride, turn right one block,
then left on Blende and stay on it."

I knew immediately why Roger sniggered.

"Okay, okay. Argent Street to Chloride Street, turn right
and up to Blende Street."

Australians had not taken up this North American habit of
referring to streets on a first-names basis. This was a curious
reversal of the Australian compulsion for cutting everything
down to the smallest possible size.

What had appeared to be a small miner's cottage turned
out to be only the two front rooms of a large house. A long
row of bedrooms stretched back on one side. Below, there
were more rooms. And at the back of the concrete yard, more
units. From the side, it would have the appearance of a motel.
In fact we'd passed few motels with so many people coming
and going.

Shearers and rouseabouts came and went. Some of them
were obviously Maoris. (In Canada they would be "visible
minorities", or "viz mins" in bureaucratic shorthand – a
term to make you shudder whether you were one yourself or
not.) Some were probably not, though all were New Zealand
born. Like grown-up family members still dependent on the
folks, they stepped in, watched television for a while in the

living room, grabbed a bite to eat from the kitchen, and slipped out again. The true children of the family — or at least the two youngest — stood shyly by at first, eyeing the strangers. They had such delicate features, and eyes so large and dark that even the most literal portrait painter could be accused of sentimentality.

These children seemed to be fascinated with the foreigner. They came closer, squinting up from beneath their shiny black hair.

"Jeck?" It was barely whispered.

"Yes. That's me. And I know who you are too."

They fled back, giggling, to hide behind their mother.

And to peek out from either side. "Jeck." "Jeck." Perhaps they knew no other Jacks, perhaps it was a name found only in fairy tales and school books. Perhaps it was only that they could not quite fathom that I had come, as Roger explained, from a country in the northern hemisphere.

I became a toy. One of them hopped up on my knee and put a hand on either side of my face and squeezed. "Jeck." The other swung back and forth by the chair, bright eyes promising mischief.

The adult conversation was a matter of catching up. None of my business. How was X? What happened to Y? Was it true that S and D were in trouble with the police again? It seemed they were. They'd spent the night in jail. S had been inside a shop and saw someone attack a dog which was tied up outside the door. He ran to rescue the dog but defended the animal so energetically that he was charged with assault by the very person who had been assaulting the dog. When D ran out to defend her man, she was charged with assault as well.

"And it looks like they're gonna get married."

Rewi took us downstairs to the company office, a long narrow room with a cluttered desk, a bench along one wall, a couple of stuffed armchairs at the end farthest from the screen door. A Grazcos calendar hung on one wall — a pale watercolour of the sort of plains we'd driven through on our way up

from Wentworth, landscape to hammer a writer's prose flat
to the page.

Roger had told me of his admiration for these brothers. Of
his affection for them. This admiration and affection — and
fascination — were, in fact, one reason he had thought of
doing his book. As a cook, he had worked for Rewi, a bright-
eyed man in his thirties, tall and good-looking with dark curly
hair — a Hollywood producer's idea of what a Maori should
look like if he was to be the romantic or heroic lead in a movie.
It was obvious he was eager to please, it was equally obvious
that he liked Roger. But he did not hesitate to make it clear
how busy he was, how many things he was doing all at once,
how he ought to be doing something else this minute. Hemi,
his brother and second-in-command, was a great wide happy
young man (who looked like the Hollywood producer's idea of
what a Maori should look like if he were to play a comic sec-
ondary role). Although he was much more relaxed in his body
language than Rewi, he too was a bit edgy, anxious to get this
thing started, uncertain what was about to take place.

If Rewi gave the impression of being something of a work-
aholic, it was clear from his conversation that he devoted his
energy to making the shearing go well, keeping the shearers
happy. To improve the lot of the shearer was his goal. He
wished, he said, that someone would write a magazine piece
which gave shearers a few good role-models to emulate. They
needed to hear, he said, about "shearers who've climbed up
and made somethin' of themselves."

Of course he was providing something of a role-model himself, though he did not say as much. When Roger asked him
what he considered the most important thing he and his company had to offer the shearing industry, he spoke of principles. It was important to make sure the customer was aware
of the company's principles — trustworthiness, consistency,
honesty. There was no question that these were his private
principles as well, and his family's.

In some cases, Roger had been glad to have me with him
while he interviewed. I could ask the stupid questions only a
foreigner could ask and it sometimes led to information that

might not have been disclosed without me. But there were times when my presence was not at all useful – a listener-in whose credentials were untested and unknown. I sensed almost immediately that this was one of those times. I made appropriate noises, stood up. Roger wondered aloud if I wanted to take the truck back to the caravan park. I did.

The town, of course, was closed down tight. Another Australian Saturday afternoon. No-one was in the streets. Where had they gone? This place was even quieter than what I remembered of Sundays in the town nearest to where I'd grown up, when Eaton's department store hung sheets over the display windows to save viewers from a temptation to covet on the Day of Rest. (A habit long discarded; now shops consider Sunday just another day for business.) I saw no children playing in this city of Broken Hill. I saw few other travellers – even at the tourist information centre, which turned out to be mainly a shop selling predictable gifts.

True tackiness of the Australian bush variety. Mugs, coasters, place mats, aprons, tea towels, t-shirts, sweat shirts, singlets, matchboxes, tins of tea, pieces of rock – all were emblazoned with kangaroos and emus and silhouettes of the Broken Hill mining towers.

Out on the street, it was hot. Someone in Adelaide told me it had been over forty shortly before I'd arrived. To me it felt over forty still, though I hadn't seen a thermometer since and imagined it had actually been somewhere in the late twenties or early thirties most days. "Over forty" was what I loosely tossed out in phone calls home, to those accustomed to adjusting my exaggerations for themselves. How else to convey how it felt?

At least I wasn't wearing black leather, like the hefty couple getting off the motorcycle at the curb. They took off their helmets, shook out their hair. He ran fingers down through his greying beard. She checked her face in the mirror. He leaned forward, brushed dust from the corner of her mouth. They both laughed. Then they went inside.

The Ulysses Club again? Instead of enjoying a chill down

my back and imagining murder and mayhem, from now on whenever I saw a motorcycle gang swarming across the dusty plain it would be impossible not to think of the kangaroo tea towels stuffed in their saddle bags, souvenirs for the more conventional folks at home.

I decided to go back to the caravan park and read. The cool of the rustling cottonwood, the quiet of the campsite, and the alternative world of a book seemed a good idea — Australia was sometimes just a little too much, too difficult to absorb.

Kate Grenville's *Joan Makes History* was the next on my pile, since I'd decided to leave both Keneally and Niland until I'd got away from the landscape which had intruded upon them.

This novel had been commissioned! A bicentennial project. I should probably have been offended by the very idea. The idea of commissioning a novel for a national celebration would never occur to anyone in Canada — perhaps because, if any such thing were proposed, a Royal Commission would be required to hold hearings from coast to coast before an author could ever be chosen. It would be unanimously agreed that no-one was good enough. (Unless someone from New York should say otherwise.) No-one would be representative enough either. No-one was at the same time male and female, heterosexual and homosexual, white and black and brown and yellow and red, rich and poor, newcomer and indigenous, with property in all ten provinces and two territories and a habit of writing novels set everywhere at once. That such a thing had been done in Australia, and not only done but done in such a way that Kate Grenville was still alive and writing, provided one more reinforcement of my notion of this country as a land filled with wonders impossible anywhere else.

I hadn't read long enough to discover the secret of Kate Grenville's survival, though, when I became aware that I was being observed. A blue sedan crept slowly down the far lane, across the bottom gravel, and turned to start up the lane in front of our site. It came to a complete stop in front of me.

Hemi was behind the wheel — his face split wide by a grin.

Others grinned too – the back seat was filled with happy teeth. I was introduced all around. Hemi was still waiting his turn to be interviewed. "So Oi come down to puck up these fillas." (I was barely aware of the Australian accent now, much of the time, but the sudden arrival of New Zealand vowels re-awakened my slothful ear.) These "fillas" were shearers, living in the campsite for the weekend, before setting out to a woolshed for Monday morning. They just wanted to see what sort of gear the writer and his travelling mate had set up.

The next morning Roger returned to the Taurau household to conduct his interviews. I drove the truck to a nearby service station for an oil change and lube job. Then I walked up to the house to put in time until I could pick up the truck and drive myself out to Silverton, the ghost town which has been used as the setting for a number of movies.

When I arrived, Roger was downstairs in the Grazcos office interviewing Kere, the third Taurau brother. Hemi was in the living room watching surf lifeguarding competitions on television. His huge thonged feet rested on a footstool. "Hey, Jeck," he shouted through the screen door from the far end of the room. "C'm unn. Y'want a hot drunk?"

Travel with a nonfiction writer doing research and you would be welcomed with such a great delighted smile that you almost forgot it was someone else who had earned it for you. Admittedly, you might attach yourself to writers who inspired a far less enthusiastic welcome than Roger McDonald.

Though Hemi admitted that he would watch any sport at all on television, he confessed that he had seen little Canadian hockey. He'd heard of Wayne Gretzky. He knew (he said this with relish) that Canadian hockey was violent. The important thing for this man who looked so huge in his chair that you might think he was there for good was that there be plenty of action. Surf lifeguards on the screen, dressed in the typically Australian rubber swim hats and tight swim trunks, rowed and swam and ran through the surf with displays of furious energy.

In this house, the telephone was the life-line to the world and especially to the world of work. At one point Hemi picked up the telephone to get in touch with someone in the state of Victoria whose number he didn't know. He dialed Information and asked for the numbers of everyone with that surname in that certain town. Then he started at the top of the list. "Is that X?" It was, first try. "Be here at 3:30 tomorra mornin'. You got yer gear? Y'll be out at Mulyungarie." Presumably, getting to Broken Hill by 3:30 the next morning was not an unreasonable demand to someone who'd been waiting for a shed.

A young pakeha New Zealander named Ian came in and sat looking at the television for a while. He joined in our conversation, though as a rather shy man he looked as though he were weighing the moral and physical implications of each word he uttered. To tell me he was raised on his father's sheep farm in New Zealand was a painfully serious business. His goal was to save enough money to go home and buy a sheep farm of his own.

Throughout this time, Marama was preparing a hot lunch. Being transplanted from another country was not always easy, she admitted, but she loved the clear Australian sky. "In New Zealand, there's always clouds."

We spoke briefly of my visit to Wellington. She was interested to hear that guest writers at the Wellington Writers' and Readers' Week had been taken to a Maori *Marai*, where we were given a long elaborate welcome. She spoke of her grandmother and of her mother and how they had taught her the old ways, the traditions. She agreed that it was a fine thing that the Maori culture seemed to have succesfully impressed itself upon the New Zealand consciousness but she had little use for the militants. "There's some that would push all the pakeha into the sea! Take back all the land. I'd hate to see the mess they'd make of it then."

When it was time to pick up the truck, she insisted that I come back and eat with them before I leave for Silverton. I protested weakly – surely in this house full of shearers she didn't need an extra mouth to feed – but she insisted. This was different. "It isn't often we have real visitors."

"The mechanic told me to tell you to keep an eye on the differential," I reported to Roger when we'd gathered at the table. "And the gear box. He thinks they're both leaking. He had to fill them up."

This news – that the truck had problems which had not been discovered in its pre-trip check-up nor suspected during the stressful times since – initiated a conversation about the next leg of our journey. News of rain in Queensland affected everything. Rain? How was it possible here to believe in rain? Yet an Easter weekend in the Flinders Ranges was no longer a possibility because that would be putting more distance between ourselves and the volatile situation ahead. We needed to be closer in order to respond to the changing circumstances. We would probably drive north to Tibaboora and stay in the National Park, then keep on going up across the Channel Country to Quilpie, where arrangements had been made for the next interview.

Rewi was skeptical about setting off into that country without a four-wheel drive, especially amidst rumours of rain. (Little reliable news crossed state lines, it seemed. The radio stations in New South Wales did not seem to care that a place called Queensland existed.) "You want to borrow a radio?"

He got up and fetched one from somewhere – a two-way radio made for a vehicle – and made it clear he thought a person would be a fool to go anywhere in that country without either a four-wheel drive or a radio. "You get bogged up there without a radio – you're out of luck."

Apparently there were only two kinds of road in this country – paved (sometimes referred to as bitumen, more often as sealed) and dirt. On sealed road you were more or less safe, on dirt road you were not. I could see on the map that there were far more kilometres of dirt road than sealed. It seemed there was no such thing as gravel road, or any unsealed road that had been built up and made sturdy.

Roger agreed that a radio was probably a good idea. An inaccurate fuel gauge, temperamental headlights, a taxed water-cooling system, a leaking differential, a leaking gear box, a bonnet that had taken to popping up while we drove, an ageing truck, a two-wheel drive — maybe it wasn't a good idea to head up into the Channel Country without a means of calling for help. He looked at the radio, however, with an expression on his face which suggested disgust for all of humanity — including himself — that allowed itself to become dependent upon such gadgets. Nevertheless, it was decided that once we had spent Monday with one of the Maori crews across the state line in South Australia, and Tuesday with another up the Darling River this side of Wilcannia, we would return to Broken Hill and equip ourselves properly before setting off into the dangerous and isolated north.

Milparinka. Tibooburra. Thargomindah. The "jump-ups" and sand dunes and red kangaroos and the Great Dingo Fence and Sturt National Park. I could already taste the heat and the magic and danger of the place.

7 Camels, artists, and a disgruntled cook: Trying to cope with the dust

There wasn't much magic in Silverton. I don't know if there was danger. There was, however, plenty of heat. And dust. The camels lounging in the paddock of the camel farm wouldn't know they weren't in Saudi Arabia. The camel train kneeling in the dust outside the Silverton Hotel, waiting for tourists to climb on their backs, didn't seem to care much where they were. Inside the walled courtyard of the Hotel, tourists seemed happy to have found a reason for driving all this distance – they drank beer and listened to a barefoot singer crooning love songs on an elevated corner stage while an infant crawled in and around his legs.

Even the buildings seemed built of dust – they were the same colour. This was not a town at all, just a few surviving buildings of a former town, all of them spread out across the sandy plain at peculiar angles and distances. You could see where dozens of others might once have filled in the gaps. A group of buildings might have quarrelled bitterly and decided to put as much distance between themselves as possible – without risking the loss of visitors who'd expected something cohesive.

This "old gaol" too was a museum. Was it the habit of these descendants of convicts to make museums of all their jails? Perhaps they intended you to believe they were no longer needed in this paradise. The school house sold arts and crafts. One small stone building up the slope near the church might have been a bank once, but was occupied now by an artist. He seemed to have fallen in love with emus, but found them ridiculous. His Volkswagen Beetle was decorated with them – exaggerated cartoon figures. Inside, the walls were covered with paintings of the same type. Emus with startled faces stuck their long necks up into every sort of scene – all of them the reddish-brown colour of the dust outside, the building itself, and all the plains and hills around. A group of tourists from the US South exclaimed over them. "Oh, Harry. Come look at this! Ain't it adorable?" They were so fat and so loud that even though there were only six or seven of them they took up all of the space, not to mention the oxygen. And all of the artist-salesman's time, as well. "Now take my picture in front of this one, George!" They were treating the paintings as if they were just more of the scenery to be photographed. The salesman took one painting after another down off the wall so that someone could have her photograph taken with it before he returned it. Perhaps it hadn't occurred to him yet that these people did not intend to purchase a thing.

Nor did I. Emus looked bizarre enough in real life. They needed no-one to turn them into cartoons. Though kangaroos had long ago ceased being a novelty – their pricked-up ears or bounding progress a common sight – an emu, or a pair of emus, or a family of emus, still caught me off-guard every time. Still wandering around trying to figure out how they'd got themselves onto the wrong planet.

On the drive back to Broken Hill, the several "dips" and "floodways" made the road across the flat plains an occasional roller coaster – presumably to create places where rainwater might cross. Not that you could imagine rainwater here. White upright stakes along the side were marked so that you could see how deep the "water" would be. It seemed there may be another, invisible Australia hidden behind appearances. These "dips" hinted at it, but you wondered if they were not simply some madman's paranoid fantasy, terror of the very opposite to what so obviously and permanently was. As though an Innuit in Tuktoyaktuk were to become obsessively afraid that his white frozen landscape might suddenly be transformed into a scorching desert of sand.

I stopped at the Ant Hill Gallery on Bromide Street. If art

had become the town's second industry as the brochures suggested – threatening to become its first – I wanted to see what kind of art it was. More cartoon emus? It seemed that every second person here was an artist. The town was filled with galleries. Even a department store featured an artist's work in its window. Beneath his photo was his name and the information that he was "a naive artist". I wouldn't have thought it was the kind of thing you'd want to advertise. "A fumbling violinist?" "An ignorant novelist?" I realised, of course, that I was being told that the painter was untaught, unsophisticated, unruined by education. But I was uncomfortable all the same, on his behalf.

No-one would call Pro Hart naive. This ex-miner was sophisticated enough to suspect that if his style of painting could earn him a fortune, owning the gallery that sold them would earn him even more. The Ant Hill Gallery was perhaps the best-known of the galleries devoted to "The Brushmen of the Bush", as they'd decided to call themselves.

I didn't need to be inside long to suspect that every expanse of flat landscape, every rolling hill, every chenille-spread of pale green saltbush, every wedge-tail eagle and every dingo and every shorn sheep had been painted forty times over. I shuddered to think of the tonnes of orange-red-brown paint which had been spread over canvas here.

Two moods dominated. Whimsical and awe-stricken. Amongst the whimsical were country weddings with pregnant brides and drunken guests. Also shearing mates having a smoke while the billy boils and skulls lie frying in the sun. The awe-stricken type included wide fierce blazing landscapes, lonely and harsh, with perhaps the occasional animal prowling through. Apparently tourists liked both types. They poured into Broken Hill and, finding nothing else they wanted, snatched themselves up some original art to take home – much as those early industrialists snatched up the silver, making the fortunes of those who had it to sell. A new sort of mining, this.

Ant Hill Gallery indeed. Artists worked with red-brown materials, building, building.

I wondered what my younger son would think of this. Perhaps this was because I'd called him yesterday morning before he set off for his graduation ceremony – three years of art college behind him. What would he make of this phenomenon, art as a growth industry? Artists actually making money. To be a parent of grown children is to see the world from several quite separate points of view all at once. You couldn't enter the Ant Hill Gallery and simply think "Now I like this" without also thinking, "Tyler'd raise questions about mass-production, I suppose. And wonder if the landscape had been too obviously sentimentalised, catering to the tourist looking for decoration." (Similarly, you couldn't watch stage drama in Adelaide without wishing that Gavin were there to discuss what made this particular actor so much better than the others – or, for that matter, without a knot of anxiety in the stomach on behalf of all parents of actors. And you couldn't overhear parents in Hay complain about having trouble teaching their nursery-school children to share their toys without trying to recall what anecdotes Shannon might have to tell, showing how she would handle this sort of thing at her school.)

When I'd asked the clerk about one of the prints, she said, "You're from America!" Since Australians invariably referred to the US as America, I denied it – "From Canada." My suggestion, once, in Sydney, that Canadians and Peruvians and Panamanians were American too had received only blank looks. The US revenge upon Canada for its refusal to join the Republic in the nineteenth century has been to render us invisible, inconsequential, and practically impossible.

Not entirely invisible. People had asked if I was a Canadian, but later confessed that they made a habit of doing this, knowing that Canadians were often insulted to be mistaken for Americans while Americans didn't seem to mind being mistaken for Canadians. (Once, in Adelaide, I'd said only three words before the gentleman pointed a finger and said, "You're Canadian." When I asked him how he knew, he said it was because one of the words I'd used was "out", a dead giveaway. He went off saying it to himself: "Oot, oot, oot.")

Two customers overheard our exchange and ruffled up with interest. A rather urban-looking couple with accents obviously cultivated in boarding schools. "Oh, Canada! A wonderful country. I have a cousin in – somewhere. Where is it, Herbert? Montreal?'

"No," said Herbert. "It's in the east."

"Montreal is in the east," I said. "It's probably Toronto."

"No . . ." The woman stared hard at me as though she might find a map of Canada on my face. "It's a big city." (Toronto did not qualify?) She closed her eyes to stare at her own map. "Where are you from?"

"Vancouver Island. The closest part of Canada to Australia."

She shook her head. "No." That just wouldn't do. "It isn't there. Oh, where is it?'

I thought she might insist that I list off every Canadian city until I came to one she recognised but, since neither Herbert nor I was any help, she gave up the search all at once. Her cousin was lost to us all. However, "It's a lovely country," she allowed, before dismissing me from her acknowledged field of vision.

Herbert had business to attend to. He'd come into the gallery with a mission. One' lousy Canadian who did not even know which city his wife's cousin lived in was not about to get him off the track. He was a teacher, he said. And he was ecstatic about this small painting he owned, given to him by one of his students. He lowered his voice to employ terms both sacred and scholarly to convey the content of this singular painting, and its impact. A painting of a dog, it seemed. (I imagined the thousands of dog paintings done by eight-year-olds.) He'd worked so hard himself to encourage this boy to paint, and it had turned out that he possessed genius. He lowered his voice even more, almost breathless. "And it is brilliant. I can tell you that it's – better than anything in this gallery." He glared around, daring any of the displayed paintings to challenge this.

Aha! I flashed Herbert a knowing glance (which he did not acknowledge). He wasn't fooling me. The clerk would now beg him to part with this spectacular painting. He would name an impossible price, and then brace himself to negotiate.

But Herbert was not so crass as all that. He had better plans. (And was very well dressed, I thought. He was wearing what may have been the only dress suit I had seen on this continent.) He and his wife must run, they were expected somewhere. A flurry of goodbyes and smiles and waves, and then they were gone. The clerk was left to stew overnight, presumably, devising her own plot for separating the gentleman from his work of genius.

Indeed the clerk looked stunned. She felt all over her hair for give-away signs of her battle-shocked state. Finding no escaped locks or stray hanks of hair, she stood and stared at cards on the counter, and pushed them around. Then she said, "Did you find what you were looking for?"

In fact I decided that I quite liked some of what I was seeing. Words like "naive" and labels like "Brushmen of the Bush" might put me off, and certainly you might call some of them sentimental, but the paintings themselves could do to me something like what the world outside was doing. The great red landscapes were frightening, even as they made it impossible for you to resist the urge to explore. The crowd scenes were busy, both funny and sad, in a sort of bush-Brueghal manner. You could put together the lives of an entire town by staring long enough. Naive and untutored and unsophisticated these artists may be, but their work − or some of it − would probably be gathered in by the scholars and teachers one day so that future painters, sophisticated and tutored and anything but naive, would be imitating them in warehouse studios all over Melbourne and Sydney.

To get to Mulyungarie we drove west on the Barrier Highway across the state line into South Australia. Then, on the far side of the Barrier Range (low scattered red hills, imagined mountains collapsed to feeble peaks of rubble) we drove north for another hour on a dusty road. Dust boiled up behind us as we raced across the surface of a table-flat world – over several grids, through several open gates, past strutting emus, across the railroad tracks which linked the east coast to the west. Dust got in to settle on the dashboard and everything else inside. Dust was in our nostrils and on our lips. Dust was thick on the tarp behind us. Dust storms followed in the wake of one sheep truck after another that bore down upon us and passed us, leaving us shuddering by the side of the road. One, two, three road trains, each of them loaded with four tiers of sheep. Someone was in a big hurry.

Another road train was being loaded when we arrived. The station manager and the truckie were wielding sticks and beating the sheep who balked at climbing the ramp to the penthouse tier. When the truck had been loaded, the manager came over to welcome us. That was the sixth truck to go out this morning, he said. Each of them with 450 shorn sheep bound for Adelaide.

"And what'll happen to them there?" I wanted to know.

"Shipment to the Far East. Probably Kuwait." James, the owner-manager, grinned from beneath the brim of his Akubra. "They want them shipped live, so they can face Mecca and slit their throats." He was a young man, perhaps in his thirties, with the emblem of an agricultural college on the front of his dust-streaked sweatshirt.

At $25 a sheep (I remembered this from our friend in Mungadal) six truckloads of four hundred and fifty sheep would bring in $67,500. Why did I bother figuring it out – I had no idea whether this represented a decent income or not. It was probably pocket money salvaged from rejects – rather like a sawmill owner charging someone a few dollars for the slabwood that would otherwise have just rotted in the pile by the mill.

Dust was powdery underfoot, rose up in clouds when you walked. There were few trees around, except beside the small houses at a distance from the shed – all of them up on stumps in the style I associated with Queensland. The corrugated iron of the woolshed and the nearby cookhouse and the long verandaed shearers' quarters radiated both heat and light as they baked in the sun. Horses whinnied on the far side of a fence; horses on this side ran to meet them, whinnying too. Dogs lay panting in shade, chained to trucks. Unseen dogs barked in the distance.

In the cookhouse, the cook complained to Roger of the dust. "Eating dust all day and cooking with crook equipment." She said that dust came rolling in under the door the whole day long. "Last year this time we had wool sacks packed in under there, trying to keep out the water."

It was hard to tell what the point of this comparison was. Did she prefer the water or was she presenting it as another thing to complain about in this job?

She couldn't complain that she hadn't known what she was getting into. "My grandmother was a shearers' cook, my mother was a shearers' cook, and I'm a shearers' cook." She raised a hand in the direction of a teenaged girl who'd come into the room with a broom. "Debbie there – that's my daughter – she wants to be a shearer! Her grandma must be bangin' her head on her coffin lid!" She addressed Roger; hardly glanced at me.

A slight woman in slacks, the cook moved about her kitchen as she talked, making small gestures towards preparing a meal but never quite accomplishing anything. Perhaps she didn't want an audience. She lit a cigarette and leaned back against the counter. There was a sort of washed-out look to her – her angular features were pale, her skin was dry. She reminded me of that honeymoon bride at Lake Mungo Park, though there was a touch of amusement which never quite left her Irish eyes. She was about as different as it was possible to be from the bare-shouldered upbeat cook at Thelangerin.

She and her family had got out of the shearing business altogether a few years back after a long time at it, she said. Then one daughter decided to work in shearing. Then a son announced he was doing the same. Then her husband started to talk about doing it. "Whoa, I says. If you're goin' back then so am I. We might as well all be in it together."

And yet, there were these little dissatisfactions. The owners wouldn't get you what you wanted. Nobody defended you when the shearers acted up. The shearers complained if the food was too expensive but complained if you cut back on the meals. She was fed up with them all. She had cut back to necessities and didn't care what they thought. No more ice-cream. No more pudding. She'd cut right back to the bone.

"What have you got it down to?" Roger asked.

"Four fifty a day." I understood this to mean four dollars and fifty cents a day per shearer. I already knew that Roger had managed to get his cost down to three fifty a day before he'd quit cooking. His food, he said, was "imaginative, plentiful, and cheap."

It wasn't only the dust and the water and the owners and the shearers this cook was fed up with. One cookhouse she'd worked in had been haunted. You heard noises at night. You woke up in bed with someone sitting on your chest, trying to choke you. It had happened to her mother, it had happened to her, and it had also happened to her daughter – all at different times. She would never work there again.

The cook was not the only one fed up with the dust. It preoccupied the overseer as well. Dust and its opposite. This was a short man in khaki, named Bob. "Hard to believe that last year this time they were takin' us out by helicopter." He looked out across the dusty yard, the dusty plain, and painted a picture of rising water, waterlogged sheep, humans clinging to the rope ladders of helicopters. He seemed an ordinary trustworthy man but I wondered if the heat hadn't done some damage to his memory – the cook's as well. Like the people who'd built those "dips" into the highway to Silverton.

Inside the wool shed, Roger began to take photos of shearers at work. There were only five of them today, down the outside wall of a shed so narrow that there was hardly room for the rouseabouts to operate – they seemed to have to coordinate all movements. An improvised choreography. Nobody's elbows bumped anyone else's. Nobody tripped over a shearer. Roger stood back against the wall, his elbows pulled in, careful not to get in the way. To make things even tighter, the shed was also occupied by a number of station hands running tests. The "maiden ewes" were being shorn today, we were told, and being control-tested at the same time. The fleece were weighed, various data was recorded. All this would help them choose which ewes would be best for breeding rams.

Pakeha Ian was amongst the shearers, working silently and seriously, no doubt dreaming of the little farm he would buy on his emerald isle.

The third Taurau brother was shearing as well – Kere. He was steady, quick, intense. He wore a sweat band around his head. When he stood up and turned for a drink of water I commented upon his evident skill. "I guess you must really know shearing by now."

He looked at me, friendly enough. "Yeh. I know shearin'." He paused. "I know accountin' too. And thet's what Oim goin'ta do right after Chrussmess." He turned again, stuck his cigarette in the middle of his mouth, and went in through the little gate to grab himself a sheep.

One more shearer who dreamt of getting out!

When it was time to break for lunch the station hands jumped down out of the shed, threw their legs over their motor bikes, whistled up their dogs to sit on their laps, and took off in separate clouds of dust. These boys – none looked more than twenty – were modern jackeroos. Once they'd have gone galloping off on their horses. It must be hard to feel "tall in the saddle" when you're sputtering across the dirt on a Yamaha 250, however shiny and new.

The manager pulled up in his Toyota ute and invited us to eat our lunch at his house. Somewhere on his rounds he'd picked up a dead sheep which had rotted to the point of falling to pieces. Not surprisingly, it stank.

This and all other unpleasantness was banished to the world outside the high board fence which surrounded the house and its lush flowering garden. This broad screened-verandaed house was up on cylindrical concrete stumps. A hallway ran right down the middle. The kitchen was large, with a great wide table in the middle, covered with oilcloth.

Snapshots decorated the door of the refrigerator. Although the adjoining room was the office, there was a sink in it for washing up. A practical touch. The dust had become mud around James's collar and — with his sweatshirt removed — down the front of his shirt.

James's wife wasn't home. They were expecting their first child, he said, and she was down in Adelaide for an appointment with her doctor.

James was the heir of a squatter family. Brought up in Adelaide the son of a barrister, he was educated in agricultural college and was now managing this, one of three stations in the family. It was about twenty miles wide and reached from the Dingo Fence in the north, I understood, for about 300 miles to the south. This did not seem so huge as it might have once, before I'd been given some idea of how much space each sheep needed — ten acres — in order to find enough to eat off those little grey saltbushes that grew in the rust-red dust.

People had been lost on the property. This was one reason that James, like others we'd met, hated the Easter weekend. Everyone took to the roads, went where they had no business going, didn't know how to prepare for the trip, caused no end of trouble for others.

Roger dreaded the coming Easter weekend for much the same reason. Too many people. "We'd planned to meet with friends in the Flinders Ranges," he said. "But the place will be swarming with holidayers. We may go north to Sturt National Park instead, but that could be just as bad."

I tried to imagine the all-but-deserted roads turned suddenly into freeways filled with carloads of city people madly racing towards the few scraps of Outback space not already occupied by those who got there first. But did not succeed.

To demonstrate his contempt for these hordes of unwelcome Easter travellers, James told us about a couple of bush-campers who'd got lost up at the north end of the property just a year before. They hadn't asked — nobody on Mulyungarie knew they were there. The wife of one of the missing men telephoned one day, she knew only that they were in the area somewhere and hadn't come home when they should have. A station hand eventually found them. Lost, hungry, frightened.

Stupid bastards, his tone of voice suggested. They ought to have known better.

Ungrateful too. "Never phoned to say thank you. Never wrote." There was no question about the contempt with which the station manager viewed all those town and city folk who thought this country was put there for the sake of their fun. Or adventure. They deserved what they got; they ought to stay home; you had to understand this country if you wanted to get out of it alive.

The station hand who'd found the lost weekenders was one of the several kangaroo shooters the station kept on permanent staff.

"They shoot many?" I thought maybe it was a sort of honorary employment. A kangaroo now and then just to keep your trigger finger in shape.

"Last year they killed five thousand."

That many. "Big reds, I guess — out here." To show I knew something — that we'd entered the territory of the truly big ones.

He nodded. "Yeh." Smiled. Probably thought he'd shocked me. He hadn't. Or hadn't so much as he'd hoped. I'd already discovered for myself how kangaroos could make enemies. In Adelaide, guest writers were driven out to a wildlife sanctuary, given a boxed lunch, and marched off to eat it inside a fenced paddock populated by several dozen of these hopping beasts. Once the animals realised that we had food, it became necessary to dance about, climb trees, perch on stacks of posts, and even engage in physical force, to keep them from wrestling our lunches from our hands. A few hours later we were treated to a banquet of kangaroo steaks.

I didn't ask James what was done with the five thousand corpses. South Australia was the only state in the Commonwealth where eating kangaroos was legal, but would gourmet appetites take care of such an impressive slaughter? This was one of those situations where I had no business raising questions. Australians were still fighting about this themselves. And anyway, I didn't want to have Newfoundland's seals thrown in my face. Or, for that matter, Vancouver Island's forests, if anyone had known enough to do so.

We made sure we were back in Broken Hill before the shops closed. In a three-day visit, it would be nice to see the town once, however briefly, while it was open for business. For me this meant a chance to visit the bookstore on Argent Street, in the centre of town. It seemed unfair to the writers of serious fiction to be trying to read their novels with only half a brain. I would save the unread Keneally, and Niland, and Grenville (as well as the Thea Astley still at the bottom of my bag) until I was home. In the meantime, I would try something light. Roger had mentioned a thriller named *Wake in Fright* which was supposed to be set in Broken Hill.

Wake in Fright. Could be about campers terrorised by bike gangs. Not the Over Forty Club, surely. As several members roared past on their shiny motorcycles, creased faces happy as children, one of them briefly caught my eye and nodded a greeting. A pale, simple face. He might have been the tax accountant from next door. Just another middle-aged man enjoying himself. Fellow traveller.

I wondered if the Ulysses Club had been inspired by Homer, Joyce, or Tennyson?

... Come, my friends,
'Tis not too late to seek a newer world.
Push off, and sitting well in order smite
The sounding furrows; for my purpose holds
To sail beyond the sunset, and the baths
Of all the western stars, until I die.

The shop did not have *Wake in Fright*, however. Nor had the proprietor heard of it. She was new to town. *The Lemon Tree* was set in Broken Hill but I'd already ordered one in Sydney. By now it ought to be crossing the Pacific, heading for home.

If not a thriller, something useful then. Patsy Adam-Smith's *The Shearers* would undoubtedly fill in some of the enormous gaps in my background. I'd seen Patsy Adam-

Smith on a television program at home, talking about Australia in this century's wars. She seemed gritty, and tough, and intelligent. The book included a number of photos along with the text. There was the One Tree Hotel. A barge loaded with wool bales heading down the Murrumbidgee. Though I doubted that Jacky Howe and these other legendary gods would be as interesting to me as the living breathing shearers I'd been talking to today, this was obviously the sort of reading material that I needed.

Roger agreed, when he came in from making a series of calls from a phone box down the street. It would be good for my education. At the moment, though, he was more interested in meeting a shearing contractor he'd just spoken to on the phone. He would do so tonight. "This fellow's office is a table in a hotel bar. He's 'open for business' there one hour a day." Quite a contrast to the 24-hour commitment you sensed at the building across town which provided the Taurau family with a home, Grazcos with an office, and the New Zealand shearers with admirable role models as well as a Home Away from Home.

8 *So this is what it means to be bogged*

I'd heard altogether too much talk about rain. As we drove east from Broken Hill, heading for a station near Wilcannia on the Darling River, the sky was a glaring blue. It had been a glaring blue every morning of the trip. The day was already hot. Ahead we could see another optical illusion – trees grew above their own reflections on the far side of what appeared to be a lake but which of course was no such thing. This obsession with imaginary rains, or rumours of rain to the north, was – like the optical illusions – probably just one more effect of the heat, so much sun and dust.

And anyway, for someone who had lived his life in the rainshadow of the Vancouver Island mountains, it was hard to imagine why the thought of a little moisture should cause such tension.

The tension on the driver's side of the truck increased when dark clouds appeared on the horizon ahead, just an hour out of town. Not content to stay where they were, these clouds were hauling themselves towards us, dragging great dark sagging underbellies that made them appear as though they were looking for somewhere to settle down. "Oh hell, Jack, I think we're going to see a little rain."

We were seeing it already: rainclouds ahead sent down solid shafts to earth, like space ships beaming down some extra-terrestrial power. Road trains swept by in a roar that left us not only shuddering in their wake but surrounded by mist.

And suddenly the rain fell upon us with a terrible weight.

Dust on the windscreen was a smear of mud for a moment, then a series of curved disintegrating streaks, then gone. The road surface shone from beneath an instant lake. We were thrashed and beaten.

Within moments, pink puddles were expanding to fill in the spaces amongst the pale green bushes. Whole stretches of land seemed to have turned into swamp. A few sheep huddled beneath a gum tree. A cow shook its head. Ragged roadside scrub seemed to be torn violently out of my vision as we raced on past. Everything might have been screaming for help.

Off to the left, the flat red land stretched north into the world we intended to cross in just a few days. The occasional dirt road disappeared beyond a mail box into the low bush — one of those was the road we would take. (I could still not quite get it through my head that these modest tracks that looked like private lanes belonging to the abject poor were actually public roads recorded on the map.)

Roger pulled over, looked at the puddle that stretched across the entrance to a road, then turned around. "Better go back to that roadhouse and use the phone."

The tattooed man behind the roadhouse bar at Little Topar didn't mind sharing his phone. At least we weren't expecting him to abandon his newspaper and serve us. The road from Wilcannia, Roger was assured, would cause no difficulty. The rain hadn't got that far. If things got bad once we were there, we could simply stay the night.

As we passed through the little town of Wilcannia, black faces watched us from the veranda of the hotel and from inside the open doors of little houses. A few drops of rain had just begun to fall here. The road out of town, though dry enough, was not easy driving. It was built up with chunks of rocks, many of them sharp. We cringed, winced, empathised with the tortured tires. But things got worse when the rain started to fall and the road took on the softer smoother texture of peanut butter. We slipped and slid on grey-pink grease. So long as we stayed on the high central crown we could keep going, but this wasn't easy — gravity wanted to drag us out of that perfect balance and down the slope to one side.

This was called "black-dirt country", though I couldn't guess why – dirt here was as pink as everywhere else. Pink and slippery. We travelled twenty kilometres or so on it – Roger constantly battling with the wheel, regularly overcorrecting as though he were piloting a boat on turbulent water. Then, suddenly, something threw us altogether off balance, we slid to the left, fishtailed, turned sideways downhill, slipped around backwards, and came to a stop with our rear tires in the muddy trough at the side of the road.

"Oh, shit."

The truck refused to reconsider. A new petrol gauge, repaired lighting wires, a new radiator, a new grease job, a new oil change, and still it was being stubborn. Tires spun. We got out to consider possibilities. There were none. In all this wide expanse of flat wet land there was not a sign of human life. No farmhouse hid behind those scattered gum trees. A tufted muddy world fled out in all directions under too much pearl-grey sky.

The only movement: three kangaroos grazing fifty metres away. They looked up, twitched their ears, and decided to ignore us.

I folded back the tarp. As The One Who Know Where Things Are Kept, it was up to me to find the rain gear. Roger's drizabone was precisely where it was supposed to be – scrunched in a ball and shoved down in the well of a spare wheel. My hooded rain-jacket had to be got from inside a suitcase, which was under the folding table, which was beneath the foam mattress, which was getting wetter every moment I kept the tarp peeled back.

We tried pushing. That is, I put my foot against the bank and leaned into the tail-gate while Roger released the clutch. Futile.

"This is ridiculous," I said. "It shouldn't be any different than getting out of a snow bank."

"Well here's your chance to put your Canadian skills to use. Get us out of this mess – if you can."

From a nearby eucalyptus we collected twigs and limbs
and put them under the rear tires. But Australian mud was
not Canadian snow. The sticks shot out from under the tires
as though from a sling. The rocking technique sometimes worked in greasy West
Coast snow — ahead a little, back a little, ahead a little, back
a little — but it didn't work in the greasy mud of New South
Wales. Not far away the kangaroos had come out onto the
road and started jumping up and down. Did they enjoy playing in this muck, like children? I suspected they were mock-
ing us: "Nyah nyah, why don't you simply hop out of this
mess? Here's how it's done."

The rain seemed to have altered the very make-up of the
dirt particles. Parts of the surface looked dry, yet you discovered if you put your foot on it that everything beneath had become three or four inches of lard. Your foot broke the surface
and sank, the mud surrounded your shoe, then you raised the
foot and brought a heavy coating of the mud up with you.
With each step the coating got thicker, heavier. You would
soon be rooted. Meanwhile, it continued to rain. Our own ruts
were long ribbons of milk chocolate water. The ditch was a
milky unmoving creek.

I did not say: I guess we should have taken Rewi's radio.

I certainly did not say: I suppose a four-wheel drive would
sail right over this.

The silence had hardly had time to get awkward when a
yellow Daihatsu 4x4 came whining down the road. It stopped.
A grinning young man stepped out to look us over. Rain
poured down from off the brim of his hat but he didn't seem
to mind. He didn't seem to mind anything. This sort of thing
might happen every day in his world. He attached a thick
chain to the front of the truck and pulled us up the slope to the
crown of the road, then towed us up the road to where we
could turn around and start getting ourselves out of this
place. He followed while we slipped and slid and fishtailed for
a kilometre or so. Then we went out of control again and into
the ditch.

At least we'd brought our rescuer with us. Or so we

thought. But this time the Daihatsu had broken down. The driver could not get it started. "No worries." He threw up the bonnet and peered in. He wasn't grinning any more. He climbed beneath. He started taking things apart.

"I reckon I know what the trouble is," he called up.

But when everything was back together again, the engine still wouldn't start. He scratched his head. It was a mystery. This whole world had become a mystery. We stood about, feeling guilty, trying to look as though we'd be glad to help if he'd only tell us what we could do.

As if we weren't already part of something absurd enough, an entire parade of vehicles was soon whining down upon us from behind the Daihatsu. Drivers hopped out and came up to see what was going on. One of these (the broadest grin) was Hemi – the little blue car was his girlfriend's. He was not wearing his gigantic thongs today; he was barefoot, his great wide feet encased in layers of mud. He leaned for a moment against our tailgate and you could almost believe that a man his size might move it – might pick any one of these vehicles up and carry it beneath his arm to safety.

The truck behind his girlfriend's car was filled with the shearers Roger had come to photograph. Had they been planning to escape? They stayed where they were and waited. Nothing that was going on was of any interest, apparently. The driver of the little white Suzuki Sierra at the rear of the queue was curious enough to come up and investigate. Then he went back and got into his truck. He roared down into the ditch and up into the bush and came whining up past everyone to bounce down onto the road again in front of us. Within moments he had us up on the crown again, facing in the right direction, and attached himself to the troubled Daihatsu.

Now we were a true parade – a little blue sedan, a large four wheel drive truck full of Maori shearers on their way to town, a Suzuki pulling a Daihatsu, and – leading the entire pack – ourselves in the Holden.

We did not lead the pack for long. Across a dry creek bed a "side track" had been made to avoid a condemned wooden bridge. Here the mud was even softer than in other places.

We slipped to one side, slithered, swung sideways, slid towards the bank (a metre-high drop) and came to a stop only a hand's breadth from the edge. Bogged for the third time today.

We were not, however, rescued for the third time today. We were abandoned. First the farmer left us, pulling the original rescuer behind him. Then Hemi and his girlfriend, who was anxious to get out on the proper road for home. Then even the truckload of shearers who were our reason for being here. They were going only as far as Wilcannia on some errands, they said, but would be back immediately to rescue us. They would pick us up and take us to the woolshed, leaving the truck where it was if the road had not improved. We stood and watched the last of civilisation drive away.

We should think about what we absolutely must have with us, Roger suggested. "In case we have to leave the truck here and sleep in the shearers' quarters."

This was so appropriate that it seemed inevitable. What better way to imagine the life of an Australian shearer than to spend a night on the bedsprings of an Australian shearer's cell? Nonfiction research at its best.

We waited, leaning against the truck. Then we paced – in opposite directions – mud building up on our shoes. We met to consider how long it might take to get to Wilcannia and back, how long they might take to do whatever it was they had gone in to town to do. The approach to the old bridge was packed down with gravel and uncut by recent traffic, but its surface was seething with millions of tiny red ants. The bridge was best of all, but you had to watch your step – there were some rotted planks, and dangerous gaps. Under the bridge was dry but you couldn't listen for the sound of approaching rescue from under a bridge, or feel you were actually doing something about the situation.

"Maybe Hemi is finding it hard to say goodbye to his girlfriend."

"And to his girlfriend's car."

"The shearers are probably feeling sorry for us, but find it hard to tear themselves away from the bar."

"That Suzuki farmer's had time to leave the Daihatsu in town and come back."

If we listened hard enough, we believed we could hear his dogs barking to welcome him home, off in the riverside trees.

"He's about to put his feet up by the stove and have a good laugh, telling his wife about us."

At least this was an opportunity to observe. An Australian classroom. Roger pointed out a cloud of black cockatoos passing over, making sure they were heard. All around, crows were making their terrible deserted-child sound – something North American crows had never learned. The magnificent tree in the dry creek bed was a coolabah. "As in 'Waltzing Matilda.'" That was a red gum by the bridge, with black and white patchy bark. These low prickly bushes along the bank did not deserve a name – they were merely "woody weeds".

These flies had little regard for our special circumstances, and worked as hard as flies everywhere at their job of driving humans mad.

Darkness was in the habit of falling suddenly at six o'clock. At six o'clock we had been here for half a day and it seemed we had indeed been deserted. So great had been our trust that we had not even considered the possibility that now stared us in the face. We could be here overnight.

"Jack, we'd better build ourselves a fire."

"Here? Out of what?"

"And we'll have to think about setting up the tents, if that rain lets up for a while."

Where could you set up camp in a wet flat muddy world like this? "Under the bridge?" Roger wondered this aloud. For under the dilapidated bridge was the one dry place in our universe.

"But what if there's one of your famous flash floods in the night?"

I did not really consider this a sensible question, but had begun to believe that on this continent the impossible happened all the time. I remembered reading a newspaper article about sardines raining on the town of Ipswich. No explanation given. When it came to news from Australia, Canadian newspapers assumed the bizarre was normal in this inverted world. In view of this, a house-high wall of water slamming down that narrow depression like something in a Cecil B. de Mille movie didn't seem all that unlikely.

Roger grunted, and looked elsewhere for inspiration.

"Not on top of the bridge either," I said, since there would be no place to drive in the stakes. And anyway, a condemned bridge could not be trusted to stand up all night under unaccustomed weight.

We walked up onto the approach to the bridge and shone our torchlights down between our feet at a sea of scurrying ants. If you stomped your foot they went mad; if you stood still, they took this as an invitation to run up your leg. Presumably a pair of tents would not encourage them to evacuate.

Only one small patch of mud was free of ants and clear of saltbush and yet still relatively solid – an ordinary sort of mud that showed no signs of wanting to imitate the road. It was perhaps seventy-five metres from the truck – a long trek back and forth with torches, carrying our gear, while our feet insisted on going out from under us without warning. This way, then that, then both ways at once. It was not unlike trying to walk on a black-ice-covered Ottawa street. (The last time I'd tried that, I'd ended up making my way home on all fours.)

So we moved our gear to the chosen spot but did not set it up. We would build a fire first, and wait until the rain let up before unpacking. To go out gathering firewood in this soggy flatland seemed a hopeless task. With torches we scrounged around in the riverbed after twigs and shreds of bark. We broke dead branches off the "woody weeds". We found newspapers in the truck, and tore splinters off the planks of the dilapidated bridge. A sour smell rose from the earth.

"That still doesn't seem like much." Roger raised his eyes to the horizon, still filled with hope.

"Well, there's the bridge railings. Some of them looked pretty loose."

We wrenched loose railings off the bridge and dragged

them up to our fire, where we laid them out so that they crossed one another above our little flame. It was soon possible to boil the billy for tea while we sat on our plastic-covered folding chairs in the dark, reassuring ourselves that the rain would let up any moment or the shearers come back or something happen that we hadn't anticipated. The slight breeze shifted its direction often, so that every time you thought the mosquitoes might drive you screaming across the darkened surface of earth you were suddenly engulfed in a cloud of smoke which drove them away, and that every time you thought you would expire from the smoke getting into your lungs the shift in wind direction brought fresh air and the mozzies back again.

"Can you hear a dog barking?"

"I can't hear anything."

"There's a car somewhere. Listen."

"I heard it. It's gone. It was going the other way."

"There's someone over there with a loudspeaker and a recording of sound effects, hoping to drive us mad."

Rain off and on. A bit of moon between clouds. A single star to the north. Then solid rain again — we'd waited too long in hopes of a clearing. We would have to set up our tents in the wet.

At eleven o'clock we crawled inside, but lay with our heads out the openings, watching the fire and listening for that inevitable sound of the shearers' approach. Surely even Wilcannia pubs must close when the law required it. Since Roger was about to immortalise them in a book, it seemed to me they could put themselves out a little to rescue him from this mud.

"Maybe the road's been closed and they aren't allowed to come in and get us."

What if it rained for weeks and NO-ONE was ever allowed to come in and get us? What if the whole world was being evacuated out there, racing south ahead of a gigantic flood, and nobody was allowed to come and tell us of the fate that was on its way?

"I think the rain's letting up."

"You think so?"

"Well it isn't as bad as it was."

The fire licked at the white paint scales on the bridge rails. Wet branches sizzled below. Our voices seemed as strangely naked and crookedly etched in the silent night as the silhouettes of the eucalyptus trees against the moving sky. You wanted to whisper – but why?

"Who was the person on the phone who said it was all right to come down here?" (Probably said, "She'll be right, mate," without even looking out the window.)

Nobody came. Silence was as heavy as a quilt laid out in all directions. Where were those cheeky kangaroos now? Watching. Laughing at us. I remembered when a friend and I (both ten-years-old) spent the night in a little cabin we'd built ourselves of trunks of young green alder; we lay awake the entire night listening for the bears we knew were sneaking up from all around in the woods. We'd have been disappointed to think that none considered eating us.

"Time to get up, Jack."

"What time is it?" *(It was still dark, for crying out loud.)*

"Five o'clock." I could hear the grin in the words. I could sense him standing outside his own tent, grinning at the world. "The shearers'll come through about six to start work. We've got to get our gear ready before they get here."

Why? We seemed to have waited all night – or most of it – for them. Now let them wait for us.

"How does it look?"

"Drier, I think. The road looks a little drier from here."

I would believe anything of this place. But Roger's eyes were telling him what he wanted to see – on closer examination the road was every bit as wet as it had been the night before. Long ditches of milky mud defined our tyre ruts like claw-marks down the road-face; cocoa puddles lay in every footprint. There were even a few drops of falling rain to disturb the ugly surface.

Who could lie in bed? My sleeping bag had got wet where

it touched the wall of the tent. My feet were wet. The clothes I'd rolled up near my head were wet.

By six we had our muddy tents down, our wet gear packed away, and dry clothes put on, but there was no sign of the shearers. If they were going to work today they weren't going as early as Roger intended them to. Magpies started their warm-up exercises in the trees to the south, along the imagined river. A group of children with reedy flutes, piping random notes.

By seven we'd cooked ourselves a little breakfast. The fire had survived the night. But there was still no sign of the shearers. Except for the magpies, this desolate place was as silent in daylight as it had been in the dark.

After breakfast we began hauling rocks up out of the ditch, to pack them in front of the tires. Then we inched the truck ahead on its cobbled road. We did the same again.

"Jack Absalom would have his inflatable bag attached to the exhaust pipe by now," Roger said. "He'd be up and out of here in no time at all."

Jack Absalom, Jack Absalom! Once this famous air bag had lifted your truck up out of the mud – what was supposed to happen next? Did it float up, like a helium balloon, and come down somewhere on dry rocky ground? It seemed a rather stupid idea to me.

By eight o'clock we'd moved the truck a metre or so closer to Wilcannia and the sealed road. Give us a year or so and we might finally get there! But the wheels had slipped a little closer to the edge. The bank was sliding out from under it. Still no shearers.

At eight-thirty we boiled the billy for coffee. Flies were trying to make up for the periods in which they'd been thrown out of work by the rain. My dark-blue hooded waterproof jacket was decorated with a map of several pink continents.

Eventually, a distant and persistent whine could be heard which could not be anything but the sound of an approaching truck.

Indeed it was the shearers' four-wheel drive. Rewi was at the wheel. Shearers grinned out at us from the backseat but did not offer any explanation for their desertion. Nor did anyone ask if we'd had a comfortable night. Wiry Ihaia leapt out, a happy perpetual-motion machine, to begin doing something about our truck. A boy named Chris leapt out behind him to help. Rewi gave us a hot meat pie to share. "Some breakfast." He'd had to call the shearers back to Broken Hill for the night, he explained. He would take the crew in to the woolshed and then come back, so that he and Ihaia could get us out of this mess.

Rewi took charge. The man of principle was also a man of practical ideas, as well as a man of action. With his jack and our chains and a come-along, the truck was coaxed away from the edge of the road. First the jack was established on a piece of sturdy board, the rear end was cranked up, the chain to the four-by-four tightened, pulling our truck's tail through the air until the tilted jack collapsed and the truck's back wheels dropped to the earth again. Then the process was begun all over again, easing the tail end of the Holden towards the crown of the road. Jack Absalom should have been there to witness this.

When Ihaia took over, Rewi stepped back beside me. He grinned, and shook his head. "Quite a place, enn't it."

"A country of extremes, that's for sure."

He was an outsider here himself, or had been. After several years of living in Australia, he confessed he was still not used to the surprises it could throw you. He also had some advice to give me. When this country got to you and you started to get irritable, "you have to go off by yersilf and loi down and have a smoke or somethun." It was something he'd had to do quite often, I could tell.

I was not irritable at all, and I would not go off and lie down and miss any of this if I were. (Lie down where?)

Eventually, a chain was attached to the front of the Holden and Rewi's truck pulled it out onto the crown and along the road until it was free of our churned-up mud. Roger drove off then, towards Wilcannia, where he would leave the Holden locked in a mechanic's compound. Rewi followed, and brought him back, and picked the rest of us up so that we could go sailing off, at ninety kilometres an hour, over the mud like a hovercraft over water, towards the woolshed we had been trying to get to for more than twenty-four hours.

Evening. Nyngan. We checked into a motel for the night so that our gear would have time to dry out. Sleeping bags, tents, and wet clothing were laid out across the floors of both units, hung from doors, draped over shower curtain rails. Brick-hard mud was hammered and chipped away from shoes in heavy clods; what didn't fall away turned to gumbo again beneath the bathroom hot-water tap; white Reeboks eventually revealed themselves to be a uniform rose. Shirts and jeans had acquired patches which looked suspiciously like the results of a blood bath. Cowpokes might be cleaning up after a gunfight.

The motel was called The Alamo.

The Alamo! Synonymous with ignoble defeat after long siege. Heroic deaths − a slaughter, in fact. "Remember the Alamo!" is an American cry demanding revenge for humiliation. The neon logo above the wet parking lot suggested Davy Crockett or Daniel Boone or John Wayne − one of those men who wore dead raccoons on their heads. Was there something appropriate in the name today? I had a feeling there was. I had a feeling, in fact, that the kind of journey we'd been on until now had come to a sudden end.

It was all the fault of the rain. It was the rain − and the news of even worse rains up in Queensland − that changed our plans. By the time we left the sheep station in the afternoon, it had been decided that we would not go back to Broken Hill after all, as we'd earlier planned. Nor would we risk taking the short cuts on dirt roads across the Channel Country to Quilpie. Instead, we would play it safe, take the sealed roads, the long way, up to Charleville. If the rains had not let up by the time we got there we would keep on going up to Roger's brother's cattle station north of Clermont.

Earlier that afternoon, once Roger had taken his photos and cleaned out the cookhouse abandoned by a cook who'd been fired the day before, Rewi had driven us to Wilcannia where the Holden waited in the mechanic's compound. We weren't sorry to avoid spending the night in the ramshackle sleeping quarters with their rough unpainted little rooms and rusted bedsprings, their muddy yard littered with bones and half-decayed animals and scraps of machinery. We filled up with petrol and went into the attached cafe for hamburgers before setting out for Nyngan. "I didn't want to say anythun before," Rewi said, his dark eyes twinkling as he was about to take his first bite of his hamburger. Whatever he hadn't wanted to say before he could hardly wait to say now. "The road is closed."

"Whaddaya mean, closed?"

It had been closed, he said, before we went in. "There's a sign. If the cops seen you come out you could hev been booked."

"Booked?" You were "booked" into a cell in the city jail.

But "booked", like other words, had its own meaning here. "Fined. $1,000 a kilometre."

Roger and I looked at one another, calculating. $20,000! Even split two ways it was impressive. After all we'd been through, to be insulted by a $20,000 fine!

I'd noticed their stupid sign, I remembered now. Of course I'd noticed it. Small and white and up on a post on the left. It had never occurred to me to draw it to Roger's attention. Small and white! What race of people is this that think small and white is good enough to stop people from straying into dangers? Yellow and large, maybe. Bright scarlet stretched right across the road would be better. Besides being small and white, this sign had been ambiguous − to say the least. "Road to Menindee Closed." We were not going to Menindee. I'd understood it to mean: If you want to go all the way to Lake Menindee you'd better not try, because eventually you will run into a scarlet barrier across the road that will stop you from going on. Obviously the sign had not been meant for us. Anyway, if the road was "closed" why wasn't it indeed closed? A foreigner could get into trouble around here, taking things too literally.

Roger and Rewi seemed to understand this matter in a way

that I could not. I could be sure, they explained, that the threatened fine was not because we had foolishly risked our necks, our axles, and our sanity by going down that "closed" road that wasn't really closed. The substantial fine would be because we had messed up their road. When the sun came out again and sucked the moisture out of the dirt, turning it once again into hard-packed dust, our footprints and tire tracks and bog holes would all be hardened into permanent features of the surface.

You could only decide to let a foreign country have a few peculiarities. A motel called The Alamo was an appropriate place to spend the night.

9 *"Please call again soon":*
The siege of Charleville

Not only were we still alive when we left The Alamo the next morning − an historically unique accomplishment − but we took our time about doing it. The sky was still an unpleasant sight, the parking lot was one large puddle reminding you of what damage the sky could do. And we − despite everything − were heading north. Bourke, the Queensland border, Cunnamulla, and finally Charleville, our immediate destination, 650 km up the Mitchell Highway. A long day of driving.

The rains had turned everything green. Grass grew along the shoulders. Trees and shrubs seemed alive and healthy. Out in the scrub, abandoned cars seemed to be emerging from beneath the verdant earth, nosing up to smell the fresh new world which had replaced the drought they'd burrowed to escape. For me, after the dust we'd left behind, this was like driving down a long avenue through a botanical garden. For Roger it was a disappointment: "I wish all this green would stop so we could see the rich redness of the soil."

Before leaving home I'd read a hitchhiker's account of his travels through this part of the world. He'd referred to this stretch of land as "dry and dusty and dull as muesli without milk." Well, the milk had just been added − bringing about a miracle.

For a while I mused over a story idea Roger had mentioned last night in a conversation about stories begun and abandoned. We had both abandoned plenty. This one seemed too good to be thrown back − I wished it were mine. Something that grew out of his period as a new teacher, when he'd lived in a small town hotel. A Criterion Hotel. The characters he'd mentioned, the situations he'd described, even the name of the hotel all seemed (to me) too good to drop. I imagined how I would structure a novella for it. Then I rewrote it as a stage play. It would eventually make a superb movie – making me rich. The Criterion Hotel – it even suggested the theme: young people searching for criteria upon which to base their adult lives. I had everything – structure, characters, mood, theme – everything, that is, except the details that would make it work. Roger had those, and he was keeping them to himself.

In Bourke, we crossed the Darling River again – at its source this time, as Wentworth had been its destination, swallowed by the Murray. We drove up and down a few residential streets in search of the house where Roger had lived for a while as a child. Several towns claimed to be the "gateway to the Outback" but Bourke's claim had been one of the first, and remained loudest. "When I was a boy here," Roger said, "the Outback was just whatever was farther out than you were yourself. Now it's a fashionable term, for the sake of commerce."

As a Presbyterian minister's son, he'd lived in a number of houses in several small towns in New South Wales. This one may have held more memories than others, since it came later. However, the house was not to be found. Where it once stood, a modern motel displayed its VACANCY sign. One more piece of childhood had been erased. This sort of insult did not encourage us to hang around but we stopped at the row of telephone boxes outside the post office – our last town before leaving the state. Once again, Roger had calls to make.

Quite a few, I think.Once I'd visited the nearest butcher shop and the nearest grocery, I still had some time in the truck to observe the street activity. Shoppers came and went, looking much like shoppers anywhere. Clerks dashed out of shops and ran to the Post Office, then ran back. Not far away a crowd of Aborigines seemed permanently attached to a small part of the pavement in front of the open door of a hotel bar. A scene, I realised all at once, I had been seeing again and again as we passed through the towns of New South Wales.

Two white women pushed baby prams down the footpath in front of the hotel. For a moment they paused. One of the black women — a girl really — held a baby. Words were exchanged amongst mothers, while around them old men, young men, boys, were busy assembling, parting, reassembling, consulting, going in and out through the door. A constant tentative restless tension between breaking away and returning, as though they were all connected to one another by invisible elastic strings.

I recalled one afternoon in Alice Springs when Dianne and I were walking in to town from our hotel. It was some time before we understood that what we were walking beside was a river. Bridges spanned what was a wide but only shallow depression, completely dry. Those great white trees were growing off the river's sandy bottom. It was even longer before we realised that the river's bed was more than the peculiar habitat of several hundred trees; it was a passageway as well — dark figures moved along it, in clusters of two or five or seven, in the direction of town. In wool caps and dusty clothing, they seemed to drift slowly — how could I guess whether they were moving up-river or down? There was something about the way they walked that suggested wading — bodies leaned back, hands dragged across the tops of low bushes, slim legs moved as though pushing against water.

On the streets of Alice Springs, whites and blacks passed without seeing one another, I thought. Eyes were not averted, or even careful; they looked at different worlds. When an old black woman with a shopping bag suddenly started shouting at another black woman a block away, none of the whites between them even seemed to notice. Even there, where sand and pavement had both been covered over with the interlocking paving bricks of someone's idea of a city, they walked paths that seemed as separated as the black-topped roads and the dusty river bed coming in to town.

After dark, as we returned to the hotel, there were voices and campfires along the river bottom, amongst the pale ghosts of the beautiful white-barked trees. To return to the hotel room was to be left out of things, but no alternative suggested itself. Life in the river sand was as foreign and indifferent to my existence as the pattern of stars in the sky.

I felt similarly excluded in Bourke, but more troubled. Those black faces in Alice Springs had seemed content in a separate world, I thought. Here, as in Wilcannia and other towns along our route, they seemed to have collapsed in a heap around the open doorways of the pubs. Old men sat on the footpath with their backs to the wall, sleeping. Young women with babies in prams stood talking. Young men came out the open door, went back in, came out again. Half-grown children were part of the crowd and yet not – they stepped out to watch shoppers pass by, walked out to look into a shop window and come back, ran off in pairs to go into a shop and run back. There was an urge here, I thought (or imagined) to be part of something that excluded them.

From my view inside the truck, this small untidy cluster of human beings had the appearance of having been swept into this heap by a giant garden rake – like autumn leaves gathered up and left in a pile against a wall until someone had the time or energy to haul them away.

The owner of the station we'd visited the day before – after we'd been un-bogged – had given me his frank opinion of the blacks. While I sat on a wool bale watching the Maori shearers at work, he came in from outside and joined me. Raising his voice to be heard above the blaring rock music (something Maoris insist upon, he said) he expressed his admiration for these dark-skinned Kiwis. He used to hire Aborigines as station hands, he said, apparently making some link between the Maoris and the native Australians, "but the government has ruined them." They'd all become drunks, he said. "Nobody'll hire them now. The welfare system has turned them into bums."

This was stated like an original insight but it sounded all too familiar to me. Another continent had already worn it out.

I was disappointed to discover that the Dingo Fence which

followed much of the Queensland border was nowhere to be seen when we crossed. The crossing, in fact, was without drama. But not without change – the most noticeable being in the condition of the road. First it got narrower, bumpier. Then, it narrowed right down to a single lane of pavement. When another vehicle approached, you dropped your left wheels onto the dirt shoulders and hoped the other driver would do the same. Considering the muddy condition of things, they might decide to play chicken with you, just in case they could avoid taking the chance of sinking up to their axles in Queensland grease.

This possibility didn't come up very often – which perhaps explained the lack of attention given the road. This was supposed to be a major thoroughfare, but we seemed to be almost alone in using it. Maybe if you lived in a country as flat and bare as this you always knew (in decent weather at least) that if there was no decent road to where you wanted to go you could simply drive across the plains.

People who lived amongst mountains did not have that option. People who lived on an island of mountains could barely imagine such a thing. Coming from a province whose political survival has depended upon the building of super highways linking communities through monstrous mountain passes, I wondered that so little attention had been given to roads where construction would be so much easier. Maybe a shortage of voters made the difference. In parts of British Columbia you could sometimes tell when you were approaching a town that hadn't voted for the party in power. You could find places, once, where wide paved highways set off into wilderness on their way to nowhere, and where bridges sailed across rivers without any connection to a road – simply because the few isolated residents of the area had thrown their crucial votes in the direction of a particular cabinet minister. However the Queensland government rewarded its supporters, it wasn't with shiny wide black pavement.

The floods we'd been hearing about were more than rumour. Muddy water stood reflecting trees and sky on either side. We drove from floodway to dip, from dip to floodway, creeping through long stretches of water with the doors open, watching the level rise, concerned for the distributor. It seemed that the narrow strip of sealed road was a living amphibian which had to dip beneath the water every once in a while in order to keep itself alive.

The Queensland air was charged, it seemed to me, with danger. The threat of something. At any moment our progress could be stopped — by rains, floods, whatever. We'd be blocked, sent back, our journey interrupted and brought to a premature end. All it would take was one flooded stretch too deep to cross.

I found the emptiness of the road a little eerie. Not Roger. There couldn't be few enough people around for him. After watching for quite a while for a place where we might pull off the road for morning coffee (without sinking out of sight in the mud) we finally spotted a modest track up ahead which would lead into a small clump of trees. We slowed down to turn in. Then, suddenly, Roger put his foot to the floor. There was a car parked there already — two gentlemen sitting in it. A crowd like that could spoil everything.

In Cunnamulla, the fellow who served us petrol (muscles and fat bulging out of his singlet) seemed to take a good deal of pleasure in telling us we would never get to Charleville. The road, he said, was out. He didn't seem to care whether we turned back or simply stayed where we were; he'd had his pleasure. Glancing around at the wide flat spaces, the row of modest houses, I guessed that if you lived here you were glad of any excitement. Or maybe, as a service station attendant, you resented the number of people who were on the move.

This added some interest to the journey: would we make it, or would we be stopped in our tracks? More than an hour north of Cunnamulla we met our first approaching car and Roger flagged him down.

"How's the road ahead?"

"No worries yet."

"The road's still open?"

"As far as Charleville it is. The problem comes when you

get there. River's flooded. Road's out. Water's coming right
up the main street of town."

We approached Charleville, then, with some apprehension. At one spot we were required to wait while a road train
was being pulled from a watery gully. The earth up the slope
was gouged and scarred. The driver had been caught off
guard, we were told. Hit the water and went out of control. A
crew had spent most of the day hauling the truck up to where
it could lie on its side, waiting for whatever equipment might
be powerful enough to take it away for repairs. So much damage had been done that you could imagine future travellers
wondering whether a meteor or a falling space shuttle had
ploughed up the land.

Workmen looked up to watch, without interest, as we
passed. I knew they were workmen, though they did not look
like workmen to me. Singlets. Shorts. Elastic-sided boots.
Akubra hats. This habit of going to work in holiday clothing
had given me the impression that few people in this country
were seriously employed. They may be doing a job at the moment, but that was only an interruption in the ongoing world
of play. In my world, shorts were meant for the beach and singlets for teenaged musclemen on holiday. The ubiquitous
Akubra had no equivalent at home, except for the stetson
worn by Calgary city-slickers come down to the Coast to
swagger and pretend to relax.

Ironically, it was the children of Australia who wore working clothes, poor souls. Uniforms for school! Where their Canadian cousins would be free to wear any sort of play clothing
they might wish, Australian children were dressed like little
soldiers or little business people or little shop clerks and
marched off in identical rows to school.

Once you've crossed the railroad tracks in Charleville, the
road turns sharply twice and becomes the main street, head-
ing down a slope towards the river. The Railway Hotel, the
Warrego Motel, the School of Arts Hotel, a row of shops, the
Corones Hotel, the bus depot, the Charleville Hotel, Australia
Post, an Ampol station, the river.

For the time being, this was the end of the line.

This time the ROAD CLOSED sign was where a Road Closed sign ought to be – blocking your way. Not only was it unambiguous but it was also a bright, noticeable yellow. It was also unnecessary. The road wasn't merely "closed", it had disappeared. Muddy water rushed across below the petrol station. It seemed the river was at least two hundred metres wide, and racing fast. Somewhere out towards the middle, the road surfaced for a moment and then again sank out of sight. Water passed around large gum trees; flowed through a thicket of trunks; broke into rapids as it errupted off the side of the rising pavement. There was no way of knowing where the river belonged – somewhere lost beneath this racing flood.

Several cars were parked near the barrier. People sat and stared through their windscreens, or stood outside and looked at the flood. Several of the row of public telephones outside the Post Office were in use – travellers sending messages ahead? "We're stranded! We may not get there in time. What're we gonna do?"

Right at the edge of the water, a tall sign by the petrol station declared: AMPOL WELCOMES YOU TO CHARLEVILLE. Not far away, another sign with legs right down into the lapping water's edge requested that you PLEASE CALL AGAIN SOON. It did not need to add: "If you ever manage to get out."

The couple who ran the motel seemed far too pleased to see us. Not just pleased, but smug. Knowing. Sitting on the doorstep to their office they grinned the grin of people who were thinking, "We know what you want, and we know you're at our mercy."

Indeed we were. We could share the only room left (the only room left in town, the tone implied) but only because of a recent cancellation. The alternative was to put up tents in the dark. After driving all the way from Nyngan in a state of tension, we did not feel like putting up tents in the dark.

There were several weddings planned for this weekend, the woman explained. But the rising river was making a difference – some guests couldn't get here, others were fright-

ened of trying, people were cancelling reservations. That was
the only reason we could get a room at all.

She couldn't lose. She would be filled up with people who
came to the weddings, or she would be filled up with people
who couldn't cross the river. She was filled up with something else, too: power. There was a fine swagger in her movements, a tone of gloating in her voice. I think I recognised
both – small town people had suddenly been put in a position
of giving or withholding favours. She was giving a favour to
us, but could take it back, her manner implied, in a minute.
The road behind us was filled with people who would kill for
her room.

(The idea of an Australian road being "filled" with
travellers was a ludicrous one. Outside of Sydney I hadn't
seen a road yet that couldn't be descibed as "almost
deserted" by standards I'd become accustomed to, even living on an island considered underpopulated and largely rural.
This sense of being uncrowded was one of the things I liked
best. The illusion of having the road to yourself, even sometimes the world, created a sense of freedom I had never experienced before.)

"Oi've bin wytin' all dye for my boys," she said. "Oi've
been down to meet the bus three toimes already. But the bus
from Brisbane hasn't come in. Nobody knows where it ees."

For dinner, she recommended the barbecue at the Railway
Hotel. The food was good. More important, it was the only
restaurant open.

"Catchya lyter," she said, disappearing into the living
quarters behind the office. "See yuz in the mawning."

"Jack, have you seen my notebook anywhere?" Roger was
still rummaging around in the truck, though we'd taken our
bags inside.

"It's not on the front seat?"

"No. I've looked everywhere." He went to the back of the
truck and began to sort through the boxes beneath the tarp.

We stripped back the tarp and began a systematic search
through everything – boxes of smoko essentials, cooking
pots, damp camping gear. It seemed unlikely that a notebook

would find its way into any of this. Roger was clearly agitated, but not yet alarmed. We adopted calm for the time being, certain the notebook would turn up in some unlikely place. A matter for joking: Whew, a close call! Yet it didn't turn up in any of the unlikely places. Roger was soon less calm about it.

"This is the notebook you've been scribbling in all along, right?"

"Everything." Silence. "Of course there's the tapes. But you know how you write down things that don't get said."

He did not have to tell me that this was a matter of some importance. What happened to a research trip when the accumulated research went missing? Roger had begun to look a little grim. The gaze that probed our belongings seemed to be looking inward as well.

One more search through the bags in the motel room. Nothing. The notebook was not in the office where we'd checked in. Or anywhere on the parking lot pavement. Obviously it had been left behind. Somewhere.

"The Alamo?"

"The Cunnamulla petrol station?"

While Roger used the telephone, I imagined the man who'd told us we wouldn't get to Charleville tapping one finger on the notebook and smugly smiling while he tried to decide whether to tell the truth right away or let Roger sweat awhile.

"Not there. They didn't know what I was talking about."

"Were you writing in it when we stopped for coffee?"

Roger's face lit up. Almost smiled. "The telephone box, in Bourke!"

"Does it have your name on it?"

A quick death to that smile. Roger flinched, as though sideswiped. "Damn. Damn. Damn. It doesn't." He bit down on his impatience. "There's other people's names. Telephone numbers. I'm sure I never put my own on it."

Clearly this emergency could no longer be confined to the truck and the motel room. "I'll phone the Post Office in

Bourke – the telephone boxes are just outside. Maybe someone will go out and look."

Too late. The Post Office was already closed.

This precipitated a telephone blitz any detective would
have approved of. Within the next few moments, Roger had
spoken to the Bourke police, a Bourke taxi company, the Post
Office manager at his home, the Bourke radio station to offer
a reward, and the Taurau family in Broken Hill (whose phone
number was in the book, if a finder cared enough to use it).

On the patio at the rear of the Railway Hotel we ate our
barbecue dinner of steak and barramundi in a cloud of gloom.
Mostly silent.

"Dammit. This sort of thing happens too often."

"It happens to some of the rest of us, too. More often than
it used to." I felt in my pocket, to make sure the extra truck
key was still there.

"I hate it. It makes me feel stupid."

I didn't want to insult Roger's right to be devastated, but it
seemed a little too soon to give up hope. "At least no-one who
finds it will want to keep it," I ventured. "It's no use to anyone else."

Roger was not about to give up despair so easily. "Of
course they won't keep it, they'll throw it in the rubbish."

Silence. Young couples talked cheerfully around us. Everyone here was young. Every young woman had beautiful
teeth. Every young man had a stud in his left ear. Everyone
had long tanned limbs. Everyone was blond – Australian
taffy-blond. Much beer was consumed, under the strings of
coloured lights. No one said "Right!" here; everyone said
"Ow-kye!"

"Well," I eventually said, "somebody could be turning it in
to the police while we're sitting here. They'll phone the
motel."

No telephone messages at the motel. While Roger waited
for a local shearing contractor who'd agreed to be interviewed, he made a few more telephone calls. The Bourke police again. The Bourke taxi company again, in case the
notebook had been spotted somewhere by one of the drivers.

At this point I would be phoning home, I thought. For better ideas from a clearer thinker. Or for sympathy, at least. Evidently, Roger felt the same – he phoned Rhyll at Spring Farm. Then his brother – to check on the weather to the north of us. ("Gavin says the creek's up. We may have to be rowed across.") And then his mother in Rockhampton – to check on the weather at Carnarvon Gorge. ("Lorna says I have to show you the Jacky Howe statue in Blackall.") He also telephoned the Grazcos office in Broken Hill again, in case they'd heard something. He phoned the shearer who'd been expecting us in unreachable Quilpie. ("His wife says, Don't even try it!") And he phoned a husband and wife shearing team who lived just out of town.

I knew that losing something of importance could make you feel abandoned and lonely, but I wondered if all Australians were this addicted to the telephone? Suspicious of the instrument myself (an amoral invader, it could turn your life upside down in a matter of seconds), and living in a household where everyone hated the phone, where everyone waited for someone else to respond to its ring, I'd been astonished at the number of calls Roger made – even before this crisis.

Perhaps everyone in this country kept in touch with everyone else, as Roger did, almost daily – creating a small town out of an entire continent. I could understand that, I suppose, if I didn't happen to know that Telecom was not required to itemise your bill. That this was tolerated by those who paid the bills was either an indication of incredible trust or proof that the phone had become an uncontrollable addiction.

There were times when I wondered if Roger weren't privately panicking a little about how far we had got from everyone else but was determined not to let me suspect. On the other hand, since I didn't have to talk on the phone myself I rather enjoyed the feeling that we were connected by wires to any number of people who knew what we were doing, and presumably cared.

I left Roger to his calls and set out on foot to re-visit the rising flood. At the bottom of the street, in front of the petrol station, two parked cars were gleaming wet. Had their owners decided to wash them while they awaited a miracle? People were wringing out soaked clothes.

What was going on, I asked.

Look for yourself, I was told.

A Toyota 4x4 utility truck towed a car up out of the river. When they stopped, and the Toyota driver had unhitched his chain, the driver of the sedan got out and lifted the bonnet and removed her distribtuor cap. She dried it out with a rag, then replaced it, closed the bonnet, got back in the car, started the engine, and drove off.

Others came together to consult. Should they take the chance? Things could get worse – if the river got deeper this way of crossing would not be an option. But things could always get better, too. "By morning – who knows?"

"The driver isn't charging a fee. He just takes whatever you offer."

A local hero.

Much later, when the crowd had lost interest in the continuing spectacle and had mostly drifted away, I walked back up the main street towards our motel. A sign in a butcher shop window invited me to buy an entire sheep for $24. (Escaped the queue for Saudi Arabia only to be butchered in drowning Charleville! Absurdly, I imagined dragging a dead sheep behind me through the rest of the trip. "Too much of a bargain to resist.") On a small patch of grass to the right stood an awkward piece of machinery which I imagined was the infamous Steiger Vortex Gun, invented as a desperate attempt to end the drought of 1902 by shooting the sky.

The bar in the Corones Hotel was noisy. This grand old hotel was a two-storey block-long building with stained glass windows and glass doorways in each of the upstairs rooms. Someone was up on the second-floor veranda. In all a row of darkened upstairs rooms, one stained window was lighted, the door beside it open; I could see the figure of a man leaning on the railing while he smoked a cigarette, the silhouette of a woman leaning in the doorway behind him. Then, suddenly, she stepped back inside; disappeared. The sort of split-second image that could spark the imagination into story.

(Was this where she had got to – my Charlotte C. from the Victoria Street hotel? Was the cigarette smoker one of the youths who'd turned on her at Mungo? Or was that her husband – the two of them now on the run from those others? One way or the other, she was a prisoner of sorts, stalled in her flight by that river. She was also, unlike other fictional characters who'd come along on previous travels, determined to keep her distance. Apparently she was not at all interested in horning in on my trip – just in giving me the nod from a distance once in a while, to remind me she was still having her own. Maybe we would have the opportunity to compare notes later.)

At one end of a little bridge across a ravine, a solemn hymn drifted out from a stucco church; at the other end of the bridge, cowboy music swirled from a bar. On the bridge itself two small boys played together – one of them Aboriginal, one a freckled blond. On the outside of the bridge railing, with their toes on the deck, they gripped the top rail and ducked and danced and bobbed and laughed together, above the muddy water of the ravine.

The school wore its hallways on the outside of its walls – verandas – making an altogether more attractive structure than the formidable-looking schools at home. Many of the houses along this street were up on "stumps" – some high enough to stand over the parked family vehicle, some squatting over a crammed-in collection of junk. Exotic and ragged tropical plants leaned against unpainted lattice-work screens.

Roger had only begun to interview a contractor who worked out of Charleville. This was a young man in his twenties, with a blond crew cut and the meaty face of a former athlete. Five empty beer bottles sat on the table in front of him. One empty beer bottle sat in front of Roger, beside an open notebook. A new one.

Too young to be much affected by the wide-comb dispute which had shaken the industry, this fellow had had other problems to deal with. Because he looked so young, he sometimes had trouble being taken seriously. To make things worse, when he'd first started out – as a shearer – he'd got along just fine with the others "until they found out I was a cocky's son." He helped himself to another beer from the fridge. "This bloke wanted me sacked, because I was 'depriving' another 'worker's' son of a job! The worker's son just happened to be his own."

Now he was a shearing contractor – one of six or seven in town. Naturally he'd sometimes employed New Zealanders. "We're lucky here. We've got good Kiwis."

And yet, New Zealand shearers seemed to fill him with disgust. "Over home is always better. I hate that. What the hell are they doin' here? If over home was so much better what are they doin' over here? That pisses me right off."

The interview was put on hold while I reported on matters down at the river. Roger's smile said, "Good. Jack's found something else to get excited about in what others only see as everyday routine."

"And there was this fellow in a Toyota 4x4 pulling people across!"

"That was me!" said the young shearing contractor, his face breaking into a gigantic grin.

Frankly, I doubted this. I'd noticed no-one down there wearing clothing anywhere near as "flash" as this fellow's garb: pink and white patterned shorts, blue and white striped rugby shirt. Your eyes hurt to look at him.

He may have taken the time to change, however. Because the famous Toyota, I saw, was parked outside on the street. Roo bar, spotlights, aerials. I had passed it, had heard its radio talking to itself, and hadn't realised I was in the presence of a one-in-a-million vehicle.

And would drive that Toyota myself, several hours later, when the local hero had brought the interview to an end but did not want to drive himself home. Local police had little tolerance for drivers who'd been drinking, even when they'd spent part of their evening doing good turns for strangers.

More phone calls in the morning. Still no word on the notebook.

Although Roger had made no advance plans to include

Charleville in his research, being stalled here had allowed for all sorts of unexpected interviews. Last night's contractor had been only the first. There was a husband and wife team waiting to meet him. Two young women shearers from Wales had agreed to talk with him after they'd attended church. What had begun as quite a sharply focused project seemed to be taking on a larger perspective.

I walked down to the foot of the main street again. The river was still up. It seemed that everyone else in town had come down as well. One couple sat on the white wooden fence, bare toes tucked back behind the lower rail. Travellers complained that Easter holidays were being ruined. Tourist families took pictures of themselves in front of the rushing water. At the top of the block, several men leaned on the upper verandah railing of the Charleville Hotel, looking down at the water – local shearers who were out of work because of the rain. Just below their elbows, a long yellow sign said XXXX our beer XXXX beside a long white sign saying FOSTER'S LIGHT which was beside a long green sign saying VB: FOR A HARD-EARNED THIRST – all of them above an even longer dark blue sign saying FOSTERS counter meals FOSTERS. You never ran out of reading material in an Australian town.

Out on the pavement, a group of young workmen paced up and down, uncertain whether to take a chance and drive their Toyota four-wheel drives across.

Their trucks sat parked at the curb, loaded with equipment. The men stood out on the street, staring at the river. Two of them were barefoot, two wore elastic-sided boots, the youngest – a lanky adolescent – wore running shoes. They exchanged opinions, shook their heads, walked off a ways and came back, then gathered around a fat man who'd wheeled a bicycle into their midst.

As a group they watched as a freight truck came across the river, ploughing up waves of mud. When the truck had gone up past them, they listened to whatever the fat man had to say, then swung all at once and ran for their trucks. The lanky teenager, looking as delighted as he was nervous, said,

"Shit", and hopped in to sit amongst the equipment in the back of the lead truck.

First one, then the other, drove down to the river's edge, and paused. The second waited while the first set off slowly into the flood.

I moved in closer to the cyclist to watch. "I told 'em," she said. "I told 'em, no worries. I done it myself. Plenty of times. Once in a Ford sedan. I got a bunch of them boys that was playing around out there to hop up on the bonnet. Some on the boot. Up to the windscreen it was. Yeh. Up to the windscreen. A regular petrol motor too."

The first of the trucks was approaching the deepest part. "Oh, I forgot to tell those fellas," the fat man said. "See that little spot out there in the middle where there's no ripples? I forgot to warn them about that. The road's washed away at that spot. Big hole. Yeh. Big hole at that spot."

We watched in silence as the first truck passed the dangerous spot and began to rise up out of the water on the far side. The second truck plunged in to follow.

This gentleman on the bike seemed to have set himself up as some sort of counsellor here. When one car pulled down to the water's edge and then swung around to go back up the slope, he hollered to the elderly lady in the passenger seat, "Not tryin' 'er?"

"Naw," she said, and waved the idea away.

"Stupid bloody bitch," he said, looking off towards the farther shore. His tone suggested that he'd expected nothing else. Apparently she was someone he knew.

And yet, to another car paused at the water's edge, he shouted: "Don't try 'er in that or you'll fuckin' end up in fuckin' Cunnamulla!"

He took a swig from a large amber bottle and continued to look across the flood. "Don't know where all that water's comin' from. Four miles an hour. Four miles an hour. Don't know where it's comin' from."

"Isn't it up Carnarvon way?" said a gentleman who'd joined us.

"Yeh. Carnarvon's the top of it." He thought for a moment. "Yeh. Carnarvon's the top of it."

He hadn't left the seat of his bike since arriving, but had kept one foot on the pavement, the other on the raised pedal, as though to suggest he was merely pausing on his way to more important matters. In fact, as he let the bicycle roll a little distance ahead, he raised the bottle for another gulp and – still not looking at either of the two strangers who'd come in to listen – announced: "I was gonna swim out to the island with this beer and spend the day drinkin' and writin' up my orders."

Orders for what? Was he a shearers' cook?

"There's an island out there?"

"Oh yeh. Look. Just after the dip, there's that little clump of trees. There. A park. Toilets and everything."

When I went down to the river in the afternoon, while Roger was interviewing the husband-and-wife shearing team, the upper verandas of both the Corones and the Charleville were populated by even more people than they had been in the morning. Several leaned on the railings, just looking down at the river. Some stood about in groups, talking. Some came out and went back inside, and then came out again.

(I did not see Charlotte C. or her companion in daylight.)

The river, this time, seemed to be full of children. In bathing suits they waded, they rode tubes down the current, they floated on slabs of foam, they swam. A group of them hopped onto a cream-coloured utility truck with a small wooden boat on its tray and rode on it, like people on a parade float, raising their arms in triumph when they rose up out of the flood onto pavement on this nearer side. Then they hopped off and ran back into the river.

Amongst the folks standing by the water's edge was a middle-aged man in a short-sleeved dress shirt and dress pants. If this costume was unusual here, his hat was not – a tan Akubra. With him was a young man in his twenties who wore a t-shirt and shorts, closer to the local costume but so clean and colourful as to set him apart – a visitor.

He was from Sydney, where he worked for an airline company — visiting his parents for the Easter weekend. This was his first time in Charleville, he said — his father having been posted here only thirteen months before.

"You find this different from Sydney?"

"Yeh." He did not venture into reasons.

Charleville, however, was a nice enough little town, according to the father. As a pastor he'd lived all over the place, though he'd grown up in Victoria — Ballarat. He'd just now come from preaching a Good Friday morning sermon, which may have explained their dress. I'd been in Australia long enough now to think of clean t-shirt and pressed shorts as Sunday best.

What would this man have preached in his sermon, I wondered. The world was certainly supplying him with enough material. Some of it was in front of us now, and distinctly biblical: floods, bodies submerged in water, a town in siege, out-of-work shepherds on every side, neglected sheep.

"A tough life," he said, when I mentioned the shearers we'd met.

I confessed that I'd been so filled with admiration for their skills I'd taken it for granted they had the same pleasure in their work as, say, a dancer might. "But now here I am moving through the country, free, and those fellows are still spending every day shearing wool off the backs of an endless supply of sheep. Most of them plotting escape."

"Not much work for the shearers now," the pastor said. "Not here. There's seven thousand sheep out there waiting to come through."

"Out there" was in the direction of the far shore of the river. Presumably, mustering had been interrupted by the rains, and the risen river had become an obstacle between the range and the woolsheds.

Neither father nor son was surprised to learn that I had met two women shearers at lunch. "Quite a few women shearers here," said the father. "One of the lasses we know, her husband he's a wool classer, but sometimes he stays home and looks after the baby while she goes out rouseabouting."

Had his sermon addressed the anxiety of people who lived so close to an untrustworthy force of nature? When I suggested that coming down to the river seemed to be the main entertainment in town, that people seemed to be in a state of some excitement, he assumed that by "excitement" I'd meant "having fun".

"Not a couple of nights ago they weren't. Everybody was worried. Thought it was gonna come right up. It didn't come as far as they thought it would – they were getting ready to evacuate."

Then the pastor gave me a glimpse of perhaps one more reason Charleville people came down several times a day, like me, to look at the water. "You see, we're on the main tourist route from down south. Up to Longreach? We're on the main Melbourne-Sydney route – people come up through Dubbo, Bourke, Cunnamulla, Charleville on their way to Longreach."

Of course, I'd been fooled by the narrow road into thinking we'd strayed off onto a back track and into some out-of-the-way bush town. If Charleville people thought of themselves as located on the main route linking Australia's most important centres they must think of themselves as watching the world come to them, if only to pass them by. In the present circumstances, then, they could observe how the world that usually passed them by was handling the surprise of being stalled, for a change, on their doorsteps.

At dusk, most people had left the street for their homes or hotel rooms, but a crowd had gathered inside the pale green corner bar, and small groups stood out on the darkened veranda above, talking in lowered voices.

Few had gathered towards the farther end of the upper veranda. Only the dark figure of a man in a white t-shirt leaning over the railing to smoke a cigarette, which flared up crimson when he sucked on it and glowed tightly red when he let it hang down from his fingers below the railing. Behind him, light shone from a narrow window. Light shone from an open doorway as well, where a woman in silhouette leaned against one side with her arms crossed at her breast. She was, I thought, in a slip. The man and the woman were talking – their voices only murmurs to me on the street. The air was still warm, still humid. The river – I turned to look back at what they might be seeing at the foot of the street – the river roared past like a racing tide of molten silver.

More travellers stalled because of that river? Lovers, probably. Travelling north to some large station where he was employed as a drover, mustering cattle. They were returning from a honeymoon in Sydney. Taking advantage of this unexpected hitch in their plans to spend day and night in a hotel room bed. I had caught them, I thought, cooling off, allowing their passion time to regenerate.

I was about to get back in the car. I took up Charlotte's camera from the seat of the car and aimed it just as the man put the cigarette to his mouth and drew on it. The automatic focus whirred but brought the woman, not the man, into clarity, just as she raised a hand to her hair and turned towards the light from the room.

The shock of seeing a stranger about whom you have begun to invent a life turn suddenly into your own wife is enough to make all the blood in your veins turn cold at once, and every muscle in your body lose its strength. For a moment you aren't entirely sure who you are yourself.

The bar was so crowded that its customers had overflowed into the lobby. So many men stood about that I had to push my way through a confusion of shouts and laughter and a low rumble of continuous palaver. Everyone, of course, was talking flood. You were scared to take your eye off that goddam river for a minute, one fellow in a black Akubra said, in case the bloody thing swelled up and took you away. "Y'd be down in fuckin' Cunnamulla in a minute, swimmin' like a barra-fuckin'-mundi for yer life."

"Shoulda gone straight to the Gold Coast and laid in the bleedin' sand fer the duration."

"Excuse me," I said. "Excuse me, please."

I fought my way through and went past the reception desk where an elderly woman looked up, calling, "Sir? Sir?"

Ignoring her, I ran up the stairway and down the hall. Dull lights. Threadbare carpet. An impression of dark peeling wallpaper. These rooms were probably not used except in times of flood, when people with no desire to stop in this town were forced to spend the night.

Second room from the end. I don't know how I knew this, I certainly had not taken the time to count windows while I was outside. Some sort of instinct had taken over, I suppose. I hammered on the door, and called her name.

I stepped back from the door, expecting to have to duck a fist. But it did not open. Instead, Charlotte's voice called out: "Eric?" Such a sad voice that it nearly broke my heart.

When she opened the door she looked at me as though she weren't sure who I was. She'd pulled her flowered duster on over her slip. Then she gasped, believing it was me, and for a moment she rested against me. Gratitude, pleasure, relief. Perhaps I wasn't living in a nightmare after all.

"You're all right?"

"Yeah. Yes, I'm all right."

"You haven't been hurt?"

"I'm all right. I'm fine."

"Who's the man outside?"

She looked up at me, puzzled. "What man?"

Still later in the afternoon Roger came down to the river with me. Between a bonanza of unplanned interviews and a blitz of unwished-for telephone calls, he'd been missing out on the drama. We were just in time to see a road train poised on the far side of the flood, contemplating the crossing. It sat, huge and dark and square, on the hump just beyond the deepest part, like some strange metallic animal weighing the pros and cons of risking the plunge. The muddy water had risen more – racing by at its steady speed, smooth as marble across the road and then breaking into rapids past the giant coolabah.

It was as though people sensed a moment of some importance here. Various cars came down and stopped. People got out and stood looking across the water at this monster looking back. I imagined townspeople looking across a moat at a dragon about to attack. Some were clustered behind the white fence rails, some stood in the roadway by the ROAD CLOSED sign, the water slapping past their feet. Some, like us, stood up on the curb below the petrol station.

Then, as though a decision had been made, or prayers completed, the monster suddenly moved down and into the water. It ploughed forward, towards us. Water piled up before it. Waves ran out on either side. The engine roared. Water rose up its broad flat nose. Its tires disappeared. For a moment the monster was half-submerged, crocodile-snouting its way across. Watchers were silent.

Up the slope it eventually came, shedding sheets of water, even more gigantic than it had seemed at a distance. It wore

the sign ROAD TRAIN on its front bumper, in case you might
mistake it for something else. (We'd been through towns
whose main streets were smaller.) The enormous blue cab
pulled two long semis behind it – one of them with two
empty semi-trailers stacked on top of it, the other carrying an
ordinary truck and an ordinary car. It went on past us without
pause, shedding water like a risen sea-monster, as though it
had not accomplished anything splendid. It turned the corner
at the Post Office and disappeared.

I felt as though we'd been visited by some half-god creature out of myth. There ought to have been applause. But
there was none. No sense of community had been accomplished here; people were experiencing this in private. Less
sentimental about this giant's triumph, most turned away to
stare across the water again, this time at a Toyota utility
truck which was paused, on the same hump the giant had so
recently relinquished. A small rodent planning to go where a
dinosaur had gone before. Perhaps they would prefer to witness failure – an over-confident 4x4 swept downriver, or
stalled in the deepest part – punishment for those who
thought of Charleville as merely a place to pass through. Perhaps, on the other hand, they were only thinking of the ruined
Easter weekend.

10 The invasion of the prickly pear

When we checked out of the motel we noticed that the proprietors had posted a BUSINESS FOR SALE sign on the wall of the office. Perhaps the river coming up the main street made them nervous. Perhaps the daily habit of watching others leave town had made them restless. They wanted to check out themselves. In the meantime, they promised to relay any telephone messages about a certain notebook up to Roger's brother's station.

In the truck, Roger handed me an opened bottle of dark brown soft drink and opened one for himself. "Something we used to drink when we were kids. It may be something new for you."

I recognised the smell, or thought I did. "Root beer?"

"Sarsaparilla."

Sarsaparilla? In Australian fiction, sarsaparilla was what "wowsers" ordered in bars, earning them sneers and perhaps worse. A word to provoke brawls.

But it was root beer, of course. Or something close enough to provoke a few childhood memories of my own. "I used to make root beer when I was a kid. Dozens and dozens of bottles. You bought a kit." We drank root beer with our picnics after swimming lessons. We drank root beer while peeling the bark from cascara trees for spending money. We drank root beer while playing pirates inside the hollow pasture stumps. "One batch exploded all over the basement ceiling."

As soon as we'd turned the corner and headed east, I unfolded the map and held one corner in place with my sarsaparilla bottle. We would drive to Morven on the Warrego Highway, then north-west to Augathella to get back on the road we'd been on until the river had cut us off. Then north and north-west farther up to Tambo, Blackall, Barcaldine on what they called the Matilda Highway. (This was because it led, eventually, to the town of Winton, which took credit for hosting Banjo Paterson at the time he wrote Australia's most famous song.) From Barcaldine we would not continue on to Longreach (the Stockman's Hall of Fame) and to Winton and Mount Isa ("largest city in the world" – 41,000 sq km) but would turn right and travel along the Capricorn Highway through Jericho, Alpha, Bogantungan, and on to Emerald. A total of eight hundred kilometres.

We would be passing through land encountered by some of the great explorers, who might have been glad to sit for a day in our truck. Landsborough, Mitchell, Gregory. Burke and Wills had perished not far to the left. Leichhardt had disappeared not far to the right. Not encouraging. If some of these kangaroos had read the history books they might have thought twice about trying to cross the road – we passed through waft after waft of ripe carrion smell.

This first stretch, heading east, was mulga country. Charleville bragged about being in "mulga country". Roger thought this was funny: every place vying to claim something natural as its own distinctive emblem. Apparently one town up ahead bragged of being the centre of "meat ant country".

"You can imagine a meeting where all the mayors got together," Roger said. "One says, 'What you got down your way?' 'Oh, just a lot of mulga.' 'Right – you're mulga country. Who else?' 'We got a whole lot of mallee.' 'Right – you're mallee country. What about you, Rex?' 'Oh, we got nothin' up around our way, just a lot of bloody meat ants.' 'Right – you'll be meat ant country then.'" Meat ant country clearly had Roger's vote, for facing the facts.

A wonderful perverse streak ran close to the surface in this man. He chuckled at the silliness of town's competing for distinctive tags as he chuckled at any story which put city folks in a bad light, put scholarly writers in their place, or made pompous fellows of every stripe look like fools. He was not the type who would fall all over the place howling about the absurdities of life, but he maintained a constant readiness to chuckle softly and make a gently ironic comment about the ill-fortune of someone who ought to have known better than to take himself so seriously.

After a certain amount of "mulga country" – the mulga being the thick forest that grew right up to the road, throwing shade down across the more interesting sights like rusted cars half buried in creek water – we turned left onto what looked like just another back road to me but which was unquestionably the dark black line on the map which indicated bitumen. We began to pass through wide expanses of rolling grasslands.

"Downs," Roger said. These paddocks had not been cleared by man, apparently. Downs were natural – perfect grazing land. After all the rains they were an astonishing green.

Light here, like the heat, was oppressive. You might think the light had its own kind of weight that lay on your head, pressing down. All this green (I felt) was not meant to be seen in this light, which was more appropriate to browns and rusty reds. Green was intended to be seen through a gentle watery light. Otherwise it seemed like a startling unnatural thing laid upon the world.

Tambo was our immediate goal on the map – 116 km north of Augathella – but by the time we got to it Blackall had become our immediate goal in its stead, just another hundred k's ahead. Larger print. A place of legend. A couple of reasons to stop. Within moments of passing through Tambo I had already forgotten what I had seen. A few buildings? (I felt guilty. What had poor Tambo done to deserve this instantaneous disappearance?) I had also lost all sense of where on the map we had finally crossed the Great Dingo Fence – in fact it was a grid where I'd expected a gate. For the first time, there was some danger that the map I'd opened out on my lap was becoming more real than the world outside the truck. The Dingo Fence was not marked; Tambo was only a name at the conjunction of the Dawson Development Road and this continuation of the Matilda Highway. A name and a black dot. An Australian map could be as interesting and peculiar as the world outside the truck windows. Strange and magical names of towns: Grong Grong, and Urandangi. Place names which were not towns at all but private properties, such as "Yallara" or "Annandale (ruins)" or "Planet Downs (abandoned)". Dots identified merely as "tanks". Roads which looked like roads on the map but were actually a set of tyre tracks on the ground. Rivers so crinkled and scribbly that you could tell they were moving without much assistance from gravity. Contradictions like "Dry Bed Creek". Red warnings: "Avoid planning a motoring holiday during the summer months." Capitalised expressions that could only make you wonder: INUNDATION. Once started on an exploration of this paper world, it wasn't easy to pull attention away. No wonder Tambo was missed.

I noticed the occasional cactus growing by the side of the road. Prickly pear. A surprise – though I knew better than to be surprised by anything in Queensland, the state where magic realism is kitchen sink. I'd thought of the north as one giant solarium, a steamy observatory of exotic jungle plantlife and violently coloured raucous birds and lush decaying fruit. So far I had had to abandon any expectation of jungle – this was flat dry cattle country, grassy "downs" and wide stubbly paddocks – but still expected to see the unexpected, including a plant which should have been in the deserts of Mexico or Nevada.

In fact the prickly pear was more of a surprise to Queenslanders than it was to me. Or had been at one time. They were not an indigenous plant, Roger explained. They were, as they say, "introduced".

"An invasion."

"An invasion of prickly pears?" It made you think of a science fiction movie.

"Someone brought a plant home from America or Mexico or somewhere. Back in the 1830s. One plant – but it spread. Someone took cuttings. Someone else thought it would make a good fence. Before long it had spread to cover the state. Cattle died, because they couldn't get to their feed."

"Are you sure? This sounds pretty bizarre."

"Check the book."

Since the glove box door would not stay closed for more than a minute or two before dropping open on my knees, I'd decided to leave it open permanently. I sorted through the maps and guide books inside and drew out the one that might help. Indeed, Roger had not been inventing fiction. The prickly pear, which had begun with a single plant brought home by a traveller, was found to make excellent hedges, but eventually spread to cover twenty-three million acres. Pastoralist properties had to be abandoned because of the alien intruder.

"Listen to this. Apparently while it lasted some people tried to make the most of it. In drought times, they fed it to cattle and sheep. Someone tried to use its oil to make petrol for machines. Someone else invented recipes for prickly pear jelly." I imagined people lying awake at nights, thinking they could hear the prickly pear multiplying outside their bedroom windows, desperately trying to think of some new way of putting it to use. Fertiliser? Coat racks for dwarfs? Prickly pear sandwiches? (A woman stands over a man who doesn't want to bite into a sandwich with spikes poking out in all directions: "Just try it. It could solve the state's problems and make our fortune at the same time.") In the 1920s someone came up with the idea of introducing a natural enemy, the cactoblastic cactorum insect, and the prickly pear's invasion was quickly halted.

The few survivors along the roadside looked a little smug. Even as defeated aliens they knew they hadn't gone down without showing what damage they could do. This wasn't a science fiction movie, it was a South American novel.

(Newspapers at home, when they mention Australia at all, prepare you for this sort of thing. SARDINES RAIN DOWN ON IPSWICH! BEER-DRINKING AUSSIE MEN PASS RECORD VOLUME OF WIND! ABORIGINES FIGHT OFF POLICE WITH FROZEN KANGAROO TAILS!)

No wonder Australia insisted on spraying you and your luggage and the entire fuselage of your airplane with poisonous gases before you were allowed to set foot on their soil. They knew what could happen once foreign things got rooted. Rabbits had overrun the place. Cacti had run wild. Cane toads had, apparently, grown to monstrous proportions. Did they think there were people out there plotting to set things loose in their land? Rampaging Canadian beavers gnawing down their few trees?

I wondered if human immigrants – or "migrants", as they were called here, perhaps implying that they should not feel encouraged to stop in one spot – reacted with the same sort of fecund abandon as plants and animals did. These empty roads suggested they didn't over-reproduce – but did they become exaggerations of their former selves, did they indulge in excess? I may have discovered a reason for Australia's famous historical stinginess in immigration policy, willing to risk racism rather than a mistake. If rabbits and prickly pear could exhibit such frightening fertility and menace as soon as they'd been set loose on the continent, what might be expected of "New Chums" from peculiar lands?

The occasional bottle tree began to show up a little later than the prickly pear but it was not an alien, nor had it ever threatened to take over the country. In fact it was a protected species. Where paddocks were cleared, bottle trees were left standing. They looked like handfuls of greenery shoved into the swollen vase of their own trunk.

We stopped at Blackall, but not for long. I'd thought the statue of Jacky Howe at the very centre of town was a natural attraction for a man who was writing a book on shearing. So had Roger's mother, who'd done research in this area for her own book. I would not have been surprised if he'd decided to make the great shearing champion's statue a sort of symbolic end to this part of his research, a kind of pilgrimage end. But no. All I got was a glimpse of the statue as we sped past. The legendary shearer stood holding the two front legs of a sheep from behind, in a posture that suggested he would carry it forward. Not only that, he was holding the sheep a good foot off the ground. Was this a sculptor's poetic license, to suggest we were looking at no ordinary man? The shearers I'd watched would back out of the pen, dragging their sheep along the floor. This man was clearly a giant.

According to the postcard I bought while Roger was buying the *Sydney Morning Herald*, Jacky Howe had broken his own record not far from this town. This was in 1892. After a week of shearing three hundred a day, he was challenged to keep it up. His response to the challenge was to shear three hundred and twenty one sheep in under eight hours – with blades, or hand shears. This record was never beaten by anyone else and led to the naming of the working singlet as the "Jacky Howe".

By the time I'd read this information we'd started down a narrow road in search of the first scouring shed. Another spot where wool history had been made. We found the building eventually – a great sprawling woolshed which looked as if it had been abandoned unexpectedly all at once by people who'd never come back to clean up behind themselves. Heaps of fleece had been left to rot. Half-filled sacks toppled over. A cart that seemed to put you instantly into the nineteenth century was loaded with filled sacks. Rows and rows of connected machinery composed of wheels and shafts and teeth stood rusting above long narrow rusted tubs. This whole complicated process had been invented to scour the wool once it had been taken from the sheep, to get away from the impossible working conditions for those who scoured the wool while it was still attached – standing up to their waists in water trying to scrub out the sand and the clots of dust.

Outside, a complicated maze of roughly fenced sheep pens stood empty. An artesian bore shot a steady stream of water out the end of a pipe to sink into the ground. Electric motors hummed inside the buildings of the neighbouring pet food plant.

At Barcaldine (beautiful to the ear, Bar-CALL-din) we turned right, onto the Capricorn Highway, only a short distance south of the Tropic of Capricorn. We stopped, as all travellers must feel compelled to do, at the Tree of Knowledge, a thick, twisted white gum growing at the side of the road in front of the railroad station. (I did not think to ask Roger what kind of eucalyptus it was, and I knew better than to guess. Red gums weren't red, yellow wood wasn't yellow, nothing in this country was what it seemed.) A monument marked the spot in case the tree was not enough. This was where the ruling Australian Labor Party had come into being, when a shearers' strike against non-union labour had ended with the arrests of its leaders. Once again I thought this might be an appropriately symbolic climax to Roger's research trip, since we'd come north of all the shearers he'd lined up to interview. But he refused to let me take his photo here. He would have nothing to do with anything that might appear staged, or phony, or important. As much from an uneasy modesty, I suspected, as from conviction.

Now we were fleeing east. Emus watched us pass. White ghost gums stood close along the road, their trunks so smooth and full they invited you to bite, or caress. Roger drew my attention to the gidgee, whose heady fragrance was aroused by rain. Wild horses whirled away as we approached, but turned back, uneasily grazing. We plunged into one stretch of flood that went on for so long that we couldn't see the far shore until we were well into it. Rust-red ant hills stood up all around, waist-high pinacles, thick spike-ends thrust up as though from below-ground. Somewhere we passed through the Great Dividing Range, but did not notice anything that you might call a summit, or even a hill.

It looked as though the people of Jericho had taken inspiration from the numerous ant hills that populated the forest floor throughout this area. For a moment, as we aproached, I thought a number of exceptionally tall ant hills had been removed to the town for display, but when we stopped to admire them we discovered we were looking at works of art. Tall stylised ant hills created, according to the plaque, by volunteer labour under the direction of a single artist. Even the elongated boulders which formed a wall around it were the colour and shape of the ant hills.

I wondered if we might express our admiration to someone. Ask a few questions. But there was no-one in sight. No-one – not even a dog – was out on the street. No-one appeared in windows. This was not the first time Australia had given the impression of having been evacuated.

Come to think of it, we had seen almost no-one all day – not since Charleville. Towns were collections of buildings, empty footpaths, deserted streets. Roads had been built only for us and a half dozen other vehicles, to pass us through an abandoned landscape. That it was a Saturday afternoon may have been part of the reason – I'd learned that much at least. That this was the Easter weekend might have something to do with it as well – but I'd expected to see more, not fewer, cars on the road. Perhaps the rains, the floods, had driven everyone indoors to watch themselves on television.

Whatever the reason, this only served to deepen my suspicion that the whole of Australia – outside the great cities – was inhabited by just enough population for a single small town. They moved around, to fool visitors into thinking there were more. Obviously they'd lost all interest in fooling us.

Too bad we hadn't found anyone. We might have got the real story on that public sculpture. Apparently those wonderful ant hill sculptures of Jericho weren't really sculptures of ant hills at all. Or so we were told that evening in Emerald, over the telephone, by Roger's mother in Rockhampton. As a writer who scoured this country doing research for her PhD thesis and subsequent book on the Queensland cattle industry, she ought to know. "She says those ant hills weren't ant hills at all," Roger reported. "They're supposed to be the walls of Jericho."

"The walls of Jericho?" I looked at my map. Jericho was on the Jordan River. Lake Galilee wasn't far to the north. This was a bit too much for me. (Dismal Creek wasn't so far away either.) If these people were so determined to surround themselves with the Bible, you'd think they'd know what happened to the walls of Jericho. What they ought to have been out there building in this weather was Noah's Ark.

That night my reading began and ended with the books page of the *Australian*, where a guest columnist berated Australian novelists for writing yarns instead of something more intellectual. He seemed an intelligent writer himself but I wasn't in a mood to be understanding. I get as excited as anyone about brave experiments in prose – so long as they serve an original vision – but something in me rose to the defence of the yarn. To begin with, I love the word, which is rarely used in Canada. I associate it with both Australia and the American South – rural and lengthy and full of preposterous anecdotes. For me it implies a strong sense of narrative, some exaggeration, humour, and a hint of the oral in the narrative voice. Spinning out an ever-surprising thread from the promising but unmanageable mass of wool that is life. For someone who'd travelled through the preposterous landscape I'd just been through – where an invasion of prickly pear had spread through the land and routed the pastoralists, and where a man who once shore three hundred sheep in a day stood forever on the main street of town holding a sheep a foot from the floor while his nation uses his name for a sleeveless shirt, and where people in a town called Jericho erect statues that look like ant hills but are really the Walls of Jericho which everyone knows fell down after a few good blows from Joshua's horn – it was difficult to imagine any other sort of narrative meeting the challenge. After meeting a few of the people and listening to some of their tales, I suspected that the rich humorous sprawling novel may be the natural literary form – perhaps the only possible form – for writers who have been either nursed or haunted by all that lies west of the Great Dividing Range.

11　Cassiopeia and the dreaded parthenium

Easter Sunday. A final telephone call to Cassiopeia. The creek was still up; we would have to be rowed across. At the Emerald bus depot, Roger picked up a machinery part Gavin had ordered. Then we drove north on the Gregory Developmental Road to the little town of Clermont. Twice flooded, it had decided to move to higher ground. Roses bloomed in the tiny central park. Rock music pulsated through the open door of the cafe. A few citizens thumbed through magazines in the news agency. I saw no Easter bonnets or fancy dresses. Divorced from a northern hemisphere spring — new grass, nesting birds, lilacs, lighter clothing, signs of rebirth — had Easter been deprived of significance altogether? I'd heard no church bells ringing out of the bush.

Since much of the narrow pavement north was under repair, we were forced to drive on a red dirt "side track" alongside the road. For long stretches the woods on either side had been recently cleared. Trees lay as though uprooted by a hurricane. In fact, Roger said, they had been cleared by a farmer, probably using a drag-chain — the usual manner of clearing land.

Appropriately, an Australian singer named John Williamson talked about the environment through our radio's static. He was especially emphatic about the need to save the trees. His most recent record was played — a song about woodchips. It was, I gathered, at the centre of some vigorous controversy. A popular singer of ballads, Roger explained, Williamson had been getting a lot of people stirred up with these latest songs. One minute an admired singing star, the next a reviled enemy of various industry interest groups. Pastoralists who'd been clearing the land for more than a century weren't willing to let someone suggest they'd been doing damage to the continent. Or tell them to stop.

At one o'clock we came upon the large sign we'd been looking for. Our turning-off place.

SHIPFIELD PASTORAL COMPANY
SANTA GERTRUDIS STUD
Elgin Downs
Cassiopeia
Moray Downs

"This is it," Roger said. "Another forty k's to go."

These forty k's were rougher driving than any we'd encountered yet. Red-soil road was rough with a surface of rocks of various sizes, most of them with sharp edges. Cattle of a deep red colour, obviously a Brahman mix, looked up from patches of grass amongst the slaughtered trees. Some came trotting down towards the road to see us better. We whined uphill past a gravel pit, then curved and wound through rough terrain and down into a flooded creek. Much farther on we came to a second creek, this one so much wider that we knew instinctively we shouldn't try to cross. Our destination. Mistake Creek. A Toyota utility truck and a blue sedan were abandoned, side by side, just up the slope.

Roger's timing was close. Five minutes to two. At two o'clock, as planned, we heard the sounds of metal scraping on rocks behind a thicket of trees.

"That'll be Gavin. Putting the boat in the water."

The scraping was replaced with the sound of oars. Ka-thunk, ka-thunk. Eventually, the aluminium punt appeared from behind the trees and swung in our direction. Ka-thunk, ka-thunk.

The man who stepped out of the boat and came up with his hand out to greet us wore a wide grin which suggested much more than just the pleasure of finding us there. You knew even before you met him that he would find you amusing; also that you wouldn't mind. He shook hands with us both, reset-tled his cap, and stretched his long upper lip even longer as he contemplated the creek he had crossed. Unlike Roger's long-sleeved shirt and full-length pants, Gavin's shorts and shirt had let his bare arms get as dark as his face.

We carried our gear down to the water's edge and put it in the boat. Then, when Roger had parked the Holden in the highest spot available – the gravel pit – where it was pre-sumably safe from even the deepest flood, we got into the boat and crossed the swollen creek. On the far side we hauled our gear up to Gavin's parked utility truck and drove off.

A short distance down the road we stopped at Elgin Downs to pick up Gavin's daughters, the ten-year-old twins, Kate and Sal, who'd been visiting with a friend. The whole family came down out of the large white modern house – blinding white in this sun – to see the girls off, the man walking with the aid of a crutch. He wore a cast on one leg. While Gavin spoke with his wife, Roger asked the husband what had hap-pened.

"Fell off a horse," he said. But was more interested in talk-ing about the level of the creek, the weather, the forecast. As the farmer who lived closest to Mistake Creek, he felt respon-sible for making sure he knew these things – so that he could pass them on, over the radio, to others.

We did not stay long. Kate and Sal climbed up into the back of the truck amongst our things and we set off down one more long red road.

"Russell's got that place looking pretty good, Gav," Roger said.

"Yeh, that's right, Rodge. He's got some good men workin' for him."

Driving, he sat up close to the wheel, his short forearm laid against it, steering from the top. The peak of his cap was pulled down low so that he had to keep his chin up a little in order to look out upon the road ahead. When he spoke, he turned his head to look at us, then quickly turned to face the road again.

"So Russell fell off a horse?" Roger said. Ready to have a laugh at poor Russell's misfortune.

"Naw!" Gavin said this as though he were speaking to a child — a wide grin, an ironic eye. Meaning: Where did you hear a preposterous thing like that?

"That's what he told me."

"He didn't fall off a horse, Rodge! He fell off this little old can he was standing on." Gavin took obvious delight in telling this — the joke was on two people: Russell for telling the story and Roger for believing it. "He's just embarrassed. Old Russell just wanted you to think he fell off his horse." A quick sawing of the head from side to side proclaimed the silliness of humanity. Here was someone who got up in the morning already grinning, I thought, knowing that the day would provide him with proof after proof of humanity's endless ability to entertain him by being ridiculous.

"You're getting the grass seed in?"

"Yeh, Rodge, that's right. That's what we're doin'."

"This rain hasn't slowed you down?"

"Can't stop for it. We're working right through the night."

"Maybe you could give us something to do, to help."

Apparently Gavin found this an amusing possibility. "You think so, Rodge?" He looked at me when he said this, his grin broader than ever. "You reckon you could go without your sleep, do you?"

You reckon you can handle my kind of work? was what I heard. Perhaps every male writer in the world with a brother who worked at a normal job had heard this. I imagined my own — a fire chief — trying to think of something he could trust me to do without causing the entire Okanagan Valley to go up in flames.

We seldom got out of second gear. It was like riding in an armoured tank across a heated landscape. There might have been no destination, only an endless dirt road wandering past stands of eucalyptus trees and clusters of curious cattle.

Eventually, however, we came upon a stretch of white board fence and turned in through a gate. Huge corrugated iron machinery sheds were the most noticeable, amongst the trees. Horses grazed in a nearby paddock. Two small cottages and a caravan sat in long grass, amongst shrubbery and flowering bushes. The family house – long and white, up clear of the ground on short posts – stood amidst a fenced-in expanse of lawn and shrubs.

Cookie came out to greet us, and invited us in. A quick, cheerful woman, she had a way of making you feel you were a gift from the outside world. Where Gavin was all khaki brown, she was all crisp and white.

Despite the afternoon heat, the house was cool inside. Helicopter blades turned in the centre of every room's ceiling. Windows were open, and screened. The living room opened onto a screened veranda. You walked into one sort of world from another quite its opposite – which seemed, all at once, to cease to exist. The surface of your skin responded: this is more like it.

After cold drinks at the kitchen table, Gavin said he guessed he'd better take the new replacement part for the tractor's air-conditioner out and help Ronnie install it.

Mention of Ronnie caused a stir in the family. Gavin grinned his wicked grin. The twins giggled.

" 'Ronnie Ragweed' is what the girls call him," Cookie said. "Kate? Sal?"

Apparently "Ronnie Ragweed" was such an eager worker as to be comical. Someone who'd been on the skids, he'd been hired and given a chance by Gavin and now he was so grateful he couldn't do enough, or do it fast enough, to show how happy he was.

Cookie seemed delighted to fill us in. This Ronnie Ragweed was obviously a special possession, like an eccentric pet. "He's only happy when he works." When he took his holiday, he just went into town and drank, waited for it to be over. He never really wanted to leave the place. "He'd work all day and night if you let him."

"Long as you keep an eye on him," Gavin said. "He's fine so long as you're there to say 'Now do this, Ron – okay?' and 'Now do that, Ron.'"

He picked up the radio transmitter from the counter. "You there, Ron?" He grinned at us.

"Yeh."

"Not getting tired?"

"Naw. I'm right."

"I guess you'll be glad to get that air-conditioner fixed, Ron."

"It's pretty hot out here, yeh."

"Well we got the part right here. You bring the tractor round, will ya, Ron? Bring 'er over to the near corner and wait. We'll be right out."

We drove – Gavin and Roger and I – through a vast paddock which, while it was waiting for seed, had sprung up in a brilliant green blanket of parthenium weed. "That damn stuff," Gavin said. "Y'know it's good soil when you see that. It'll take right over. Just look at it!"

"Cows won't eat it?" I asked.

"No good for anything. But it'll spread! You'll have nothing else if you don't watch out."

What he was planting was something called buffel grass. This was a North American hybrid of some kind, apparently better for the Gertrudis breed than even the native Mitchell grass. He needed to get it in while the soil was still wet from this latest rain, so that it could get a good start and overwhelm the parthenium.

Beyond a thicket of trees we came to the vast paddock which was currently being seeded. The tractor was parked, waiting for us. This machine was as tall as a two-storey house, on man-high tyres, with a glass-enclosed cab up top. Behind it was a sixty-foot wide scarifier to loosen the soil. And behind that was the equally wide seeding machine. From a huge seed hopper a pipe arched out to fork and run along the top of the row of long curved pointed seeders.

"Ronnie Ragweed" was a bearded, wild-eyed skinny young man with a hat pulled down to his eyes. He manifested, as we'd been told, a manic eagerness and cheerful enthusiasm. He jumped to this task, leapt to another. Grinning through his bushy beard. Obviously he worshipped Gavin, who treated him with a combination of amused patience and business-like gravity.

"Just about ready for some sleep, I guess," Gavin said. He looked at us as he said it, grinning. Watch this, he meant. Ronnie Ragweed's elbows jerked, he leapt to help. "No. No. Not me. I could work all night – it don't bother me."

The sun had set; it was getting dark. We left them to install the part for the air-conditioner and walked through clouds of mosquitoes towards the house.

Ronnie Ragweed was not the only hired man to enter the conversation at dinner. Hired men and their wives. The wives of the hired hands were sometimes the biggest problem on an isolated station like this. Cookie was trying to think of ways to involve the wife of the newest arrival. "Once the wife gets restless you've lost your man."

The wife of a recently departed hired hand was a case in point. "Constantly threatening to kill herself."

Every time you saw her she was talking about it. She made sure you never relaxed, she kept you on edge waiting for her to do it. She tried to get the help of doctors by insisting on this or that operation she didn't need until sooner or later a doctor would be talked into it. But she always pulled through to go on threatening suicide another day.

"But I shut 'er up," Gavin said at his end of the table. From the size of his grin you knew this was going to be good.

"How'd you do that?"

"Oh, lord," Cookie said. She looked as though she would like to tell this herself. Smiling, she hugged her arms.

"Well, I had one of these body bags given to me by this policeman friend we knew in the Territory. You know, they have them to bring in the bodies after a motor accident. Or one of their murders. He said I might want to use it one day for meat – if you kill something way out in the bush it'd be good for bringing it home. Well I got tired or her goin' on and on about killin' herself so I went out and got the body bag and put it outside the door of their cabin over there."

He paused, grinned at the twin on his left, then at the twin on his right, confident of his effect. Cookie's hand fluttered about her face a little, as though she would like to grab the end of this story and display it for us herself.

"Yeh? And?"

"Well Bill he comes over and says 'What you got that body bag for?' 'Oh that,' I says, 'I reckoned if I had it right there when she finally does it I could just throw 'er in and haul 'er down to the rubbish tip right away.'"

The girls raised dark eyes to their mother, who gave them a special look which suggested We know this story, don't we? And it's funny every time. She employed this special look often – widened eyes, drawn-up shoulders – as a way of including the twins in the fun. Their own shy looks swivelled from their father to their mother to one and then the other visitor.

"She stopped threatening after that?"

"Yeh. They moved away. That was the end of them."

"But she didn't go without –" Cookie leaned forward, eager to tell this. "She left a reference letter behind for the next hired man's wife. She hid it in the broiler tray of the stove. I was out there cleaning the place up before the new people arrived and I pulled out this tray. There it was."

"What did she say?"

"Oh it was all quite nice! She told them they'd like it here. She said Cookie's just fine but she likes you to stay on your side of the fence while she stays on hers. She was right, too. You have to be like that or they'd be over here driving you crazy."

She had too much to do to waste time sitting around listening to the complaints of discontented wives. As the wife of the station manager her jobs included keeping house, cooking the family meals, doing the books for the station, looking after the "stores" for the hired hands, looking after the lawns and plants in the irrigated area around the house, and of course spending four or five hours a day with the girls in the little caravan-classroom, supervising their Distance Education classes. This last task explained the effort she made to include the girls in everything, I thought – those special looks.

Her role as their mother was inseparable from her role as their teacher.

It wasn't an easy life. Occasionally she got so "aggro" she just had to escape. Weekly pottery lessons a three hour drive away in Clermont served the purpose most of the time, but once in a while she got down to "Rocky" for a week or two. Whenever she could be spared.

Yet she was not one of those drawn and saddened weather-beaten women we'd seen in every place we'd passed through. However hard she worked, however tough the life, however unforgiving the climate and the isolation, apparently she had something that helped her not to succumb. Her own energetic and lively intelligence had something to do with it, no doubt. And the sort of man she worked with.

I thought of the cook at Thelangerin, putting her life back together after a disastrous marriage. I recalled those Mother's Day wives in Dimboola, waiting while their husbands played with tools under the bonnet. Any one of them might have been Drysdale's puffy-eyed giantess looming in *Woman in a Landscape*, a painting which had apparently caused a row when it was first viewed – "an insult to Australian womanhood" which would "discourage emigrants from coming to the country."

Was dried-up loneliness all that awaited the woman who moved to Australia? I knew women students who'd come home from travels with their own opinions. "Never again!" They had never been treated like that before in their lives! Australian men were animals! They treated you as though you didn't have a brain in your head. They harassed you, insulted you, abused you. Never again would they allow themselves to be treated with such disrespect.

This wasn't good for any of us. For months, all Canadian men were viewed with suspicion, as though they might be covering up the Australian who lived inside. Maybe the ghost that tried to strangle the Mulyungaree cook while she slept (and tried to strangle her mother and her daughter as well) was no ghost at all but only the facts of life for women in rural Australia.

It was evident that however hard Cookie was expected to work on Cassiopeia, she suffered from nothing for which Australian men were being blamed. She was one half of what looked to me like a healthy partnership.

After dinner, Gavin went out to take over his shift on the tractor. He would seed all night. It had to be done while the soil was still damp from the recent rain. "See you fellas at breakfast." *See you pampered sluggards after you've had your sleep.*

When he came in from his night's work the next morning, Roger and I had been for a long walk down a trail to a water-filled dam, the sound of the far-off tractor a steady hum in the air. Flies were already out, hungry for human flesh. Kangaroos ignored us. Cattle stared. Had every morning begun with this sound of invisible magpies? I think so. They daily startled a pleasant thrill of anticipation somewhere in my diaphragm. What did it matter if they still hadn't found the tune they were looking for − they played their music on my ribs.

After breakfast, instead of going to bed, Gavin suggested he drive us out to deliver an inner tube which one of the neighbouring farmers had asked for over the radio. "He knows I keep two of everything here. I've got to. What's the point in having only one? Soon as you use it you got to turn around and order another."

After delivering the inner tube to the farmer, who had rowed himself and his two children across Mistake Creek to wait for us, Gavin drove us through various parts of the forty thousand acre station he'd once owned himself but now managed for the American company which owned the two adjacent stations as well.

At one point we got out to admire a seven hundred acre paddock which had been cleared and made ready for planting next year. It stretched all the way to the base of a pale blue hill. A kangaroo stood up to watch us, twitching its ears, but did not run away.

"I won't allow the fellas to shoot them. They know they're pretty safe."

This one carried a joey in her pouch, the protruding head so small that we could see it only through binoculars.

We admired the long straight row of new electrical poles that marched off to the horizon. "Cost us $27,000 to bring in electricity last year." This astonishing figure was not an advance payment on a lifetime of electricity, but merely the hook-up cost.

Gavin showed us the chain which was used for clearing land. Made originally for a ship's anchor, it was two hundred feet long, with links as thick as my wrists. Dragged between two tractors, it pulled everything out that got in its way.

Here was a farmer the environmentalists would approve of. The kangaroos were not shot, since they did no real damage. He cleared no more land than he absolutely had to. Of the three adjacent stations (totalling three hundred and fifty thousand acres) Cassiopeia had been reserved for the exclusive purpose of breeding the Gertrudis bull. Once these cleared fields had been seeded, there'd be enough grazing land for the number of bulls desired. Meanwhile, some Queensland farmers were clearing more than they needed because they were afraid all the current hue and cry from "the greenies" would result in laws which would limit them.

Before heading out with Cookie and Kate and Sal to search for the pair of koalas the twins had recently seen, we threw our laundry into the washing machine and then hung it outside. It could get rained on; it could get dry. In the summer, Cookie said, her washing would be bone-dry in less than ten minutes. Moisture went straight up – disappeared. Wet or dry, my shirts and jeans and socks and even some undershorts were as stained with road-to-Menindee mud as my shoes.

At supper, we had to report to the just-awakened Gavin our failure to locate the pair of koalas. We'd taken the Landcruiser down towards the flooded Belyando (the creek Mistake Creek was mistaken for) and gone for a long walk in the woods, following Gavin's instructions: down the fence line until you came to the ironwoods, then left and into the stand of white-barked gums. We'd found plenty of sandflies (in the sun) and as many mosquitoes (in the shade) and had seen quite a few white gums with urine stains down their trunks – the tell-tale sign – but had not got a glimpse of the shy dopey animals themselves.

We'd seen a few prickly pears, however, crouching in the grass and hoping not to be noticed. Enemy aliens. Unaware, like those Japanese soldiers found forty years later in the Philippines, that the war was long ago lost.

And we'd seen brumbies on the way back. Dark, beautiful, streamlined beasts, grazing by the side of the road. They'd taken fright and galloped away. Cookie said they would have to be shot. "Trouble is, that'll only bring the dingoes around."

Prickly pear. Parthenium. Brumbies. Dingoes. This was a country of rampaging plagues. Everything was vermin.

"Are dingoes a problem for cattle?" I asked Gavin. "I know they're bad on sheep stations but I thought cattle were too large for them."

Gavin assured me the dingo could make a nuisance of itself even with cattle. "When we lived in the Territory? I saw nine of them on the back of a cow, bringing her down." The only thing good about dingoes, he said, was that they kept the wild pig population down.

Wild pigs were vermin too! I wondered if the boys at The-langerin had got themselves a wild boar that night, without us, and if they'd brought it back to Cook to prepare for their supper. Already, the shearers of Riverina were taking on mythic life.

"Your hired men shoot dingoes for the bounty, Gav?" Roger asked.

"Yeh, Rodge. Jim, he's got quite a few scalps out there, hanging behind the shed." Gavin pulled his mouth into that mischievous grin. "Old Ronnie, I think he's got one."

Roger mentioned the ant hills we'd seen in the area around Jericho – not all that far from here. "But we didn't see any today. Aren't there any ant hills on the station?"

"There's plenty of them. On the far side of the Belyando."

Cookie said they were thinking of making a tennis court. Ant bed was the material they would use. "You have to water it each time, just before using it, but it's as hard as cement." Roger was as much the learner here as I was myself. This was something new. His broad knowledge was one of the qualities that made him the perfect guide and host for this trip. He seemed to know the names of everything. "Look – a wedge-tail eagle!" "That? That's sorghum." My knowledge of my own world couldn't match it. I forgot the names of trees I'd known all my life. I could never match the birds in the air with the pictures I found in books. "Leopardwood," Roger said. "My favourite."

It wasn't only his wide knowledge that made him the ideal guide. He possessed a generous impulse to share it. This enthusiasm had made our journey through his own back yard appear as fresh and interesting for him as it was for me. He clearly loved the place.

At the same time, he never forgot he had an outsider along. Without drawing attention to what he was doing, he made sure, always, that I never felt extraneous or invisible, that I was never excluded from conversations (unless I made it clear that I wanted to be), that my wishes were always consulted – or guessed at. "Jack's probably had enough of this heat. We ought to get back to camp."

"Maybe we could have steaks for supper one night while we're here," he said now. "Let Jack have a taste of the famous Queensland beef." This, despite the fact that he considered beef – even Queensland beef – to be far inferior to lamb.

Before the meal was over, we were hearing about a family that once owned a crow named Heckle. "A real nuisance, this crow was. Would eat machine nuts? One day I was there and I didn't see him around. 'Where's Heckle?' I said.

" 'Oh, it's terrible what happened to him!'

" 'What happened to him?' I said.

" 'Well George was doin' his washing on Sunday.'

" 'George was doing his washing?'

" 'Yeh. George was outside doin' his washing, and you know how Heckle was always so curious about everything?'

" 'Yeh?'

" 'Well, he got curious about that little red dot on the wringer. Went after it!'

" 'Naw!'

" 'Did. Went right through the wringer and out the other side! Dead.'"

After supper, we helped Gavin load sacks of seed onto the Toyota, then accompanied him back to the 1400 acre paddock he would be seeding through the night. Ronnie Ragweed had brought the tractor in to the nearest corner – a whole complicated city of connected machinery, it seemed, streaming down its own bright cones of light: the high tractor cab on its man-high tyres, a great wide scarifier behind it, and behind that the seeding machine with its row of long curved teeth. Ronnie Ragweed set off as soon as we arrived, for his sleep. Not that he needed any, he claimed. In the light of the great lamps shining down off the high cab, we fed the bags of seed into the giant hopper on the top of the seeding machine, and cleaned out the clogged spouts in the long row of seeders.

Off in the eastern sky, lightning flashed – a crooked vertical stake, then a horizontal zig-zag flight along the horizon.We might have been a couple of kids staying with a farmer uncle. Roger got his turn first. I drove the Toyota along the fence line to a designated spot where I was to wait for mine. Off went the machinery like a great UFO into the night, its own huge floodlight streaming out in front for half a kilometre and several more lights pouring down upon the machines that followed – moving slowly out into this empty flat blackness. Again, the lightning flashed. And again. The sky above, however, was filled with stars.

I sat in the ute and watched the lighted monster move slowly away until it disappeared beyond a curve in the earth – then reappear to move across from one side to the other of my vision – then turn again and come back towards me. Roger's voice came over the radio, warning me to get ready to have my turn.

Just once to the far end of the paddock and back was a half-hour ride. Maintaining the right speed was important, Gavin said, because the speed affected the rate of planting. He turned the seeder off altogether when we made the turn to go back – cutting a wide swath across an already-seeded area.

"And you really will work right through the night? You won't doze off while you're driving?"

"Oh – if I feel myself getting tired I'll pull up and have a little snooze. Three o'clock maybe. But a half hour will be enough. I like it out here. Nice and quiet."

"You do all the repairs on this thing yourself?"

"Me 'n Jim. Yeh."

You learned how to do these things because you had to. Jim was on the payroll because he was a trained mechanic. Apparently there was nothing he couldn't do. When something went wrong, Gavin called him up on the radio and out he came to fix it. With one thing or another, he was busy fixing something pretty well all the time. An important part of managing a station was keeping things in good repair. You wouldn't last long if you didn't.

"I heard you say yesterday that you keep two of everything – spare parts. Does that mean two replacements for every part on a machine as big as this?"

"Yeh. Have to. Can't afford to be without. When it's time to seed you only got so much time to get it in."

Keeping this tractor in good shape was important. You couldn't afford to replace it. "I don't know how much this thing is worth now, but back in the seventies we paid $200,000 for 'er."

The next morning I got up before the house was awake and went out for a walk with my camera. Kangaroos looked up from grazing in the grass not far from the house, but were not alarmed. Magpies and butcher birds sang in the trees. Persistent sandflies were already a nuisance. Station horses neighed when they saw me coming, but didn't approach.

Roger was still not awake when I got back. Seven o'clock! I started to worry. He'd never slept this late. Maybe he'd gone out for a walk on his own? His door was closed – he left it open when he was not in bed. After the rest of us had had breakfast he was still not awake. Eight o'clock. Cookie wondered if she should bang on his door. I thought maybe she should, there must be something wrong. Since leaving Braidwood, he'd never slept past seven – rarely past six. But at nine o'clock he came out of his room. He'd had, he said, a wonderful sleep.

Maybe being out on the road with me had been more of a strain on him than I'd guessed. Now that he was back in the family circle, had he felt some of the burden fall away?

He used the radio telephone to call the motel in Charleville – just in case they'd received word of his notebook. It seemed wrong to be going on without it like this, leaving it farther and farther behind.

But, "Nothing," he reported. There must be a million notebooks like it kicking around Australia. What were the chances now of ever seeing it again? "I keep thinking of things that are in it – that I won't remember."

This was one of the very few times Roger's research was mentioned at Cassiopeia. "Putting together another book there, are you Rodge?" had been Gavin's invitation to fill him in, the day we'd arrived. But somehow, shearing and the shearing book had been set aside for the time being in favour of the cattle station life immediately before us.

For a while, the radio became the centre of life. A truckload of seed was on its way. It was important to know how high the water was in Mistake Creek. The driver wanted Gavin to tell him if he could get across; Gavin wanted Russell to go down and measure the creek; Russell thought there was a chance the truck could get across if the water didn't rise any more. Trouble was, there was thunder. Every once in a while there was a little rain. Would it hold off until the seed had arrived? Where was the truck? How much longer until he got here? If the water rose, the seed would have to be unloaded at the creek and rowed across and loaded onto the truck.

On another channel, two boys argued about their favourite rock groups.

* * *

That afternoon, we visited the little caravan classroom which stood back against the rear wall of the corrugated iron truck shed. Cookie and the twins were practising the flute with the wife of the newest hired hand – a young woman who'd recently agreed to give the girls lessons.

The room was crowded with a variety of audio visual aids: posters and books and physics equipment and calculators and drawings. Each of the girls had her own desk. Across one end wall there were several colourful posters of Australian animals, a globe, a clock, a potted plant, stacks of books, a pot of pencils and pens, a bottle of glue, a tape recorder, and, of course, the all-important two-way radio.

Headquarters for Distance Education in this district was Charters Towers, to the north. Much of the work was done in workbooks, but there was a good deal of writing done as well. Cookie sat in as teacher for four hours each day, and then put in another hour looking over the next day's lesson.

"We start at seven thirty," Sally said, "and finish at three o'clock. Two if we hurry with it."

The two girls had separate on-air teachers, though this was an arrangement that Cookie and Gavin had had to fight for. Like twins all over the world, Kate and Sal were too often treated as though they were merely the two halves of a single person.

Every school day, each of them spent one half hour on the air.

"Mine goes from 8 to 8:30," Sally said. "Kate's goes from 9:30 till ten o'clock."

And what happened during that half hour?

"They ask us questions and we have to phone if we know the answers."

It seemed a rather lonely way of doing school. I wanted to know if they had what could be called classmates.

"Yes," said Kate. "When we say good morning to the teacher we're allowed to say good morning to our mates."

How many of these would there be?

There were ten people in a class, Sally said. "But only one child at a time."

I wondered if they ever met any of the other children, or did they remain only voices?

"Yeh," Kate said. "We have Outreaches." An Outreach I understood to be a day-long, or sometimes a weekend "camp". The on-air teaching covered much more than the three R's. Occasionally the girls were involved in dramas. Recently, they took part in a performance of Cinderella.

"They sent out all these scripts," Sal said, "and we practised them each day. Some were grizzly bears and had to have a deep voice. We practise and then on the air we – on the Friday – we do it all on the air and some other classes come on and listen." They even dress in costumes for these occasions.

"And the boys have cubs," said Kate. "And we do music – we've got a recorder club." They also belonged to a Brownie group that operated through the Distance Education airwaves.

All this sounded like a lot of work for the teacher-aid. Cookie had trained as a nurse before her marriage, though she'd once wanted to be a teacher. It was hard work for her – one more demanding job amongst the many that were hers – but there was a resource person she could phone in Charters Towers whenever she felt frustrated, or wanted an explanation, or needed to talk something over.

There were some advantages to this type of education. The two girls, for instance, had become quite adept at speaking their mind. But the disadvantages were enormous, however hard the three of them worked in that little school room. For this reason, it was planned that the twins would move out to a boarding school in Rockhampton once they got to Grade Eight. This was a common practice amongst families in these remote regions, though apparently it was now possible for students to do even their high school over the air. Cookie and Gavin felt this was not a good idea, at least for their girls – too much would be missed.

Supper that night – our last – was Queensland beef. A heaping platter of steaks. The seed truck still hadn't arrived.

Anxiety had risen with the rising creek. The sky had darkened. Thunder boomed and went thumping across above us. Occasionally, rain pounded the roof, thrashed the bushes outside the windows. Cookie was perhaps the most anxious, since she hoped to get out in the morning when we did, to do her shopping in Clermont.

"You drive, Jack?" Gavin said.

"He's been driving the truck," Roger said.

"Licence good here?"

"It was good enough for the car-rental place," I said.

Gavin's smile was for the ten-year-old visitor about to be offered a treat. "Maybe Jack could drive Roy's car out tomorrow. Whaddaya reckon?"

Roy was the third hired hand, away on his holiday. When he'd left he couldn't get his truck out – a brand new utility. He'd be glad if it was delivered as far as Clermont. I would, I admitted, be glad to do it for him.

Up at 6:30 – the whole household. Gavin was already on the radio, waiting for the latest report on the creek. Cookie and the girls were getting dressed for town. We took our bags out to the Toyota.

Russell's report came in: the creek level was down to 4 – that is, 4 metres – which was a little lower than when we arrived and probably all right for crossing.

Gavin left first, in Roy's new utility truck. Then Roger and myself in Gavin's Toyota ute. Then Cookie and the twins in the Landcruiser. At the creek, which was only half as wide as it was when we arrived, Gavin attached the hired man's truck behind the Toyota and let Roger pull it across.

The old Holden was waiting for us by the gravel pit. I half expected it would punish us for our desertion by refusing to start. But it seemed that all was forgiven. Once we'd got everything into the back, we said our goodbyes and left Gavin behind. Cookie went first, this time. Then Roger. I followed them both in Roy's shiny yellow utility with the air-conditioning on.

Down the Developmental Road went the character in an Australian narrative. Driving (at last!) a ute – like any num-

ber of fictional characters I'd read about. Past those same
cleared paddocks and the same gold mine and the low blue
peaks of tiny mountains far off to the left — down the more
than one hundred kilometres of narrow pavement and
lengthy side-track to Clermont. Here we gathered on the
main street and went into a cafe for coffee. At the counter,
Roger turned and called to me where I sat with the twins at
one of the little tables: "You want a lamington with your coffee, Jack?"

"What's a lemmington?" I said.

Silence at the neighbouring tables. Doughnuts were halted
halfway to mouths. Coffee cups were put down. Had I said
something obscene? The clerk's jaw dropped. She looked at
Roger and Cookie as though she expected an explanation for
this behaviour. The twins broke into giggles. A broadly grinning Roger pointed to an example. A lamington was a small
piece of sponge cake covered in chocolate icing and rolled in
coconut. Apparently there was nothing more Australian than
this — originally an invention for disguising stale cake. Obviously, there was much I had yet to learn.

12 Queensland vernacular: It's raining in Rockhampton

At Cassiopeia I'd been told to brace myself for a human dynamo. The thought of trying to keep up with Lorna Mc-Donald made family members collapse against the backs of their chairs and shake their heads. "Just relax. Don't even try to keep up with her – no-one can!"

I saw immediately what they'd meant. Much more youthful in appearance than her seventy-some years, Roger's mother was eager to take us camping – she enjoyed the outdoors, still went on long hikes. Her every gesture, every posture, suggested an impatience with a world that would stand in the way of her plans (this rain). She was eager to get moving, to get going, to do something.

She'd been doing something all her life. Widowed in middle age – after raising three sons – she'd completed university and gone on to start her MA thesis on the Queensland cattle industry. Before the work was completed, she converted it to a PhD thesis, and later published it as a book. Since then, she'd written several commissioned histories of towns and profiles of prominent local individuals, but had recently decided against taking on more of those. Not that she intended to take it easy. She was an active member of the local heritage society. She was contemplating a history of the Archer family, original settlers in the Rockhampton area – research for which would require months and even years in the archives, as well as travel to England and Norway.

Energy. Enthusiasm. Curiosity. Wisdom. Knowledge. I believe I could see evidence of all this before we'd even got inside her house. As we climbed out of the truck to exchange introductions and pleasantries, she stood on her front walkway with feet apart, fists to her waist, a bundle of tightly-wound energy eager to be set into motion. The posture of a thirty-year-old; the energy of a child; the lively eyes of someone much older and much younger both. Fists opened and closed, opened and closed. Let's get things started here.

We got things started by going inside and considering the fate of our camping trip to the Carnarvon Gorge. It was off. Probably off, that is – Lorna McDonald did not give up easily. People had been trapped in the Gorge by rising water, but water could also subside – if this cussed rain would only stop. Perhaps some other spot could be found. She would work on it – a few telephone calls. In the meantime, we must relax. A good place to do this was the back veranda, looking out on a patch of grass beneath a mango tree.

Even while she was "relaxing", her hands betrayed the intensity of her involvement – while she talked, her fingers moved constantly, as though she were typing the text of her speech. Head tilted to one side when her point was to be made. Books and photographs were found and presented as supporting material. (The house was a reference library, it seemed. Conversations quickly became seminars. Seminars, I discovered, often became good-natured contests between mother and son. And the good-natured contests soon collapsed in laughter or exaggerated protest or elaborate dismissal or an appeal to the audience. "This son of mine never listens." "Don't let her wear you out, Jack.")

Naturally we had to bring Lorna up to date on our trip. Details mostly, since Roger had been giving her telephone reports all along. My impressions of Lake Mungo – your nose was rubbed in too much death in that place of skulls – reminded her of a recent incident. An Aboriginal acquaintance of hers had come into possession of a human skull in a box, but this woman was frightened of it. So were others of her people; they wouldn't even look at it. Not frightened herself of such things, and possessed of a deep respect for historical artifacts, she offered to keep it for them. Yet, once she had it in the house, it seemed that something more appropriate ought to be done with it. When she telephoned the university in Brisbane, experts agreed to examine it.

"Of course I had to deliver it to them!"

"How did you do it?"

"I just put the skull in a shopping bag and took it down on the train. What else could I do?"

I thought of how bright and pleasant she would appear to someone sitting beside her on the train. A slim, straight, alert grey-headed woman, cheerful and talkative, an historical expert. No-one would suspect that she carried a naked human skull in her bag. I doubt she handed it around. Apparently it hadn't spilled out on the floor, causing an uproar.

For six months she received no word from the university experts. Telephone calls only confirmed that nothing had yet been done. Then, one day, her telephone rang – the police. Evidently the university had squealed on her. She was to report immediately. The friend who'd given her the skull as well. "We were both frightened out of our wits!" Were they suspected of murdering someone? Would there be charges, publicity, headlines? They would be interrogated.

Of course they gave themselves up. What choice did they have? As it turned out, nothing was expected of them but a statement. No harassment. No night behind bars. Eventually they were able to laugh about it, but at the time they were genuinely frightened. Lorna did not explain why. Presumably there were good reasons for someone to be nervous of an interview with the Queensland police, as Australian books and movies had often suggested.

The Lake Mungo tourist brochures told you that "the oldest human skull" had been found at that location, but did not mention what had happened to the man or woman who'd discovered it. Who would suspect that an interest in history could be so dangerous?

Although the sound of rain on the roof has always made me feel like sitting down with a good book, I was no more able to read in my comfortable Rockhampton bed than I had been on

the road. Abandoned novels sulked in my luggage. I hadn't
been able to get ten pages into any of them. It may be possible
to read Hardy in a Dorset hotel and Faulkner beneath a mag-
nolia tree in Oxford, Mississippi, but the best place to read
Australian fiction was obviously as far away as possible from
the competition thrown up by Australia itself. I would take
my stacks of Australian fiction out into my own back yard
and read them beneath a gentler sun, surrounded by pale
northern flowers and lush cool greenery and dainty migratory
birds. Thea Astley, Olga Masters, Brian Mathews, Marion
Halligan, Xavier Herbert. There, I would be able to smell, in
the breeze, the salt smell of the nearby ocean that links us —
or separates us — but would keep the continent itself at a safe
distance until I'd caught up with my reading again. Then I'd
come back for more.

The next morning we relaxed over breakfast on the back
veranda. Rain had paused but the sky was overcast. The air
was humid. We sat. Read newspapers. Lorna went off to attend a funeral. We roused ourselves just long enough to drive
downtown to turn in my films for processing. Since we'd
made the effort to get out of our chairs, we walked along
Quay Street, above the swollen river. Roger pointed out men
he identified as "ringers" — cowboys — by their stetsons,
jeans, bowed legs. This city called itself the Beef Capi-
tal.Where other cities erected statues of explorers and civic
fathers, this one raised statues of giant bulls.
    The heat and humidity lasted all day. If it wasn't raining it
was just about to rain. Late in the afternoon Lorna drove us
downtown to buy fish and prawns for our supper. Then she
drove us to a Bottle Shop for Roger to buy some wine. These
"Bottle Shops" were quite a contrast to liquor stores at home.
I thought of the old blank-faced opaque-windowed government outlets which once existed in British Columbia. Pale,
urine-windowed, narrow-doored — they seemed to frown out
their disapproval of everyone who thought of entering. Inside, you lined up to approach a counter where someone
would narrow his eyes, ask for identification if age were in

question, and begrudgingly ring up the order. These old-time establishments had been replaced by glass-fronted liquor outlets set up like supermarkets – the government having decided that it was foolish to make liquor buyers feel guilty about making purchases that put so many millions of tax dollars into the government's hands. Even so, those new buildings were a far cry from the Bottle Shop – whose front wall was wide open to the world. Blazing signs in every primary colour invited entry. Reds dominated, on white. (G'DAY, said a gigantic poster, with an arrow down to today's special price, $6.99. It did not say what the price was for – though a blackboard announced that a six-pack of Powers Bitter was only $5.99.) Streamers fluttered above, from rafter to rafter. The whole thing had the appearance of a game tent in a midway. Buying booze in Australia was rather like stopping at a country carnival for candy floss.

This open-to-the-world aspect of Australian architecture was repeated in the private homes and public buildings up and down the leafy streets of Rockhampton. Queensland vernacular. Some buildings, like the Post Office, were reminiscent of Venetian palaces, with arched colonnades and surrounding arcade, and others had more than a hint of the Indian Raj about them. But private residences – pale orange or chalk white or soft yellow – were sprawling mansions up on posts, surrounded by verandas, resting cooly (and coyly) behind leafy trees and elaborate latticed screens.

I was convinced that you learned about more than climate when you looked at the architecture of a place. Indigenous architecture, that is – the "folk structures" which are to architecture (according to Frank Lloyd Wright, at least) what folklore is to literature, or folk songs to music. Perhaps it is sentimental, to have a weakness for "folk structures." The typical Vancouver Island barn, with its cedar shakes and weather-silvered planks and sagging lean-to – and its similarity to the truly indigenous longhouses of the west coast natives – tells me a story, gives away secrets about both the place and the people who came there. I had been haunted throughout this trip by the suspicion that the buildings I passed were telling me stories I hadn't been able to hear.

This habit of levitating houses had been explained to me once as an attempt to encourage cool air to circulate. What cool air? Another speculation had to do with the white ants which would eat out any wooden foundation that came too close to the ground. Whatever the reason, this was a mighty contrast to the rooted-to-the-earth appearance of Canadian homes, which often began a storey below the ground, as though attempting to screw themselves tightly into the landscape, or hide in the earth. What did this mean?

In his *12 Edmondstone Street*, David Malouf writes of the Queensland veranda: "their evocation of the raised tent flap, gives the game away completely. They are a formal confession that you are just one step up from the nomads . . ." Characters in Peter Carey's *Illywhacker* agree that the tent is the embodiment of the ideal Australian architecture. Yet even all this distance from home, verandas spoke to me of a Canadian rural childhood world – grandparents, farmhouses, summer sleeping beds, the sound of horses in the barn, and the smell of climbing roses. Verandas were half-indoors, half-outdoors, the perfect combination of bridge and barrier – offering hospitality while ensuring privacy.

Verandas were seldom added to houses in my part of the world any more. Canadians have always been quick to build garrisons, not eager to stay long in tents. The impulse throughout our history has been to indulge an instinct quite the opposite to the nomad's.

To Malouf, the open space under-the-house was "a sinister place and dangerous, but you are also liberated down there from the conventions. It's where children go to sulk. It's where cats have their kittens and sick dogs go. It's a place to hide things. It is also, as children discover, a place to explore: either by climbing up, usually on a dare, to the dark place under the front steps – exploring the dimensions of your own courage, that is, or your own fear . . ."

Some of the children of Rockhampton had been deprived of that privilege. Cars were parked beneath houses, junk had accumulated. Some of the less pretty buildings looked as though they sat on their own garbage dump. One woman, though, had found room beneath her house to practise her tai chi out of the rain.

Windows were opened and screened. Doors were opened and screened. Walls were louvred. Air flowed in, flowed out. You were not breathing a different air inside a house than you were outside. As far back as Hay, in the Mungadal woolshed, I had sensed that indoors and outdoors were not alien to one another here. Humans (and sheep) were not put in a box with double-glazed windows, doors that closed themselves, and air that passed again and again through furnace ducts.

Malouf had compared these buildings to tree-houses that children build. They reminded me of exotic birdcages. Lorna laughed. "They've always made me think of those meat-boxes you hung up in a tree away from the ants."

In case I become too impressed with these floating birdcages, Roger pointed out that this apparent openness of structure was an openness of a particular kind. Everything was carefully screened with latticework. "We can't see them, but they're sitting in there right now, looking at us."

"So much the better," I said. "The ideal writer's existence."

Roger prepared us a feast — his first real opportunity since Lake Mungo. For appetisers, we sat out on the back veranda and ate our way down through a heaping bowl of prawns, accumulating a spectacular pile of shells. Then we went inside for a delicious meal of barramundi, potatoes, and green salad. For dessert, mangoes off the backyard tree were sliced on top of ice cream. We talked of teaching, of family history, of Rockhampton and Rockhampton's position in the state. Secessionist movements had once simmered here in "Rocky," but had not got far.

History of a general nature narrowed down to the history of explorers. Lorna was halfway through reading a new biography of the explorer Ludwig Leichhardt. She hadn't decided yet whether she preferred it to others.

Roger expressed his opinion of the previous biography.

His mother would not agree. She demonstrated a remarkable ability to leap to a quick defence. The defence was met with indignation. Something was needed to settle this dispute. Primary sources were needed. "Where do you keep Leichhardt's journal?" Dishes were quickly removed; biographies and journals and diaries and histories were laid open upon the table. The new biography, however authoritative it might look in its handsome dust jacket, was made to stand up before the evidence of the last. No pair of lawyers ever searched the law books with more fervour. What was at stake here was clearly not Leichhardt's reputation nor the reputation of his biographers but the validity of opposing points of view − mother and son.

I did not sit by in total ignorance of the topic of this back-veranda seminar. (Which would go on, intermittently, over the next three days.) I knew, of course, that Ludwig Leichhardt was a nineteenth century explorer (mainly because I knew his expeditions had inspired Patrick White's novel Voss). And I knew that the man had disappeared from the face of the earth, without a trace, some distance west of here, near our recent northerly escape from Charleville. Thanks to a copy of the Newsweek-Bulletin left behind on my airline seat, I'd read a long article which traced the travels of a number of Australian explorers. According to this piece, Ludwig Leichhardt was the "most preposterous of explorers", a "strange Prussian deserter" with a phony doctorate "who yearned to solve the mysteries within by conquering the land without." Over a period of only a few years, he opened up vast areas of land to pastoralists, and traced a five thousand mile overland route from Moreton Bay to Essington on the Arafura Sea, gateway to the Indies and Europe. His second expedition had to be abandoned in central Queensland when most of his party became ill. And, in 1848 − his last letter was addressed April 4 at Mount Abundance − his party disappeared.

"That stupid Patrick White!" the current matriarch of a house where Leichhardt once stayed was quoted as saying in the *Bulletin* article. "He got everything wrong." Apparently she assumed the Nobel Prize winner had been trying to get it right. (A lesson for all novelists who make the mistake of believing the world understands or cares about the nature of fiction. Who owns history? Who owns historical figures? This challenge was not a comfort to someone about to publish a novel set in the past.)

The matriarch's vehemence had nothing on the energy with which mother and son prepared and presented their separate cases. Quotes from various biographers were hurtled from either side. Leichhardt himself got into the act – or his published words did. I began to feel as I imagine a jury must feel, given the task of weighing evidence from either side of a case. I was invited to read passages for myself. I was given Leichhardt's own words to consider – perhaps so that I would not feel neglected. Evidence piled up. My head spun.

Rain hissed and thundered down upon the house. Television newscasts told us just how bad the crisis had become. The Queensland floods were now "the worst in recorded history". The Channel Country had become "an inland sea". Helicopters were dropping food to stranded sheep and desperate farmers. Charleville had been completely flooded, its businesses all shut down. In Nyngan, citizens were building sandbag walls – the Alamo was under siege again!

In the morning we set out to explore the town and countryside, in spite of the rain. We drove past abattoirs where cattle awaited their doom, and Lorna was able to tell us something of the history of the cattle industry, which she'd spent several years researching. We stopped at an open-air chapel "built by Yank soldiers during the American occupation", where Lorna told us of conflicts between Australians and US soldiers, who were not as welcome here as they may have thought.

It was obvious that Roger came from a family of story tellers. Ask Gavin a question and you got an anecdote complete with mimicked voices, actions, and a punch line. Ask Lorna a question and you got a narrative deluge of facts and incidents explaining an entire history. Presumably a Presbyterian minister who'd delivered weekly sermons on a circuit of towns around the Outback must have been able to put together a story fairly well too, and supply it with meaning. None of this was surprising to someone who'd already listened to Roger's commentary on the passing countryside, and had observed his remarkable skill as a listener. Nor would it surprise his readers, who could see how he combined this skill with his own brand of story telling for the page. Whether there was any significance to this I couldn't tell, since my own background had taught me to suspect that most novelists, if not all, spent their childhoods listening to the voices of good yarn-spinners with whom they didn't try to compete until given a pen.

We visited a new Aboriginal museum built by a committee of local tribes along with people from the Torres Strait Islands.

To get to the front door, we had to walk through ankle-deep rainwater – useless sidewalks gleamed as though at the bottom of a lake. Inside, crowds stood steaming in puddles of their own making, fogging up the glass and wondering if they'd ever find the courage to leave.

A new guide was being trained today. This meant we had the benefit of two guides – a young woman who was more experienced tagged along to feed her cues when she faltered. She faltered often, but did not mind. Because she didn't look embarrassed, or apologise, or explain why she hadn't yet learned her entire spiel by heart, we also didn't mind. Twenty pairs of eyes watched her, then swivelled to watch the more experienced guide, then returned to the novice. Oddly, it was the easy words she forgot: "axe", "hammer". She remembered words the rest of us would find unpronounceable. Everything we were instructed to admire or understand was so unfamiliar to us that a little faltering on the part of the guide seemed perfectly natural. Hunting tools, cooking tools, didgeridoos, art work, photographs of tribes in the not-too-distant past.

Dripping tourists exuded reverence, patience, awe, excitement. If it had been explained to us that no Aboriginal woman ever went anywhere without a second woman along to make sure she got her story straight we would have been quick to believe it. The point was, we were privileged creatures, given glimpses into a mystery. The mystery was sad, of course – though this was not an exhibition of horrors, nor an attempt to develop guilt. As far as I could see, the impulse was purely educational. Here we are, folks; we've been living under your noses for centuries but you've been a little nervous about looking at us. Out there, it might seem rude. In here, you have an invitation to stare all you want.

In case we left with the wrong idea, a long series of maps along one wall told the story behind the story: the spread of the European invasion. First a tiny black bite out of the upper left-hand corner. Then another on the right. In one Australia after another the black invasion spread steadily across the pure white land. A blight. A tubercular shadow. Eventually, shadow swallowed it all.

Then, at the far right, one more map, a recent development: a small island of white had reappeared near the centre. The implication was obvious: watch this wall for further developments.

A life-sized model of humpy and campfire, intended to give some idea of the Aboriginal family's home, was impossible to see clearly through the steam which had formed on the glass. We were inside; it was out. Here was a case of Australian architecture ignoring the vernacular and suffering for it. The indigenous model – the original tent – was doing just fine outside, as far as I could see through the blur, but we, in our sealed-from-the-world sort of North American building, were severed from it by a wall of condensation. Obviously, architects had not taken this sort of weather into consideration. Or had not, like the builders of this country's roads, considered its likelihood great enough to deserve a thought.

From Aborigines we splashed on through the plunging rain to settlers. We drove into town and out again – to Gracemere, this time, the homestead of the pioneering Archer family. The house had changed little since being built in 1855 – the first in the colony – though it had been lived in by members of the family ever since. Jim Archer lived in it now — had lived in it all his life. He was a friend of Lorna Mc-Donald, and it was his family's history she hoped one day to write.

The long driveway was slithery with rainwater. Red cross-breed cattle looked up from grazing amongst the trees to watch us pass. Eventually the house came into view, at the bottom of the slope, in a grove along the edge of a lake. A tall thin man — perhaps in his sixties — came out to meet us. His long, tanned legs rose up out of rolled-down wool socks and elastic-sided boots to disappear into a pair of green shorts. His handsome bony face with its arched nose and high cheek-bones — there was Norwegian blood in the family — re-minded me of portraits I'd seen of Grey Owl. This man might pass, like Grey Owl presenting himself to the monarch, for the noblest of regal inland "redskins". (Though not for a min-ute could he pretend to be one of the natives of his own conti-nent.)

We entered the long L-shaped house from a courtyard, through the long vine-covered veranda. This was a house of planks and timbers, of uneven sloping floors, where the rows of windows contained no glass and the louvred shutters were opened, where the doors all seemed permanently held open by veranda chairs. Inside was barely distinguishable from out.

Carpet snakes appreciated this openness as much as I did. Jim Archer spoke of six foot snakes that slid in and out of the house at will, to eat rats and mice, or seek warmth. "I often find they've shed their skin out here on the veranda."

He showed us a photo of two carpet snakes mating in the grass just outside the entrance doors — as long as himself, ankle-thick, wrapped around one another.

"Once this woman who was helping around the place went into the kitchen for something and came out screaming. She'd reached for this large bowl and found a carpet snake curled up inside it. Later I went in and its mate had curled on top of it — both heads peering over the edge of the bowl!"

Ancestors looked sternly out of portraits all around the living room walls. I wondered if they had taken as much delight as their descendant in sharing their home with nature. Jim Archer's mother, who'd been born in the house and lived in it all her ninety years, had carved a wooden chair while waiting for her fiance to come home from World War I. She had carved the wooden figures above the fireplace as well. Figures out of Norse legend glowered out upon Australian hospitality.

A pathway led down through palms and bauhinia and bougainvilla vines to the swollen lake. Black swans swam by. On the far side, a contemporary housing development was visible. Fish jumped. On the way back up to the house we paused to remark upon a grave beneath a tree. Leaves were brushed aside so the faint lettering could almost be read. "The first European grave in Queensland." This was not an ancestor but someone who'd been passing through.

We settled to drink tea on the veranda that faced the lake. Perhaps because we sat on planks which seemed to be barely distinguishable from ground – a contrast to all those "birdcages" – Roger asked about the condition of the foundations.

The house's huge timbers rested on the ground, Jim Archer explained. The innards of some had been eaten out by the white ants. This didn't seem to concern him. It was easier to slip a new timber in under the house every once in a while, he suggested, than to take all the precautions necessary to make yourself safe from the ants. One reason for the raised houses in this area, Lorna told me, was so that you could walk underneath to see what damage the ants had done.

Most Australians had been happy to tell me all I thought to ask about life in their country. Few asked about mine. This was fine with me. Jim Archer, perhaps because he was accustomed to being the target of inquisitive visitors and magazine journalists, was not content to ask a few simple questions and let things go at that. He wanted details. He wanted to know about fishing on Vancouver Island. Though not a fisherman myself, I was able to talk a little about salmon. He wanted more. I described the spectacle of Goldstream Park in No-

vember, when the sockeye and chum and chinook salmon
have come upstream to spawn. Fish from bank to bank in the
shallow water, beaten and shredded from their upstream battle, lined up like cars in a traffic jam, laying their eggs in the
gravel, fertilizing them, then dying at the precise spot where
they'd been hatched four years before. Fat greedy gulls
waited to clean up the mess. For weeks on end, human families stood beneath the huge cedars along the bank, watching
this peculiar drama unfold. If you came back a month or so
later, this would be a graveyard of picked-clean skeletons.

No one here had heard of the life-cycle of the salmon. It
began to seem, even to me, like something I was making up
as I went along. These fish were how large? Did they really
return to precisely the same spot where they'd hatched? Rotting and falling apart even before they died? Jim Archer was
determined to get as much as he'd put out on this tour, and
seemed almost stunned by the information. I felt a little
stunned myself. For the first time since setting foot on this
continent of wonders, I remembered that I had left a few
wonders behind as well.

Back at Lorna's house, Roger made one more phone call.
This time, instead of the motel in Charleville he called directly to Bourke. "The notebook," he said, putting down the
telephone with an ear-wide smile, "has been found. I've
asked them to send it to Rhyll."

We rejoiced with him. But: "Found where, after all this
time?" I said.

Roger's happy smile faltered just a little. "In the telephone
box, as I suspected." The faltered smile faded further and became a scowl. "It was found soon after I'd left it – the same
day – by a street cleaner, who turned it in."

"So why has it taken so long for you to be told?" Lorna
said.

"Well – they telephoned Charleville right away, and left a
message with the motel."

Silence.

"But when you called them, they said – "

"Yeh." Roger shook his head – annoyed. Took a deep breath. Tempted, perhaps, to be angry. But soon smiled again. Research notes were safely on their way to Braidwood. The long long reach of Charleville! There were many ways those left behind could punish those who got out.

Reminded of the town in flood, we turned on the television set to see how it was doing without us. It was impossible not to wonder what might have happened by now if we'd stuck to our original plans to cross the Channel Country from Broken Hill. Stranded somewhere west of Quilpie, probably, up in the branches of a bottle tree, hoping to be spotted by a helicopter dropping packages of food.

With the sound turned up to be audible above the thundering rain on the roof, we learned that World War I veterans were being flown off today to Gallipoli, where they would celebrate Anzac Day next week. Aged craggy men who'd populated Roger's first novel in their courageous youth were being helped aboard the plane by the nurses who would accompany them.

Closer to home, sheep staggered and fell in the floods. They were dying of water where only a month ago there'd been drought.

Through the screened windows we could hear planes taking off. "Cariboo," Roger said. "Canadian-built." These Canadian-made planes were taking off from the airport at the foot of the hill with supplies for the desperate regions to the west. "Hercules jets as well."

The rain continued to batter the parked Holden out on the street, to thrash at the bushes and trees outside the windows, to pound on the roof above us. We played tapes of shearing songs –

For the western creeks are flowing
And the idle days are done;
The snowy fleece is falling,
And the Queensland sheds begun.

The combination of these lovely Irish tunes and the Australian accent worked some kind of special magic on me.

Here we are in New South Wales
Shearin' sheep as big as whales;

With leather necks and daggy tails
Hides as tough as rusty nails;

Ted Egan sang "All among the wool, boys, all among the wool", as though he knew of the journey we'd just completed and was quite happy to have supplied Roger with a working title for his book.

The ongoing courtroom battle over Leichhardt reached its climax at breakfast next morning, when Roger made the accusation that the famous explorer had expressed more grief over having to burn his specimen collection than over the murder of his partner Gilbert. One or other of the biographers was accused of overlooking this serious flaw in the Prussian's character. I wasn't sure whether this was new fuel to the old argument or a new case altogether. At any rate, Lorna leapt into battle. Food and chairs were abandoned while more evidence was sought. Passages were read aloud. Sentences were jabbed at with indignant fingers.

(The rain, indifferent to the course of justice, continued to hammer the mango tree outside.)

Finally it all seemed to boil down to something fairly simple which could be the deciding clue, or could be a red herring, or could be the beginning of quite another battle. I, the jury, unpractised in history, began to realise that Leichhardt's diaries (meant for no eyes but his own) and Leichhardt's journals (intended for publication) were not necessarily consistent. Furthermore, more heated discussion and fervent research led to the discovery that whereas Leichhardt's journal waxes sentimental about the disposing of Gilbert's specimens (after Gilbert's briefly mentioned death) the new biography makes references to Gilbert's collection of specimens as though it had survived. Was someone lying here – Leichhardt himself, or his biographer? Or were we to understand that these were quite different collections being discussed? One of the McDonald truth-seekers claimed this to be proof that the new biographer, like previous ones, ignored evidence not useful to his purpose. The adversary conceded no such thing – only that more research was needed.

The television news announcer said, "Australia's outback went under today, beneath the flood waters." Pictures confirmed this. Charleville, this morning, was completely flooded. Water was rising towards the second floor veranda of the Corones Hotel. Motor boats cruised the streets. Vehicles tilted, and slid beneath mud. Women clung to women, children wept. People were on their roofs, awaiting helicopter rescue. The town was being evacuated to a temporary camp erected at the airport.

And the Over Forty bikers – where were they now? Even if they'd gone south from Broken Hill, swarmed joyously down through dusty heat in their middle-aged freedom, they must be aware that the flood wasn't far behind. Sooner or later – like other facts of life – it was bound to catch up and put at least a temporary stop to their roaming. I hoped they were safe, somewhere. In their own homes. Polishing up their bikes for the next excursion.

A final notebook entry:

A Canadian professor is in critical condition and his wife has gone missing after a shooting incident in the small "outback" town of Charleville in Queensland. University of British Columbia professor Eric Lindstrom (42) and his wife the landscape photographer Charlotte Corbin (40) were staying in the historic Corones Hotel, prevented by the flooding Warrego River from continuing their journey north, when Lindstrom was shot in the throat and shoulder during an altercation in the hotel's lounge.

Eye-witnesses claim to have noticed the husband and wife in heated arguments during the two days they had been trapped, like other travellers, waiting for the river level to recede. Other residents of the hotel – stalled vacationers as well as shearing crews waiting for the record rainfall to stop – reported seeing two strangers, "possibly father and son" join the couple. "The lady screamed when she saw these two blokes enter the pub," said one witness, "but one of them grabbed her arm and stopped her from running away."

River water rose even higher today, reaching the second storey of the hotel. Most residents of the town have been evacuated to a tent camp set up at the airport. Dr Lindstrom has been flown to hospital in Brisbane where he was operated upon. Doctors are "cautiously optimistic" about his chances. Queensland police have broadcast the missing woman's photo on television, and have asked for information regarding the identities of the two men, but the state of emergency which is causing widespread damage over half the state is likely to dominate everyone's attention for a while yet, hindering the search.

Lindstrom, an expert on modern educational theory, was in Australia at the invitation of teacher groups, but did not show up for his scheduled lecture at the University of Sydney three weeks ago. Authorities later discovered that the Vancouver couple were checking out of their Victoria Street hotel at the very time his audience sat waiting for Professor Lindstrom to appear. Nothing is known of their whereabouts in the intervening time.

Since we had to do something we drove to the coast. The man of the plains was not impressed – *a lot of water sloshing against the shore*. This time the man of the coast felt much the same. Coastline viewed through a downpour, dark beneath low clouds, the grey ocean chopped and uneasy – all this was familiar to me. But it was picture postcard beautiful in a way that made it irrelevant. I would have the rest of my life to stare at scenery like this. The "singing ship" erected at Emu Park to honour Captain Cook – a concrete stylised suggestion of a masted ship, blinding white on a high point of land with the wind singing in the organ-pipe rigging – reminded me that there was nothing similar to mark the same man's sighting of Vancouver Island. Mangrove trees growing in salt water swamps with their little roots stuck up out of the mud waiting to take nutriments from the ocean water only reminded me that the tide those little roots were waiting for was connected to the tide that came and went over the beaches at home. This was not what I wanted. What I wanted was to go back and stare at the glaring Walls of China again, and the dusty road to Mulyungaree, and the endless red-dirt paddocks outside of Hay. I was becoming nostalgic already for the lost interior. In fact I was afraid that something new – the coast, the rain, this beautiful lacy town – would somehow try to push it aside, replace it.

If I didn't want to think about home just yet, though everything and everyone essential resided there, it may be that I knew the country itself was in serious trouble – in danger of disappearing. Federal politicians were making sure of that, by dismantling the few national institutions that were treasured symbols. Provincial premiers squabbled with one another for more regional power. The free trade treaty with the US was already beginning to show signs of eliminating jobs and causing industries to move south. People stood helplessly by. Feeling stripped, I think. And vulnerable. What would replace all that was taken away? Distance had increased my apprehension. I recalled a friend's comment shortly before I'd left home: "The way this country's going, we may all be looking for a new one to run to pretty soon. Go find yours!"

Had this been a scouting trip for a second home? So far away from the realities, it was tempting to imagine so. But – though what had most delighted me here was the wondrous beauty of the place and the fresh openness of the people and the sense of space and freedom which felt comfortable in the way a home should feel, I recognised that my response came dangerously close to a kind of nostalgia. Childhood. Rural life. The country that once was. Perhaps also, the country that might have been if we, too, had had an entire continent to ourselves, without a giant neighbour influencing every move.

Childhood. Rural life. The country that once was. No wonder these notions were surfacing now. With the trip behind us, I could see that the research journey had also been a kind of swing through the back yard of Roger's childhood – followed by visits to members of his childhood family. Naturally I'd been hearing bounced-off echoes from my own. Naturally this middle-aged boys-own-adventure had been something of a visit from station to station through the landscape of childhood.

If I didn't want to push the idea too far, or examine it too closely, it may be that a second metaphor was just as tempting. It was a fact that at the end of this experience I felt much as I felt after completing the first draft of a book. You set out in a certain direction, with certain vague notions, on a narrative journey through a world of images out of your own or someone else's life, gathering it all and examining it all but thinking, thinking, "What does it mean? What is worth keeping? What will I do with it?'' and emerging at the other end dazed and excited, with a need to look back and see what patterns there might be, what sense.

Telephone calls had confirmed that the rain was making the second-and even third-choice camping trips as unlikely as Carnarvon. (Mention of Carnarvon Gorge made me nervous. The name suggested it was the sort of place that might swallow you up. Dark shadows of claustrophobia gathered when I imagined us entering the park, spurred on by Lorna McDonald's unquenchable enthusiasm, to go where others before us had already discovered that they shouldn't have gone.) "It would be cruelty to dumb animals," Lorna said, "to take you two camping in this." The implication, I suspected, was that she would not have found it too much of a challenge herself.

I recognised that the time had come to do what shearing crews do when they've finished a shed – "cut out". This Australian narrative had come to an end. It saddened me, but it must be said. "I think we should see about buying me a rail ticket to Brisbane for tomorrow morning."

The time had come to re-pack my suitcases, turn over my key to the truck, set free my host, and say whatever one could find to say to express the sort of gratitude and affection and regret that I was feeling now. Like a character in a novel, I'd got to the final pages and there was nowhere else for me to go but out.

"A terrific trip," Roger said, "but you're right, I think it's over." He agreed to stop at the train station on the way back to the house. He would stay on a few more days himself, to visit relatives, then drive back to Spring Farm on whatever route he could find that wasn't under water.

We drove in silence for a while. Feeling – both of us, I think – a little awkward. What words could bring all this to a proper end?

"I imagine I'll keep pointing things out to you for a while," Roger said, "even though you're no longer there."

"No longer there for the time being," I said. "But you can be sure of this: I'll be back."

Before dark, and during a brief lull in the rain, I visited the '71 Holden one-tonner out on the street. Stripped back the tarp and searched for the overlooked – my Itty Bitty Book Light, and my Hay-purchased doona, used only twice, still smelling of fresh chicken manure. (As one whose childhood chores included cleaning the chicken coop, I knew the odour well. This quilt could fertilise a bed of rhubarb. Someone in Rockhampton might want it for that.) Used my own key to open the door and grab the kangaroo-hide bush hat which had been through so much with me – shrunken by the rain that fell outside Wilcannia, hardened by the mud. The brim wire had broken as well – was poking through. This hat was good for nothing now except as a trophy – or, with the dangerous wire removed, new life in my wife's kindergarten costume bag. I looked my last at the accumulated dust on dashboard, seats, and window ledges. At cakes of mud which had escaped our attempts to clean the floor mats. At the permanently-open glove box door, the erratic radio, the headlight switch – all inconsistent friends, but faithful enough in the end. Then I locked up, and went inside, and turned over my key.

Nothing to do now but go.

OTHER TITLES FROM
⟦DOUGLAS GIBSON BOOKS⟧

PUBLISHED BY McCLELLAND & STEWART INC.

WHO HAS SEEN THE WIND *by* W.O. Mitchell *illustrated by* William Kurelek
For the first time since 1947, this well-loved Canadian classic is presented in its full, unexpurgated edition, and is "gorgeously illustrated." *Calgary Herald*
Fiction, 8½ × 10, 320 pages, colour and black-and-white illustrations, hardcover

MURTHER & WALKING SPIRITS: A novel *by* Robertson Davies
"Brilliant" was the *Ottawa Citizen*'s description of this sweeping tale of a Canadian family through the generations. "It will recruit huge numbers of new readers to the Davies fan club." *Observer* (London)   *Fiction, 6¼ × 9½, 368 pages, hardcover*

HUGH MACLENNAN'S BEST: An anthology *selected by* Douglas Gibson
This selection from all of the works of the witty essayist and famous novelist is "wonderful ... It's refreshing to discover again MacLennan's formative influence on our national character." *Edmonton Journal*   *Anthology, 6 × 9, 352 pages, hardcover*

OVER FORTY IN BROKEN HILL: Unusual Encounters in the Australian Outback *by* Jack Hodgins
What's a nice Canadian guy doing in the midst of kangaroos, red deserts, sheep-shearers, floods and tough Aussie bars? Just writing an unforgettable book, mate.
Travel, 5½ × 8½, 216 pages, trade paperback

FOR ART'S SAKE: A new novel *by* W.O. Mitchell
A respected art professor and his public-spirited friends decide to liberate great paintings from private collections. When the caper turns serious and the police are on their trail, it's the usual magical Mitchell mixture of tragedy and comedy.
Fiction, 6 × 9, 240 pages, hardcover

BACK TALK: A Book for Bad Back Sufferers and Those Who Put Up With Them *by* Eric Nicol *illustrated by* Graham Pilsworth
At last, a funny book about bad backs, the prestige disease of the Nineties. Follow a layman (sitting or standing is hard) through denial, diagnosis, and The Hospital Experience and laugh your way to verticality.
Humour, 5½ × 8½, 136 pages, illustrations, trade paperback

FRIEND OF MY YOUTH *by* Alice Munro
"I want to list every story in this collection as my favourite ... Ms. Munro is a writer of extraordinary richness and texture." Bharati Mukherjee, *The New York Times*
Fiction, 6 × 9, 288 pages, hardcover

THE PRIVATE VOICE: A Journal of Reflections *by* Peter Gzowski
"A fascinating book that is cheerfully anecdotal, painfully honest, agonizingly self-doubting and compulsively readable." *Toronto Sun*
Autobiography, 5½ × 8½, 320 pages, photos, trade paperback

AT THE COTTAGE: A Fearless Look at Canada's Summer Obsession *by* Charles Gordon
"A delightful reminder of why none of us addicted to cottage life will ever give it up."
Hamilton Spectator   Humour, 5⅜ × 8¾, 224 pages, illustrations, trade paperback

THE ASTOUNDING LONG-LOST LETTERS OF DICKENS OF THE MOUNTED *edited by* Eric Nicol
These "letters" from Charles Dickens's son, a Mountie from 1874 to 1886, are "a glorious hoax … so cleverly crafted, so subtly hilarious." *Vancouver Sun*
Fiction, 4¼ × 7, 296 pages, paperback

INNOCENT CITIES: A novel *by* Jack Hodgins
Victorian in time and place, this delightful new novel by the author of *The Invention of the World* proves once again that "as a writer, Hodgins is unique among his Canadian contemporaries." *Globe and Mail   Fiction, 4¼ × 7, 416 pages, paperback*

WELCOME TO FLANDERS FIELDS: The First Canadian Battle of the Great War – Ypres, 1915 *by* Daniel G. Dancocks
"A magnificent chronicle of a terrible battle … Daniel Dancocks is spellbinding throughout." *Globe and Mail*
Military/History, 4¼ × 7, 304 pages, photos, maps, paperback

THE RADIANT WAY *by* Margaret Drabble
"*The Radiant Way* does for Thatcher's England what *Middlemarch* did for Victorian England … Essential reading!" *Margaret Atwood*
Fiction, 6 × 9, 400 pages, hardcover

ACCORDING TO JAKE AND THE KID: A Collection of New Stories *by* W.O. Mitchell
"This one's classic Mitchell. Humorous, gentle, wistful, it's 16 new short stories about life through the eyes of Jake, a farmhand, and the kid, whose mom owns the farm." *Saskatoon Star-Phoenix   Fiction, 4¼ × 7, 280 pages, paperback*

THE HONORARY PATRON *by* Jack Hodgins
The Governor General's Award-winner's thoughtful and satisfying third novel mixes comedy and wisdom "and it's magic." *Ottawa Citizen*
Fiction, 4¼ × 7, 336 pages, paperback

NEXT-YEAR COUNTRY: Voices of Prairie People *by* Barry Broadfoot
"There's something mesmerizing about these authentic Canadian voices ... a three-generation rural history of the prairie provinces, with a brief glimpse of the bleak future." *Globe and Mail*   *Oral history, 5⅜ × 8¾, 400 pages, trade paperback*

DANCING ON THE SHORE: A Celebration of Life at Annapolis Basin *by* Harold Horwood, *Foreword by* Farley Mowat
"A Canadian *Walden*" (*Windsor Star*) that "will reward, provoke, challenge and enchant its readers." (*Books in Canada*)
        Nature/Ecology, 5⅛ × 8¼, 224 pages, 16 wood engravings, trade paperback

ROSES ARE DIFFICULT HERE *by* W.O. Mitchell
"Mitchell's newest novel is a classic, capturing the richness of the small town, and delving into moments that really count in the lives of its people ..." *Windsor Star*
        Fiction, 6 × 9, 328 pages, hardcover

THE PROGRESS OF LOVE *by* Alice Munro
"Probably the best collection of stories – the most confident and, at the same time, the most adventurous – ever written by a Canadian." *Saturday Night*
        Fiction, 6 × 9, 320 pages, hardcover

PADDLE TO THE AMAZON: The Ultimate 12,000-Mile Canoe Adventure *by* Don Starkell *edited by* Charles Wilkins
"This real-life adventure book ... must be ranked among the classics of the literature of survival." *Montreal Gazette*
        Adventure, 4¼ × 7, 320 pages, maps, photos, paperback

LADYBUG, LADYBUG ... *by* W.O. Mitchell
"Mitchell slowly and subtly threads together the elements of this richly detailed and wonderful tale ... the outcome is spectacular ... *Ladybug, Ladybug* is certainly among the great ones!" *Windsor Star*   *Fiction, 4¼ × 7, 288 pages, paperback*

UNDERCOVER AGENT: How One Honest Man Took On the Drug Mob ... And Then the Mounties *by* Leonard Mitchell and Peter Rehak
"It's the stuff of spy novels – only for real ... how a family man in a tiny fishing community helped make what at the time was North America's biggest drug bust." Saint John *Telegraph-Journal*   *Non-fiction/Criminology, 4¼ × 7, 176 pages, paperback*

ALL IN THE SAME BOAT: Family Cruising Around the Atlantic *by* Fiona McCall and Paul Howard
"A lovely adventure that is a modern-day Swiss Family Robinson story ... a winner." *Toronto Sun*   *Travel/Adventure, 5¾ × 8¾, 256 pages, maps, trade paperback*